Pre-Publication Reviews for FINAL CHANCE

"A prophetic piece of fiction, and the climactic conclusion to the author's dystopian near-future trilogy ... this novel - and the entire series - shines a light of sci-fi satire on the tumultuous state of today's affairs, while still being chilling and prescient.

"Imaginative and engrossing ... this time-jumping, tongue-in-cheek narrative delves into individual psyches as easily as it unravels the frightened, recognizable soul of a nation, for an incisive and page-turning read." **-- Self-Publishing Review**

***

"A provocative dystopian novel with a science-fiction approach. The story is set in the very near future, depicting a dramatic climate change and an intriguing way to cope with it. The story has an intricate and absorbing plot, complete with unscrupulous villains and inspiring protagonists." **-- S. Sewell, Readers' Favorite**

***

"Final Chance is the third and explosive entry into the Final series by Van Fleisher, a story set in the near future when climate change and a series of deadly pandemics plague humankind.

"Van Fleisher has crafted a story that is not just realistic but hugely imaginative, weaving elements of suspense and intrigue into it in a way that is fascinating. It is the perfect meld of science fiction and political thriller ... and the superior storytelling craft keeps the pages turning in the hands of readers." **-- D. Rhodes, The Book Commentary**

***

"Final Chance is an enticing science fiction and political thriller ... a fast-paced novel laced with political satire ..."
K. Parihar, OnlineBookClub

***

FINAL CHANCE

A Novel By

VAN FLEISHER

FINAL CHANCE

By VAN FLEISHER

"The characters and events in this book are fictitious. Any similarity to real persons, living or dead, is unfortunate."

TABLE OF CONTENTS

Chapter 1 – Winter Wonderland, 2066

Camp David, Frederick County, Maryland. Friday, January 15th, 2066. The presidential chopper, "Marine One," flew over the bleak landscape, a snow-covered wasteland punctuated by domes protecting towns, cities, agricultural hubs, and an occasional forested area. There were also numerous cemeteries, a stark legacy of the many pandemics that claimed so many lives.

As the chopper approached Camp David, the two youngest first family members were squealing with delight. At eight and nine years old, the girls had been coming to the Retreat for most of their lives – five years – and they knew that the staff at Camp David would have let in the snow.

All four members of the family were looking forward to their weekend at the presidential retreat in the wooded hills of Catoctin Mountain Park. The entire two-hundred-acre retreat had been protected from the inhospitable environment under two interconnecting glass domes. The Aspen Lodge (the main residential building), Laurel Lodge (used for meetings and conferences), the swimming pool, and the one-hole practice golf course were under the main dome. The other, smaller dome covered an adjacent area of forest. The domes were connected via a secure tubed corridor, also of glass. Outside the domes, the unprotected areas were covered with a heavy white blanket of snow, artistically hiding the dead or dying trees and bushes.

The forested dome contained cleverly engineered panels that could be opened to capture a great deal of falling snow. The panels were then closed, and the temperature brought down to what would once have been normal outdoor temperature, so the snow kept its fresh powdery texture and appeal, waiting for the young family members to enjoy a good old-fashioned snow day.

After a quick change into snow gear, the president and family, along with their ever-present Secret Service detail, who were also dressed for the activity, headed to the forest dome.

Almost two hours later, all of them – including some of the Secret Service agents who had joined in the snowball battles – trudged back to the main dome and the Aspen Lodge. The president had decided to unwind with laps in the enclosed pool. The enclosure had been retained, even after the dome was erected so that it could be kept warmer than the coolish temperature preferred for other outdoor activities.

Enjoying the warmth of the water along with the calming quiet of solitude and swimming, President Bo Sanders was more relaxed than he'd been in days. That couldn't help him forget the Russian situation, however. His gut opinion, and that of his military advisors, was that the Russians were bluffing, as they'd been doing for years. But it was unheard of and unnerving that there had been no communication between the two countries' governments in over ten days.

Still, there were two positives for him to draw solace from. First, the perpetrators and architects of assassinations and thousands of American deaths were behind bars and would cause no further problems. And second, the leadership of the United States was undisputed in spearheading the effort to save the planet.

FINAL CHANCE

It was almost twenty years ago that the doming plan was conceived and announced. It was audacious and dismissed by many, at home and abroad, as an impossible headline grab. But the United States could never be counted out, as Joe Biden, the forty-sixth president, had reminded everyone when he took office amidst the first coronavirus pandemic in 2021. During World War II, he noted, a single car-manufacturing plant had been retooled to make a new four-engine B-24 bomber every hour. And on the West Coast, a group of shipyards built a new ship every day for four years.

It was with that memory, that vision in their rear-view mirror – along with the reality that there was no alternative to avoid the complete devastation of humanity – that drove three U.S. presidents to do the impossible. It was their final chance.

Sanders reflected on the successful plan, rapidly constructing thousands of domes worldwide, from Washington to Los Angeles to Beijing to … The thought was never finished, as a "Switchblade" UAV – unmanned aerial vehicle, or drone – smashed through the dome and enclosure at over a hundred miles an hour, exploding just yards away from the president. The explosion killed POTUS and the Secret Service detail instantly, even before it released its toxic gas. The gas then killed another three agents rushing to the scene before a lucky one radioed to others in the Lodge to take the family to the bunker.

***

Chapter 2 – Forty-Six Years Earlier, 2020

The "Turbulent Twenties" and "Threatening Thirties," or simply "The Lost Decades," were all appropriate monikers as the devastating combination of polarizing politics and deadly pandemics took tens of millions of lives and crippled global economies, obscuring the frightening evidence that climate change was not only real but was evolving at a rate faster than scientists had predicted.

People around the world watched helplessly as their lives crumbled as a result of the clever viruses and less-clever miscues and mismanagement by governments. As the people pushed back, their governments turned to greater and greater authoritarian tactics.

Meanwhile, in the background, the effects of climate change became much more than theories and headlines about record temperatures. Wildfires throughout the United States, Canada, South America, Europe, Australia, and parts of Asia surpassed man as the biggest danger to forests; and severe flooding impacted areas thought to be safe. Venice became almost uninhabitable except for the few who chose to hang on, using boats from their second-floor dwellings.

Closer to home, dozens of cities along the East Coast, West Coast, and the Gulf of Mexico were being flooded almost daily, including New York, Philadelphia, District of Columbia, Miami, and New Orleans.

FINAL CHANCE

Severe flooding brought about even greater devastation with major dam failures. Two of them, in California and Michigan, killed almost fifteen thousand people and destroyed over one hundred thousand homes. And while those two were the news-grabbers, there had been at least five dam failures every year. With over fifteen thousand dams in the U.S. – many of them built before 1900 – it wasn't surprising.

The jet streams were shifting, causing rain, snow, and freezing conditions in areas not accustomed to cold weather. In other areas, especially those near the equator, the summer temperatures were so hot as to make them uninhabitable. Both temperature extremes placed even more pressure on the environment through increased heating and air conditioning needs.

And then there were the health issues. First was the series of pandemics that offered scant respite between the one- to two-year plagues. And if that wasn't enough, there were the climate-related health conditions that had risen to unprecedented and worrying levels. More and more people were suffering from eye ailments, ranging from irritated red eyes to photokeratitis, pinguecula, pterygium, and macular degeneration.

Skin cancers of all types – basal cell carcinoma, squamous cell carcinoma, and melanoma – were also increasing, and not just among sun-worshippers.

Asthma and other respiratory ailments were rising right along with the air pollution levels.

Farmers throughout the world were reporting smaller yields and failed crops, forestry services shared major instances of drought and disease, and fishermen were coming back to ports with far smaller catches than normal.

With economies crumbling, tax revenues dried up just when they were most needed. These natural disasters occurred within the space of decades rather than centuries, so with not enough money, countries just continued to add debt, putting off the inevitable day of reckoning, and nose-diving their already fragile economies into the ground.

***

Unfortunately, the United States epitomized what was happening around the world. The extreme political polarization of the electorate had effectively stopped any consensus and progress, regardless of which party was in power, prompting yet another upheaval in each electoral cycle. That should have been bad enough, but each upheaval was preceded and accompanied by mass violence. Running for office also meant pinning a target on your back, and the number of candidates who were gunned down had passed the hundred mark.

***

The Beli-Tel Company. Despite the plethora of problems, the twenties were not without their share of innovations. Back in the early 2020s, Vijay Patel, a brilliant scientist who'd immigrated from a slum in Mumbai, India, to attend MIT, invented the VT2. It was a very hi-tech health and fitness watch that could accurately predict the wearer's date of death as well as tell time. A medical doctor as well as a Ph.D. in mathematics, Vijay had hoped that the watch's capability would help people get their affairs in order and say their good-byes, but many wearers used it as a prompt to take revenge, often with the help of an easily acquired gun.

Vijay and his business partner, Alek Belikov, a Russian émigré, had tweaked the VT2's capabilities to include psychological markers to help the FBI fight election interference.

FINAL CHANCE

Alek possessed a wide-open imagination and, some might add, sense of humor. In fact, it was one aspect of Alek's vision – or was it his sense of humor? – that saved his life and helped bring down the Russian agents interfering in U.S. elections. Alek had prophesied, long before it became a reality, that most peripherals – such as health monitors and smartphones – would become obsolete and that communication and data transmission would be handled by wearables or even implants. He was convinced that microchips, implanted close to the brain, could allow conversations and data exchange without devices. He did confess that the idea came from a 1967 movie starring James Coburn. Still, he had been inspired enough to design a microchip that he had embedded in his head by a veterinarian friend. And it was that very chip that allowed the FBI to locate him, along with his captors, when he was kidnapped.

Vijay and Alek worked together to help make VitalTech the undisputed leader amongst health/sport watches. Following issues with the "Final Notice" death warning, the watch was modified and improved, offering a variety of health-analyzing features, including functions that monitored cardiac issues, diabetic conditions, cancer markers, and even early-stage behavioral abnormalities. These new features were the bedrock of the upgraded model, the VT3.

The biggest boost for the company, however, as a result of a breakthrough project of Alek and Vijay's – was the ability to detect early asymptomatic infection by the series of Coronaviruses, using an even newer upgrade, the VT4. The detection accuracy, although imperfect, was almost as good as any of the much more expensive and lengthy tests available. Sales of the new VT4 to a traumatized populace more than tripled. Vijay and Alek had been on the shortlist for a Nobel prize when a couple of very effective vaccines were released, over-shadowing their achievement.

Alek and Vijay's partnership grew into a close friendship and when Alek married Sophie, the newlyweds became close friends with Vijay and his wife Jennifer. As a result of their frequent get-togethers, their children would also become good friends; but what they didn't know was that events in the future would bond them even closer.

***

During the 2020s and 2030s, Vijay and Alek continued to adjust the VT4's Coronavirus detection capability as COVID-19 morphed into COVID-21, COVID-25, COVID-30, and COVID-34. The good news was that with each version of the virus, the world got better at coping with it and developing effective vaccines more quickly.

Possibly because of countermeasures by humanity, the iterations of COVID stopped, or at least paused, in 2036. Most people might have sat back and breathed a big sigh of relief, but Alek and Vijay were different. For them, it provided the time and bandwidth to work on a project that would bring together Alek's implanted communication chip with the technology from Vijay's VT watch series. They were making progress and formed the Beli-Tel Corporation.

The communication capability of the new chip didn't work exactly as Alek had envisioned it ... yet. It needed an external device to make a call, and for most people, to hear it. Alek's vision was that a user with an embedded chip could simply think, "Call Home," or "Call John Smith," and the call would go through. The caller's voice would be picked up by their cell phone, but the inbound audio would stream directly to the user's brain via a "splice," to use a non-medical phrase, which connected the embedded head chip with the auditory nerve, bypassing the inner ear or cochlea.

FINAL CHANCE

For most people, this might seem like a strange and even risky workaround, instead of simply using a Bluetooth ear pod, but the quality of sound was far better, making issues like wind noise a thing of the past.

What made Alek's "far-out" idea a huge success, however, was the demand from the fifteen percent of the adult population who were hearing impaired. It even challenged the necessity of hearing aids, as a speaker app in the phone could stream audio from any source directly to "Gaya" – Beli-Tel's version of Siri or Alexa – which was then heard in the brain. This market alone launched Beli-Tel to the top of the trending tech companies.

Embedded chips had been in use for decades in the U.S. as security enhancements for workers in some industries, such as financial services and technology, and they were already commonplace in European and Scandinavian countries instead of credit cards. The Beli-Tel chips were different, however, in that they were designed to interact directly with their host's physiological system.

Alek doggedly pursued his dream of a user simply thinking, "Call the office," and then carrying on a conversation; but the reality – at least for the moment – was that an external device was required. And that's when his daughter, Nadya Belikov, suggested that the external device could be a VT5, rather than a phone. Nadya was seventeen.

***

Chapter 3 - Unforgettable Forties

Reap what you sow. The seeds of the 2040 election cycle had been planted twenty years before. Capping off two of the darkest decades of the country's history, the current Administration, House and Senate were in a virtual tie with the earlier 2016-2020 government to win the "Worst Government Ever" honors.

It had been increasingly apparent that the Administration would be yet another one-term phenomenon, and the vote confirmed it by a huge differential. Despite the glaring numerical difference, once again, the president and vice president, however, refused to give up their positions, citing voter fraud. Although impossible to justify, facts hadn't deterred them before.

With blind devotion from Congress along with what was becoming a new American tradition – the militias – they outshouted the saner elements while the occupants of the White House and One Naval Observatory squatted.

Surprisingly, the militias acted in an immediate and coordinated way, attacking black churches, mosques, and synagogues. Liberal governors, congress members, and senators were also targeted. As the death toll climbed into the hundreds, the United States military moved in and quite a few militias were foolish enough to fight back.

FINAL CHANCE

The outgoing president, who was extracted from the White House by Navy Seals, the vice president, Senate majority leader, eleven senators, and the chairman of their party were tried, and many were convicted of treason. It was discovered that several senators had functioned as field commanders for the militias, organizing and directing their efforts. They, in turn, had been coordinated by officials of their Party in a planned coup. They were all incarcerated at Guantanamo long enough to decide what to do with them.

In the meantime, the new Administration uncovered many serious crimes by members of the outgoing Administration, the Cabinet, and congressional leaders. Everyone expected to find irregularities, but nobody anticipated how bad it was until the post-coup audits. It was only then that people began to understand why such desperate acts were taken to stay in office.

The world watched with various emotions ranging from abject horror to uncontrollable hilarity as the debates raged about what to do with the traitors. There was no shortage of ideas that ranged from deporting them – a non-starter, as no country would take them – to execution. It took adding a few more justices to the Supreme Court to uphold the final sentence for the worst offenders – execution via a firing squad.

The argument that tipped the scales was the painful reminder that no action was taken against the unlawful acts by the Administration and Congress in 2020 when the election results were not honored, and a violent coup took place.

The outgoing president, vice president, and six other congressional leaders were executed at Guantanamo. Despite the media blackout, there were leaks and some grainy videos of the ex-president, ex-vice-president, and at least two former congressional leaders who turned out to be not quite as brave as their rhetoric.

The election results along with the vacancies created by several arrests, created a large majority and total domination of the White House, Senate, and House, by the incoming and quite liberal Democratic party, all 203 factions.

While most of the country rejoiced in having a government that (mostly) told the truth and believed that even the bottom ninety-eight percent should be treated decently, if not equally, many right-wing governors and politicians (who hadn't been imprisoned) were less than happy with having no clout in Washington.

*****

Cleaning Up. Although the Democrats were accustomed to cleaning up after previous opposition administrations, this clean-up job involved toxic waste on a level never seen before. In addition, the economy was, to use an "Olde Irish or Scottish" expression, "shite."

The new President, Angela Parkson, knew her priorities, and her 2040 Administration would be focused on the one issue that would keep everyone alive – fighting climate change. The choice was stark. To survive or not? The options were extremely limited. The gradual shift away from fossil fuels had slowed down the atmosphere's deterioration, but not fast enough.

Sadly, despite Parkson's sincerity and plan to focus on the environment, simply untangling the mismanagement and misappropriations of the trillions of dollars earmarked for relief efforts took years. Budgets had been plundered to fund unauthorized projects, leaving authorized projects underfunded.

There were also treaties that needed to be re-joined; many – mostly political – fences that required mending; and some walls that needed tearing down. The military's budgets had been plundered for pet projects and education funding was in shambles.

It took most of her first four years to simply get the U.S. back on track. A new tax code was bringing money in and the economy was thriving, both from stability as well as from the green shoots of a new program that was being hatched.

So, when Parkson won a second term, she promised that "this one would be different."

***

The State of the Union address, 2046. Exactly one year into President Parkson's second term, the 2046 SOTU was the highly visible evidence of the greatest coming together the world had ever seen. In addition to the thousand people in the House Chamber, including political and scientific leaders from almost every country in the world, more than one hundred million watched in the U.S., and across the world – in over fifty languages – almost one billion people watched or listened.

The list of attendees and the single subject of the president's address were no secret. This was simply the culmination of years of planning and a marker of sorts for a "Second Age of Reason."

2046 was a year that Vijay Patel's twenty-six-year-old daughter, Karima, would remember for many reasons, but the SOTU address would burn brightly and forever. She, Jennifer, Vijay, and her younger brother, Jason, watched it on TV. They were a strikingly handsome family, especially for a bunch of brainiacs: Vijay with his tall, dark athletic build; Jennifer with her fair, blonde "all-American" looks; Jason, a young carbon-copy of his father; and Karima, a blend of both parents – tall and slim, with long jet-black hair, neatly tied back, and a honey-hued complexion framing a pair of startling grey eyes. That night, those intelligent, grey eyes were fixated on the screen.

President Parkson was a gifted orator who was often compared with Barack Obama. After she was introduced, it took a while for the audience to quiet down, and Kari could still remember watching the stately Parkson standing quietly, her big smile and sparkling white teeth radiant against her dark skin. And Kari could still hear and remember her opening words, "The American people, and most of the world, have decided, with an unprecedented agreement – politically, scientifically and economically – that the tipping point of climate change is both real and rapidly approaching, if not already here."

As the Patel family watched the SOTU, Jennifer, who had recently won re-election to the Massachusetts State House of Representatives, explained that with control of all branches of the government, the new, progressive – and diverse – party had been able to push through unthinkable programs, new industries, and new tax codes to help pay for them.

Still, to say that everyone in every country believed in the urgency of the earth's problems would be a gross over-statement. But enough people in almost every country did. They were experiencing, first-hand, the ravages of climate change: unprecedented illness, food shortages, freezing winters, and then...

In the summer of 2045, came the horror in Jeddah, Saudi Arabia: a heatwave of such length and intensity, it killed almost half the city. The world was in shock as it watched the photos posted online by the desperate Saudi residents as they pleaded for help. The air temperature climbed to 139 degrees Fahrenheit for seven days, accompanied by a sandstorm of enormous size and intensity. People could not leave their homes. The air was too hot to breathe, and the sand made being outside impossible. (Survival time for a human being begins to decrease drastically at around 130°F). The combination of heat taxing the electrical grids and sand clogging up virtually everything had effectively shut down much of the entire country's electrical output.

Many families ran out of food and relief airdrops were impossible because of the sandstorm. Those foolish enough to attempt to drive away from this oven found themselves tragically trapped in their cars when they needed to recharge or refuel. The traffic jams turned the main roads into graveyards, complete with sand covering the four-wheeled tombs.

With hindsight, people realized that this nightmare had plenty of warning signs. As far back as 2010, Jeddah had recorded a day of 126°F degrees in the sun. But days like those were considered "isolated incidents" until this.

Worse still, when it was over, the flood of refugees fleeing Jeddah and other desert cities was overwhelming, compounding the problems, and causing the misery to spread to still more countries. Switzerland was overrun by the Saudi ruling classes, and the home countries of guest workers – who comprised more than eighty percent of the Middle East's population – struggled to accommodate the returning survivors.

Finally, leaders around the world knew they had to do something. There were a few foreign governments that were slow to engage, but as the illnesses and death tolls in their countries continued to rise – effectively shutting down their industries – they were forced to "get with the program."

Still, there was hope. The world had witnessed temporary reductions in carbon emissions during the massive shutdowns resulting from the series of virus pandemics. So they knew it was possible to make an impact if everyone worked together with a sustainable effort. But until now, each recovery was built on the use of fossil fuels.

Angela Parkson was determined to save the world, and there were some good reasons to think she could beat the odds and succeed. The stakes couldn't be higher.

***

In her address, Parkson introduced what was undoubtedly the largest and most comprehensive global program ever. A cooperative public-private partnership, administered through an effort called SHARE, would create new environmental industries to cope with the rapidly evolving climate change. The Survival, Health, and Revitalization Effort, based at CalTech in Pasadena, CA., was already underway.

She continued with details of the program while a rapt audience, both in the House Chamber and across the world, watched and listened from their disparate viewpoints.

"For years, we politicians have promised that developing new green industries would create millions of jobs. Many of my predecessors were ridiculed for what were deemed impractical dreams, and with our constant gridlocks in government, no one knew if they would work. SHARE will show the world that it can. Climate change is not a regional phenomenon; and while there are geographic differences, my fellow leaders and I, as well as a great number of scientists and engineers, believe that SHARE will work for everyone. We also agree that the global threat that we face demands that every country joins in and that we succeed."

FINAL CHANCE

It was true that nature was battering life on earth and each new year seemed to establish new records for the number and ferocity of hurricanes, tornadoes, typhoons, cyclones, floods, and heatwaves. Just last year, Kari had watched two devasting, back-to-back hurricanes on TV, "Danielle" and "Earl." Each took a different course – Danielle hit southern Florida and veered up the Gulf Coast, leaving a trail of devastation that made the previous worst hurricane to hit that area, Katrina, look like a strong breeze knocking over some lawn chairs. Hot on its heels was Earl, which decided to hit pretty much every town up Florida's eastern seaboard. And of course, they both pummeled Puerto Rico. Just last month, Kari experienced the incredible snowstorms that hit the Boston area and she heard, and shared, the fears and concerns of her neighbors and fellow citizens. Record storm size and intensity were becoming the norm in every region of the world, every year.

The president explained that perhaps the most spectacular development to come out of SHARE would be the ability to "dome" entire cities or areas, filtering out UV rays and pollution through the use of photovoltaic panels. More accurately, cities would be covered and protected by a series of domes, enclosed corridor connectors, and tunnels. She used the domes of Dubai from 2020 as a visual sneak peek into the future; however, she explained, that the technology employed in the new domes was light years ahead.

They would be temperature-controlled and were highly efficient solar collectors, generating significant volumes of electricity. Collectively, the power generated by these new domes and other innovative technologies would be sufficient to eliminate fossil fuels, helping to begin the healing process of the environment.

Injecting a practical, "what's in it for me" message, Parkson talked about job creation and the economy. "SHARE will provide millions of jobs throughout the country and the world, boosting employment and income for both families and governments.

"We intend that this program will be incorporated into university curricula to prepare graduates for the new skills required by these millions of new jobs. No one with a real desire to work will be left out."

And in a message aimed at both her U.S. and global audiences, she added, "For the past four years, the USA has been developing and consolidating our environmental expertise and we are determined to reestablish our leadership position, not as the world's policemen, but as responsible partners to help everyone who wants and needs our assistance.

"SHARE will be the largest and most ambitious infrastructure project in the history of the world. It must succeed."

***

Edinburg, Pennsylvania. Less than six hundred miles to the west, seven people were gathered in the spacious living room of Grover Nerdkist II. They were watching the SOTU, and they realized that they were also watching any hope of ever regaining control of the levers of power disappear – if Parkson succeeded.

They were strange bedfellows, to be sure, but they were united in their intent to stop this effort as soon as possible and by whatever means it took. And they had some ideas. Some very big ideas.

***

Chapter 4 - Hiccups

Washington D.C. The janitors had barely cleaned the House Chamber after the kumbaya State of the Union when the pushback began. It came from all quarters. Domes were a great idea for city dwellers, but nobody wanted to move. They just wanted their neighborhoods domed.

Industries were okay with the domes except they didn't want to ditch fossil fuel power and convert to electricity; nor did they want to stop making fossil fuel-consuming products, like cars and trucks. And what would everyone do with their cars and trucks?

Manufacturing operations within residential dome designated areas didn't want to move either, and businesses outside of dome areas feared they would be put out of business.

***

The Administration tried to explain, yet again, that there would be no life outside the domes within a few short years, but there weren't enough scientists in the world to convince everyone.

***

New York City, September 11th, 2046. President Angela Parkson left the United Nations after giving a speech to assure anxious nations that neither she nor the United States would back away from SHARE, despite the pushback, and she promised that plans were moving forward and that she would make them happen. She didn't mean to lie to them.

President Parkson arrived at "Ground Zero" to lay a wreath in honor of the "9/11" victims when a small UAV, or drone, raced in and exploded at her feet, killing her, the mayor of New York, and three Secret Service agents.

Almost immediately, across the U.S., there were echoes of the previous decade appearing everywhere, including militia activity and additional assassinations.

The all-out efforts to find the identity of the attackers yielded no clues. It was believed, based on the UAV type and explosive used, that it was possibly military, although it could have gotten into civilian hands.

The vice president, to her credit, continued to pursue the dome vision, focusing on the food supply zones. Progress was slow but steady and encountered very little pushback. It appeared that nobody cared about cows living in domes, and there was ample proof that crops were increasingly failing. The government tried to regroup, reassure and remain in power, but two years later, they lost the White House.

***

Chestnut Hill, Massachusetts. Karima Patel received her J.D. from Harvard Law School, graduating summa cum laude. She had also been Editor of the law school Review. To celebrate Kari's graduation, Jennifer and Vijay held a small party at their home and they, of course, invited the Belikovs. The two couples saw each other regularly but Kari, Jason, and Nadya hadn't seen each other in a while, other than Nadya and Jason perhaps catching a quick glance and an occasional wave at university. The "kids" enjoyed the reunion and Nadya and Jason looked at each other a little differently than they had, even just a few years ago.

Nadya had "grown up," though she still retained the slightly impish look Jason had always liked about her, with her petite frame, short "pixie" hair-cut, and warm brown eyes behind large round glasses. Jason, on the other hand, was a lot better looking than Nadya remembered. Or maybe, she just had never noticed before.

Both Vijay and Jennifer were incredibly proud of Karima. She had been exposed to both the world of science as well as politics. Kari, as she was often called, was close to her mother, but she had a special bond with her father,

As Kari was growing up, Vijay made great efforts to work from home as much as possible, specifically to allow her to get involved with his company, or at least gain a partial understanding of what science was capable of achieving. Ultimately, however, it was Jennifer, who proved to be her daughter's greatest inspiration. And, although Jennifer never pushed her daughter, the 2020s and 2030s were supercharged political times, especially for women in politics, so Kari grew up in the thick of it.

The party was a great success. Kari was engaged in serious political conversations with her mother, father, and the Belikovs, discussing her role as a member of the Brookline Town Meeting, while Nadya and Jason pretended to listen. The truth was that the two youngest party-goers were carrying out covert intelligence on one another, both visually and intellectually.

Nadya and Jason were similar in several ways. Jason was very much like his father, not just physically, but intellectually and emotionally, as well. Tall, quiet, somewhat introverted, but outspoken when required, Jason had been popular in high school with both the athletes and scholars. He was an exceptional track and field athlete, running the eight-hundred, fifteen-hundred, and three-thousand-meter races. He had taken on a science-intensive program at MIT and had just completed his MS in Biomedical Engineering.

Nadya was also popular with both the athletes and the scholars, although in her case, her popularity with the athletes was because she was extremely pretty. She was described as a "gorgeous geek" and at MIT, where "Geeks Ruled," she was popular simply because she was damn smart. She'd inherited the perfect blend of mathematical-scientific ability from her father along with the compassion and humanity of her mother, an ICU nurse.

Kari's party ended and, with the demands of academia, so did Jason and Nadya's rekindled interest in each other, until a serendipitous event occurred just before Jason completed his Ph.D. in Neurobiological Systems.

***

They both happened to attend the same college party, and neither was aware of the other's presence. Jason had just come out of the bathroom when he heard a frightened voice yelling, "STOP!" The sound came from a room just down the hall and Jason burst in. He saw, in the dim light, a very drunk guy pinning down a girl on a bed. Her skirt was pulled up and the boy's pants pulled down. Jason grabbed the guy and pulled him away with great force, throwing him onto the floor. He helped the girl up and she threw her arms around him, crying.

FINAL CHANCE

The attacker got up, realized what he had done, or tried to do, and rushed out of the room. Jason held the young woman, awkwardly, for a long time while she cried herself out. Breathing deeply, she finally released her hold on Jason and they both took a small step back, shocked to see each other. He offered her his clean handkerchief, inwardly thanking his mother for teaching him to be prepared.

Tears wiped away, Nadya awkwardly offered Jason his handkerchief back and thanked him. He smiled, accepted it, and asked if she wanted to stay or go somewhere else. She opted for the latter, so she told the friends she had come with that she was leaving with Jason.

They got to Jason's car, and he asked, "Where would you like to go?"

Nadya was upset but as she regained her composure, she began to process what had just happened. She'd almost been raped and what she wanted to do was report her attacker, but that would now involve Jason. He had saved her, but to involve a guy to report another guy, made her hesitant.

Jason picked up on her indecision, and he asked a question that would play a large part in defining their future.

"Do you want to report him? I can take you to the police station."

Nadya wanted to kiss him, but she restrained herself and simply accepted. They were both silent with their own thoughts as they drove to the station. Nadya was focused on her imminent meeting with the police, and Jason on why he'd lost track of her.

When Nadya returned from her interview with the police, she asked if Jason could take her home. She was staying with her parents in Quincy.

On the drive to Quincy, they avoided the party incident, and caught up with each other's lives. And, when they arrived at Nadya's parents' house, neither Jason nor Nadya wanted to say goodbye, so they just continued talking. The covert intelligence mounted by both of them at Kari's graduation party was immediately recalled, but now, Jason was Nadya's hero.

The conversation was easy for them both. They talked about Jason's plans for the summer and what he was going to do. He told her that he was being recruited by a major biotech firm in nearby Cambridge.

And they talked about her plans and goals after college. The time flew by and when Nadya glanced at the dashboard clock and gasped, "Is that right? One-thirty?"

Jason looked at his VT4 and said, "It's five minutes fast."

They both laughed at what had become an inside watch joke in the Patel and Belikov families, but Nadya added that she'd better go in, so Jason, being a gentleman, got out, opened her door, and helped her out. As he walked her to the front door, Nadya thanked him again for rescuing her. Jason looked at her with some confusion. Here was one of his childhood friends that he now regarded in a very different way. Hesitantly, because he didn't want to break the tenuous connection that he seemed to have with this remarkable young woman, he asked, "Would you like to go out next weekend?"

Nadya smiled, stood on her toes and kissed him on the cheek, and said, "Yes. Call me. And thank you. I am so glad you were there."

They'd been a couple ever since.

***

FINAL CHANCE

Unsurprisingly, Kari passed the Massachusetts Bar. Given her performance at Harvard, her Brookline membership, and the few other community activities she had time for, she was heavily recruited by the top law firms throughout the country who prey on Harvard Law grads. She knew what she was looking for and accepted a position in the pro bono practice of one of Boston's leading firms. Big money specialties didn't interest Kari, but the pro bono practice encompassed a wide range of the issues that were important to her.

There was no shortage of work for the pro bono practice of Ritchey, Savage and Rojas and that suited Kari's workaholic nature. It also helped open her eyes wider than they had ever been – she couldn't believe that people could treat others as cruelly and callously as her cases demonstrated. She learned that what she heard was not necessarily what was true. And she learned, one case at a time, both the positive and negative effects of law, especially upon people who were the least able to fight for themselves.

Kari was assigned eminent domain cases that foretold some of the major shades of gray that would occur with doming, including healthcare cases that were on the rise as a result of climate change. It was perfect training for a future politician.

***

Washington, D.C. Fortunately for the world, the new president elected in 2048 was a fairly moderate Republican, the Democrats still controlled both houses, and the Supreme Court still had a liberal majority. So, the next four years were more of a hiccup rather than a step back, while the growing reality of climate change made enough people remember that while the medicine doesn't always taste good, it's necessary. Summer temperatures soared to over 125 degrees in many parts of the country, and winter degrees plummeted to minus 22 degrees. Not surprisingly, there were enough people who were concerned about food to ensure that construction of agricultural zones continued at a steady pace.

Nevertheless, there was one factor that doomed the current Administration to one term, and it wasn't their fault. After more than fifteen years in absentia, COVID re-appeared, this time as COVID-51. It was contained to a relatively short time frame, thanks to the growing expertise of vaccine science, but it was particularly lethal because of the tremendous increase in asthma and other respiratory diseases. Suddenly domes became a less radical option.

So, when the White House flipped back in 2052 and the Democrats increased, even further, their domination of the House and Senate, the "Domed Generation" began in earnest.

The doming program would humble the manic manufacturing of World War II, and the United States once again showcased its greatness. With remarkable speed and efficiency, most of the country had completed their ambitious doming plans within a decade. In addition, U.S. expertise had been exported to virtually every country in the world, for both large and small projects, not only helping other nations cope with the shared environmental problem, but employing millions of Americans, as promised, and generating much-needed revenue. America's assistance and expertise, more than any past military or aid programs, brought even the most rogue nations into line, as they, too, struggled for survival in an alien atmosphere.

***

Chapter 5 – Changing of the Guards

Boston, Massachusetts. On a crisp, clear spring day in 2052, Kari met her mother at a new restaurant, Garbanzo Mediterranean Fresh, near the State House. They tried to "do lunch" at least once a month – more, if possible. Kari was the busier of the two, but she did her best to make time. She loved her mother and liked being with her – with one exception.

It had been a few weeks since their last get-together, so they caught up with the latest about Vijay, Jason, Jennifer's House activities, and Kari's cases. That conversation ended, as Kari knew it would, with her mom asking her about her love life.

Kari was thirty-two and hadn't had many relationships. To Kari, and her mother – if she was thinking with her brain rather than her heart – that wasn't surprising, given Kari's penchant for extreme (Jennifer would say, "too extreme") focus on what was important: school, Bar exam, and throwing herself into doing whatever it took to help her very needy and very many clients.

Kari gave her the standard answer, which included all of those reasons, and her mother reminded Kari of her age. This was when it got tedious.

"I know how old I am, Mom. When I find the right someone, I'll know it and then you'll know it. I just haven't found that person yet."

"I'm just afraid that, given your personality type, you'll look up one day when you're fifty and think, 'Damn. Wish I hadn't waited so long.' And then you won't have children."

Kari looked at Jennifer and asked, "Would you want to bring a child into this world? Their life would be threatened from day one."

Jennifer couldn't argue but she parried back, "No, not today, but if we can keep the White House, I think we'll rapidly address the issues."

"There's the big 'IF' again. We've had so many false starts. But Mom, if I meet the right guy … who knows."

One of Kari's abilities was observation and she had just observed her mother's expression of relief. Before Jennifer could even comment, Kari asked, "Mom. I know that you and dad have a great relationship. It worked for you and perhaps one day, if I'm lucky enough, I may have one, too. But I don't feel compelled to focus on that. I'm very happy with my life and that's all that should matter."

"I'm sorry, Sweetie. You're right. I plead guilty of imposing my values."

Kari laughed and replied, "The penalty for that is a kiss and a big soppy 'I love you'."

Kari got up and gave Jennifer a big hug and kiss on the cheek. They both sniffled a bit and settled down to finish their lunch.

Jennifer turned serious, looked around, and confided, "I'm not going to run again this year. On one hand, I was hesitating to tell you this because I'd like you to take my place, but I know that this would be another reason to postpone finding Mr. Right."

FINAL CHANCE

Jennifer's comment had come out of the blue and it took Kari a second or so to understand what her mother was saying before she asked, "And on the other hand?"

Jennifer smiled. She truly believed that Kari was destined to make a big name for herself in politics. She said, "You were born for this."

***

Two weeks later, Jennifer invited Kari to lunch and told her to dress for business and allow for a couple of hours, minimum. Kari arrived at the State House on Beacon Street, wondering why she was meeting Jennifer here, and about the dress code. Jennifer's text said that she'd meet Kari at the main entrance.

Jennifer was waiting just inside the entrance, beyond security, and she looked approvingly at her daughter's appearance. Kari was full of questions, but Jennifer just gave a quick – 'do no damage' – hug, grabbed her hand, and pulled her down the hall.

Moments later she was standing in the governor's office, shaking Governor Sally Rhydes' hand. Governor Rhydes was about Jennifer's age, petite and exuding energy and intellect.

The governor said, I've heard so much about you, Karima, and one of the things I've heard is that you're a busy woman, so let's go to my dining room, get acquainted, and have some lunch. That okay?"

Jennifer was smiling and Kari was uncommonly caught off-guard. She recovered, smiled, and said, "It's a pleasure … and an honor to meet you, Governor Rhydes. I'm a big fan."

"Well, in that case, you can call me Sally."

Governor Rhydes gently probed Kari's thought processes, views on issues, and her core beliefs, during their very informal conversation; and Kari felt like she had given up everything she held dear during the pleasant conversation. Rhydes also involved Jennifer to further disguise the interrogation and make it seem like simply a chat amongst three very smart people.

After lunch and conversation, Rhydes looked at Kari and said, "I know Todd Ritchey very well and he couldn't say enough about what an amazing job you're doing. So, before they seduce you with a promotion and more money, I'd like to make a counteroffer. I've spoken with the Party Election Committee, and we'd like you to run for your mother's seat. We all agree that if we have to lose Jennifer, we want her daughter. You probably have a lot of questions, and your mom can answer all of them, so what I want to know is, are you in?"

Kari and Jennifer restrained themselves until they left the building to give each other a high five and a big hug. Over a quick coffee, Kari asked what her chances were of winning the election and Jennifer chuckled. "State House seats are particularly influenced by gerrymandering, so running unopposed is not uncommon. But in this district, even if you have an opponent ... you'll win."

Kari continued her role as an elected member of Brookline's Town Meeting, making a name for herself as a tireless and effective working member. She also continued working at RSR although she'd given notice and was grooming a few replacements. In what was a landslide country-wide Democratic victory in November, Kari defeated her opponent by over thirty points. Thirty-two point three-seven, if you'd asked Kari.

***

FINAL CHANCE

Washington, D.C., November 2052. Alek and Vijay were called to Washington to meet with the president-elect, Rachel Metcalf. The president-elect had also invited the vice-president-elect and the likely Secretary of Health and Human Services. The election had been held less than two weeks ago.

Alek and Vijay were surprised that the three people seemed to be a lot less jubilant than they'd anticipated, so soon after winning an election. They would soon find out why.

The president-elect thanked them for coming down on short notice and then she got straight to the point.

"Gentlemen. As you are probably aware, we are in a race against time and science to retreat as quickly as possible to the safety of domed existence. The recent pandemic's harsh targeting of those with respiratory conditions proved that the decisions of 2046 were sound and necessary. The SHARE program never wavered during the past four years and we intend to accelerate the pace. The recent pandemic reminded us, too, that living in a domed existence carries risks. Substantial risks concerning disease transmission.

"Back in the twenties, you developed a monitor, using a watch, I believe, to detect those who were infected with the COVID virus, even if they were asymptomatic. What we are looking for makes what you did seem easy, by comparison. We need something that, ideally, would identify someone who has a disease that we haven't even identified yet – that first person with a new virus who enters a dome. "Is that possible?"

The three new Administration members looked at the two scientists with dread and hope. They knew the size and critical importance of their ask and they hoped that Alek and Vijay wouldn't start laughing.

After a few seconds of reflection, Alek reminded them, "Our system wasn't perfect. It was adequate. And given that what you're looking for is to identify a less defined condition, a new method might be even less perfect. However, if it was coupled with an excellent, and I truly mean excellent contact tracing system that would identify transmission, it could be adequate to quickly contain outbreaks."

Vijay added, "We'll need some time to give you some options."

The president-elect replied solemnly but ended with a smile. "Of course, but not much."

Vijay's and Alek's brains were churning and the silence between the two men in the backseat of the bouncing airport-bound taxi was deafening. As they approached the terminal, Vijay finally spoke.

"I think it's time we bring in the kids."

*****

Chestnut Hill, Massachusetts. The following day at Vijay's home, Alek, Vijay, and the "kids," in the form of Nadya and Jason, met. Vijay was sixty-seven and Alek sixty-six, but both of them could have passed for ten years younger. Their minds were at their peak, and that was all that mattered, but now was the perfect opportunity to bring Nadya and Jason into the business. It was what they were born to do.

*****

Two days later. Nadya and Jason weren't your typical new hires, nor was Beli-Tel a typical company. Both of the 'kids,' as Alek and Vijay affectionately called them, had been involved with the business, at least informally, for some time. They were naturally interested in their dads' projects and were smart enough to understand what they were doing and ask good questions.

Between the four of them, they had quickly understood the necessity and requirements of the president-elect's request. They needed to be able to identify the presence of a dangerous, but not fully defined virus. Too much latitude and they would have way too many false positives. Too narrow a filter and they'd run the risk of missing a dangerous positive.

Equally important was the need for almost foolproof tracing to immediately identify transmissions from a disease carrier.

Not surprisingly, Alek suggested an implanted chip, but he quickly added that it wouldn't need the capability to make calls … yet. That got a laugh out of everyone, but Nadya interjected, "Actually it would need to make a call, or at least send messages, to health authorities, the disease carrier, and the traced contacts."

Nadya had received her Ph.D. at MIT leading a small group of grad students at the Laboratory for Information and Decision Systems (LIDS), specializing in biological engineering. Their focus was bio-technical interfaces, along the lines that her father had long dreamt about.

Looking at a datasheet from SHARE regarding dome architecture, Jason said, "Domes will be wired for wi-fi, so sending a message should be straightforward."

Vijay weighed in. "I agree that a chip is the surest way to go. You can't take it off or leave it home. Still – maybe I'm old and thinking in the past – but will everyone agree to get an implant?"

That met with a bunch of "Hmmms," because the answer wasn't scientific.

Vijay continued, "Another option would be to build sensors into the sewage systems to monitor wastewater. Within a domed environment, it would be easy to build in numerous sensors to quickly isolate the source and trending of the virus. Of course, this would be a reactive measure and simply identify a household, at best. A chip could prevent an infected person from entering a dome and the tracing ability would be outstanding."

Nadya offered that chips were commonplace in Scandinavia and Europe and that the major reason they weren't used more often in the U.S. was there hadn't been any need. She continued, "There has also been some pushback, but if we believe that chips offer the best protection, we should say so. The next best solution would be a wearable like a watch, bracelet, or ID-type necklace. That would reduce the effectiveness, but by how much ...?"

Jason added, "That reduction would also be cumulative because it would negatively affect the tracing."

Alek agreed. "Good selling point."

Vijay smiled and said, "I agree that a chip is ideal. We need to convince the president and then all we have to do is figure out how to spot some dangerous microbe that we've never seen before."

Everyone chuckled and Jason mused, "It might not be that hard. We know what COVID-19 looked like. You two built a filter that could spot it. What were the differences between that and COVID-21, 25, 30, 34, and 51? We could build our net to capture all of those plus some additional scope consistent with the size and type of changes that the virus has already gone through. Like branches of a tree, we'll know the direction, so we just need to know how far it will grow and how many shoots it puts out."

Alek agreed. "That will be a good start. I suggest that Nadya and I look for any roadblocks using the device types we discussed, and the Patel team look into the various disease markers we need to look for. Nadya and I will also look at how those devices will interface with any tracing system developed. We should have our work completed by the end of the week."

Vijay said, "From what I remember and what Jason just said, I don't think our part will be too difficult either. Friday works for us, too."

***

Chapter 6 - The Big Time

Washington, D.C. December 3rd, 2052. The entire Beli-Tel Corporation made the trip to D.C. and the entire corporation was disappointed that they weren't meeting in the White House, but they understood. They were also disappointed that the president-elect wasn't there. They hadn't known that. The principal attendees included the vice-president-elect, the presumptive Secretary of HHS, and a new face, the presumptive Secretary of SHARE. This was a new cabinet position that would be interfacing with most of the other cabinet functions. There were also a half dozen other attendees affiliated with the principals.

They met in the same conference room in the same non-descript building in downtown D.C. as they had in November.

The "kids" had put together a pretty slick PowerPoint presentation detailing the major components of the system: The software, hardware, tracing system, reporting, and costs, but they started with the chip.

The first experiments of embedding chips into humans started in Britain in 1998. They could open doors and turn lights on and off. Later on, they'd been used for everything from accessing travel on trains, pet identification, cryptocurrency, and even contraception. They were widely used in Scandinavia and Europe and they warned that some U.S. states had enacted laws against their mandated use. Surprisingly, none of the officials in the room expressed any concerns.

They continued with the chip's broad functionality: from gaining access to a dome and identification to virus detection, tracing, and evolution capability.

When it came to the cost element, Nadya, who presented that part, swallowed hard when she gave them the cost per person and estimated total cost. The officials barely acknowledged it. All they wanted to know was how long would it take to start rolling it out. The presumptive SHARE Secretary provided a doming construction schedule, and while it seemed a bit down the road, she explained that it was important to get everyone chipped ASAP, as the process and expected pushback would take a while.

The government team asked the Beli-Tel team to send them a proposal, detailing the deliverables and timeframe. And just like that, a billion-dollar-plus deal was all but wrapped up.

Alek and Vijay were more used to high stakes transactions than Nadya and Jason, so when they were all safely out of view from their new government partners, the two elder partners of Beli-Tel shook hands, while the junior partners engaged in a passionate hug and kiss that would be more at home in Paris than D.C. This was the "Big Time!"

***

Boston, Massachusetts. When the Belikovs and Patels landed at Boston airport, Alek and Vijay returned to their homes while the younger Belikov-Patel couple returned to their modest apartment.

Despite the wealth of their parents, Nadya and Jason were doing life on their own. And while Jason made pretty good money, it wasn't enough for a lavish lifestyle, and Nadya had only recently finished her degree. Today's deal would change their lives; and over dinner that evening at Giulia, an Italian restaurant in Cambridge that they really couldn't afford – yet – they decided to get married.

The following morning, they called their parents to tell them the news and to suggest that Beli-Tel move to a real office. There was one available on Cambridge Street in Cambridge that would be perfect. Both Alek and Vijay agreed, "Let's do it!"

***

Beli-Tel HQ, Cambridge Massachusetts. Beli-Tel had until January 17th to provide the details of the contract. That was four days before inauguration day and five days before the groundbreaking of the first D.C. Dome. There was a lot of work to do to ensure that the details were accurate and complete. And if that wasn't exciting enough, they were all invited to both the inauguration and the D.C. Dome groundbreaking.

To ensure that they would be ready on time, Nadya and Jason recruited a half dozen people to help. It was explained to the recruits that the positions were initially temporary, but there was a chance that job offers would be made later. They wanted to ensure that they got the contract first, but also, they were looking for good fits.

With Jason and Vijay's medical experience and the very relevant understanding of biometrics that Vijay had mastered, their job of virus identification was fairly straightforward. Nadya and Alek's work, however, was fraught with a huge number of unknowns and variables.

Alek understood chip architecture and communication requirements, but the environment in which the chips would function, i.e., the domes, was a big unknown. He and Nadya were constantly interacting with the SHARE teams regarding dome access and wi-fi parameters across different dome types.

They also visited a Maine blueberry cooperative dome as an example of an agricultural operation. It looked like a giant greenhouse, but it was obvious that the structure was much more substantial. About eighty percent of it housed the bushes where all the farming was done. The berries were then processed and packed in the next section of the structure before moving to the loading docks for shipping. The facility they visited had already transitioned to all-electric harvesting, manufacturing, trucks, and rail. Even the roads leading out from the facility were constructed of recycled material that doubled as solar collectors.

The father-daughter team was blown away by the agricultural operation. But as impressive as it was, they needed to get a good understanding of a city dome, and those didn't exist yet.

***

SHARE HQ, Pasadena, CA. Aziz Khan was the CEO of the SHARE program based at CalTech. A Stanford grad, he'd spent twenty years at Google, mostly as a project director, managing the numerous and disparate moving parts of dozens of large initiatives. His father had worked at CalTech Labs after immigrating from Pakistan over fifty years ago.

Aziz was appointed in 2046 when the decision to proceed with SHARE was made. Very quickly, he'd put together over thirty teams to begin work immediately with the massive doming project, and despite the change at the White House in 2048, the program continued, as both the House and Senate refused to back down. In 2050, a small number of those senators and House Members lost their seats as the dome backlash roiled on, but not enough to stop the program. In 2052, with mounting evidence that people were dying as a result of climate change, those lost seats were more than recovered.

For the past – almost – six years, they had been planning and manufacturing dome components: panels, circuitry, and solar collecting road surfacing. They had also been building agricultural facilities and infrastructure. Now, the city doming phase was ready to begin and Aziz was more excited than he'd ever been.

For obvious reasons, protecting the food supply had been included in the first construction phase. A good number of agricultural domes had been built and were fully functioning. And impressive as the city domes would be, the agricultural zones took the prize for sheer size. Thousands of square miles of photovoltaic glass were helping to protect the food chain from the sun's onslaught. They were also generating massive amounts of solar energy to power the food processing and packaging plants that were typically attached to the agricultural or growing zones. These structures had been comparatively easy to construct, however, compared with the city domes that were coming next.

Aziz was just wrapping up a ZoomX session with thirty-two project managers to begin the doming of Washington D.C. He smiled when he realized that this dome would actually cover a large part of an entire state – albeit a very small one – when the District formally became a state.

His smile disappeared when he opened an e-mail from the presumptive SHARE Cabinet Secretary. She had just learned that massive protests against the doming were being planned in D.C. for the inauguration of the new president. The president-elect's team planned that immediately following

FINAL CHANCE

the inauguration, the new POTUS would take part in the ground-breaking ceremony for the D.C. Dome. The Secretary wanted Aziz on a call at 8:00 the next morning. That was 5:00 AM for Aziz, but he had gotten used to it.

***

Chapter 7 - Dome Detail

SHARE HQ, Pasadena, CA. Beli-Tel's contact point at SHARE was Tina Martinez, Chief Information Officer. She invited Alek and Nadya to a ZoomX meeting to give them a comprehensive overview of the city domes. Jason and Vijay asked to attend, as well.

Tina had been with SHARE from the outset, six years ago, and it showed. She had an encyclopedic mastery of both the overall plans as well as, it seemed, every detail. They peppered her with questions, and she just as quickly gave them the answers.

Of primary interest to the Beli-Tel team was how many domes would be built in the U.S. Tina's answer: "3,064." That would dome every town or city with more than 10,000 people.

Tina went on to explain that the term 'Dome' was an over-simplification. In many cases, multiple domes with connecting corridors would be built. 'Dome Clusters' would be a more accurate description.

They also learned that the same "8g" wi-fi network would be used across all domes and that access to all the domes could be controlled as required. Team Beli-Tel recognized that this feature could prevent – or at least detain for screening – a potentially infected person from entering a dome.

FINAL CHANCE

Another question posed by the team was in response to rumors about population control. Tina replied, "This is only a discussion item at this time, and it may be limited to financial incentives and disincentives to limit families to two children. The simple fact is that both the physical space and the fragile environment demand it."

The team wondered how that would be received by some segments of the populace, but they also realized that they were recommending that everyone be microchipped.

The inquisitive scientists had lots of questions and the responses by Ms. Martinez were impressive. But then, when she invited them into a virtual reality domed world, they were all blown away.

They realized that they were looking at a virtual reality perspective from their personalized avatars and they all laughed at their likenesses as the three men and one woman walked down the street. There were time lapses to show morning to night, and a narrator's voice came on from time to time to highlight specific features, sometimes supported by text captions.

The narrator announced, "Hi, and welcome to our showcase dome, Manhattan. My name is Nancy and I'll be your guide today."

They looked up at the New York skyline and were fascinated that some of the taller buildings stuck out above the dome. Nancy knew that this was a typical reaction and explained, "Any building taller than nine hundred feet will extend beyond the dome panels. That means that the exposed section will need to be improved with respect to the windows and ventilation. Those upper stories provide spectacular views so hold on to your stomachs! We're going to transport you to the Observatory of One World Trade Center, seventeen-hundred-seventy-six feet tall, so you can see for yourselves."

They watched their avatars as they were beamed up to the circular Sky Portal. Now, instead of simply looking down onto the streets from a hundred floors up, they looked down at the majestic curves of the dome cluster. They could also see other nearby buildings protruding out from the Manhattan Cluster. Nancy pointed out some of them; Four-Thirty-Two Park Avenue at almost fourteen hundred feet, Thirty Hudson Yards at close to thirteen hundred feet, and the two grand dames built back in the 1930s, the Empire State and Chrysler Buildings, at twelve hundred and one thousand feet, respectively. A number of nearby dome clusters were also visible, including the Brooklyn, Staten Island, Queens, Long Island, and Newark, New Jersey clusters. There were different shapes and sizes – both in height and area – and a large number of connectors and corridors were also visible. Looking at the view further away made them think of bubble wrap. They could even see planes taking off from the exposed runways adjacent to the domed terminals of airports.

Right on cue, Nancy answered their unasked question about pollution from planes. The last jet-fueled planes will be phased out before the domes are even completed. The two major aircraft manufacturers, Tesla and Airbus, are well into their conversion program to hydrogen. Tesla's H-One test flights have been a great success.

Nancy gently transported them back down to the street level, but it was a New York street they had never seen. There were a lot of (animated) people around, but they were struck with the quietness and space. Again, right on cue, Nancy explained. "Imagine New York without cars. By reclaiming the space devoted to cars, twenty-five percent more space will be devoted to people." And sure enough, there were no cars except for a few electric driverless taxis. Trams on rubber wheels carried the people on various routes and there were a lot of people gliding by silently on hop-on, hop-off electric scooters, and bicycles. There was no horn honking, no bus fumes, and no overhead plane noise from the arrivals and departures at LaGuardia, JFK, and Newark.

There were plants, trees, and even birds, at least those that could adapt to the lower dome heights, and Nancy explained, "Day and nighttime temperatures could be adjusted, as agreed by city councils."

They saw a cat sitting in a window and some people walking dogs. Tongue in cheek, Nancy predicted, "Goldfish will again become popular pets, especially as they can easily outlive dogs and cats."

She continued, "All manufacturing operations will be moved out of the dwelling domes to separate industrial domes, making more room for living accommodations. In some cities, depending on their layout and geography, connected suburban domes would also be built."

As the four viewers walked the quiet and spacious streets, they saw all the usual shops, restaurants, and coffee shops, most with outdoor seating, thanks to the absence of cars and adverse weather. It was only when their animated avatar looked skyward that they would see the soaring shape of a dome overhead.

The avatars arrived at an escalator and the group of four headed down into an underground garage. Nancy said, "Private and rental cars, electric only, of course, will be kept in underground garages on the perimeters of the cities. They can be used to drive to other domes, including the 'revitalization domes,' or 'RDs.' Let's take a drive."

The viewers watched as a driverless car approached, the doors opened, and the four avatars entered. They left through an airlocked exit onto what appeared to be a very smooth highway. Always ready to help, Nancy explained. "Most roads will be paved with composite modules containing interior circuitry to capture solar energy. Lane and speed limit information will be displayed by illuminated lighting embedded in the road circuitry. The energy collected by the modules will also power modern charging stations. We'll stop at one so you can see how your present-day gas station road stops have changed."

They pulled into a domed charging station via an airlock entry and up to a charging device. The avatars got out and it didn't take long to see that this was a far cry from the highway rest stops they once knew. Nancy said, "These stations are designed to do more than just provide fast food and restrooms during a car charging stop. They can also be used for personal re-charging – providing travelers with restaurants, hotels, shopping, nap rooms, individual or family size movie viewing areas with first-class airline type seats, office cubicles, game areas and even bowling alleys."

Some of what they saw even made Star Wars look obsolete. After "walking" around for a few minutes, an excited Nancy said, "Okay, let's go and see my favorite – an RD!"

As they drove along the smooth, composite, solar-collecting highway, they could see flashing illuminated animal footprints on the road with the words, "2 miles ahead." Anticipating their question, Nancy said, "Warnings, such as 'animals on the road' or 'accidents,' would appear as they occurred. So far, we've constructed ten thousand miles of these new composite roads over our old existing highways." That got looks of surprise from the four passengers. They remembered hearing that work had begun building roads like this, but they hadn't realized how much progress had been made.

FINAL CHANCE

Nancy added, "Sadly, however, we don't expect that the animal warnings will be seen in a few years, but that's where the RDs or Revitalization Domes come in."

The car signaled and they exited the highway toward a huge revitalization dome that seemed to house mostly trees. They entered via an airlock and saw a reception center, and behind it, many cabins and a low-profile hotel. In a particularly happy voice, Nancy told them, "Vast areas of wooded and natural habitat have already been domed and many more are planned to ensure that when the environment has healed, these areas can be re-opened to 're-seed' surrounding areas with flora and fauna. Many RDs will contain hotels and zoos to transform these critical zones into destinations for vacationers."

Their avatars took a short loop on one of the paths into the forest which passed by a small zoo containing animals that would likely live there – deer, rabbits, foxes, skunks, etc.

They returned to their car and Nancy explained that there would be two more stops. On their way, they passed through what looked like a wasteland, and their guide, now with a saddened voice, told them, "Outside the domes, almost all of nature will be dead or dying: plants, trees, insects, animals, and the seas and its inhabitants. There isn't much that can be done for the seas, but the faster we can de-pollute the air, the faster they can recover.

"We're now arriving at a manufacturing dome. As I mentioned earlier, all manufacturing will be moved from the city domes."

The dome housed large buildings, none of which had smokestacks or were emitting smoke or steam. Nancy continued, "The larger manufacturing domes may have housing, restaurants, and limited shopping and services for the workers, and will be connected to the city domes by highways or trains. Much of the manufacturing will be done with robots, but a good number of maintenance and other workers will be required. All manufacturing is electrically powered. If anyone is wondering about all the people who will be replaced by robots, rest assured, SHARE will need them all and re-training is already underway."

Nancy announced their last stop, a cattle farm. As they approached, the virtual reality changed to real aerial view footage of what looked like an endless greenhouse. She explained, "This is real footage from a cattle farm in Nebraska. There are over 100,000 head of beef cattle grazing and feeding in the 200,000-acre enclosure. Also, within the structure at one end is a dome with the slaughterhouse, packing facility, and freight docks. At the opposite end is a dome with living quarters for the operations staff. This facility was built two years ago.

"Most of the agricultural/food sites are similar in that they contain growing/rearing, processing, and packaging all in the same dome cluster, making the operations very efficient.

"This is the end of your orientation. I hope you've enjoyed it and gained a new appreciation of SHARE's activities and our immediate future. We're committed to making this work and saving our planet. It's our final chance."

The virtual reality was replaced by ZoomX reality as Tina, asked, "How did you like your tour?"

The group was almost speechless, processing what they had just seen and realizing that it would soon be reality.

***

December 31st, 2052. The first two years of the Fifties had been peppered with fear and uncertainties. COVID-51 reminded everyone that nothing could be taken for granted and there was still a long way to go. A new Democratic government would once again be in control and there had been a huge mind-shift over the past four years regarding the need for doming. This was largely a result of the dramatic increase in asthma and other respiratory illness, eye problems, heatstroke, and cancer. If the increasing number of natural disasters from floods and storms was added to that list, suddenly, domes became a less radical option.

Hundreds of thousands of Americans had been trained or were in training to help dome the U.S. and the world, and many were already actively working in dozens of countries, managing and helping them achieve their plans. Partly as a result of this, the U.S. was in good shape economically, but all eyes remained on the environment.

The world was also moving forward, and a few smaller countries, particularly in Scandinavia, Europe, and Asia, had already domed many of their cities. Massive training programs, led by American, Chinese, or European Union teams, were also making good progress. Those trainees would then become the backbone of the ongoing doming efforts within their respective countries.

Unemployment was significantly down almost everywhere; and since the doming programs were run under government auspices, all wages and purchases were "on the books," meaning they were taxed. Economies were running just like the textbooks said they could when good wages were paid. It all came down to keeping everyone alive to enjoy it.

So far, with one exception, there had been only minor disagreements within this far-flung effort. The problem had been Russia. They had been forced to go it alone because they refused to meet the very aggressive carbon emission requirements. When a good number of the richest men in the world are rich because of oil, they can have a profound influence, especially in oligarchic Russia. Still, they were showing some modest emission control results, but with the rest of the world not buying oil, the oligarchs were upset.

***

Chapter 8 - Happy New Year!

Chestnut Hill, Massachusetts. December 31st, 2052 The Patels and Belikovs, all seven of them, were together to celebrate New Year's Eve and the engagement of Nadya and Jason. Life had been good to them, and the senior Patels and Belikovs were looking forward to slowing down and watching their children flourish. And the "kids" would need to flourish to allow Alek and Vijay to slow down. But right now, it was "all-hands-on-deck." The Dome Project required it.

Vijay would soon turn sixty-eight and he hadn't slowed down yet. Well, maybe his running times had crept up, but he still won and contended in quite a few marathons, although now in the senior division. And he still spent hours every day on the Beli-Tel microchip project, along with Jason, Alek, and Nadya.

Kari was now a member-elect of the Massachusetts' House of Representatives and would take office on the eighth of January.

Jennifer's only 'for sure' plan was working with Sophie to plan Nadya's and Jason's wedding. She was looking forward to that, but still, she wished she could be planning Kari's.

Nadya and Jason were looking forward to their marriage but that was in second place behind the Dome Project. They'd been working on it non-stop, including Christmas Day, to the chagrin of their mothers. Their fathers weren't upset though. They'd been working right alongside them.

***

Vijay was in his home office, contemplating life ... and death. Both his and Jennifer's parents had passed away, and as his children grew up and carved out lives of their own, Vijay had missed them terribly. Their incredibly busy schedules relegated their connections to texts, e-mails, and the very occasional online chats. At least now he had Jason back, and he enjoyed that a lot; and although Kari wouldn't be as accessible, he knew from Jennifer's life as a politician, that she would have more time than when she worked at the law firm. That had been like twenty-four-seven.

As Vijay reflected on his past, he knew he couldn't complain. He and Jennifer had enjoyed an amazing life and their two children were not only exceptional, but were making significant contributions to the world. With both of them around over the Christmas holidays, and the world proving that the opposite of idle hands is a good thing, all was good at the Patel household on the eve of a new year.

***

Edinburg, Pennsylvania. Also gathered together on this New Year's Eve were the same group that had watched the 2046 State of the Union address. They weren't here to party, although a number of them would be toasting their plans throughout the evening, some with vodka.

Since the last time they were all together, Grover Nerdkist II had domed his estate to include his fifteen thousand square foot house; the stables; a garage containing almost fifty, mostly antique, collector cars; and the staff house. As his guests marveled at the dome, Nerdkist joked that by doming everything, he'd saved the cost of a separate air conditioning system for the garage.

One point of irony is that Grover got a substantial government grant to build his dome – including materials, systems, and expertise. SHARE wanted to gain practical experience and Nerdkist's application was approved by the outgoing president in 2050.

The irony was definitely not lost on Georgi Volkov, who burst out laughing. "I like dat. You complain and stir up shit about making people move to domes from comfort of own dome!"

The others joined the laughter because it was true and also because it was a good idea to go along with Georgi.

Now, once again, Nerdkist's guest list included:

The afore-mentioned Georgi Volkov. One of the three richest Russian oilmen, he was often simply known as the owner of a three-hundred-foot yacht, the Poseidon. His father had benefitted greatly from the "privatization" of the Russian state oil business and Volkov used his inherited wealth, connections, and power to assist the Russian leadership in their nefarious acts of aggression against neighboring countries. His income had taken a hit from the move away from oil and he was still bitter at the sanctions imposed by the U.S. on his company, which had cost him over a billion dollars. He was angry, too, at the mostly American-inspired protests against his company's exploration and mining, which was destroying a significant reindeer habitat. Somehow, despite being banned from entering the U.S., Georgi was in Edinburg.

Naresh Argawal. Considered to be one of the richest men in the world, Argawal had combined shrewd business acumen, favors from the Indian government, and a huge inheritance to become a major force in chemicals, pharmaceuticals, and oil. He was educated in the U.S. and understood, better than the Russian sitting next to him, the American mindset. The world's weaning away from fossil fuel was greatly affecting his income and influence. Plus, he was still upset that his company was not selected to make any of the COVID vaccines for the United States.

Prince Ibrahim Al Saud. Prince Ibrahim, known as PIS, was also known for his lavish spending. He'd bought a six-hundred-million-dollar A380 Airbus, a five-hundred-million-dollar chateau in Monaco, and dozens of paintings valued at one million to five-hundred-million dollars each. With no investments other than oil, he was in the same (large) boat as Argawal and Volkov. He was also the recipient of a sanction by the U.S. government and had a few hundred million dollars frozen in the States. He had not been banned from entering the country, however, as a favor to the Saudi family.

Gerald Failwell. Failwell's father had been a legend in the world of Evangelicals. Gerald claimed to represent them, too. He also represented most things that weren't Christian, according to the numerous lawsuits and criminal charges against him. Spurning scientific advice during one of the pandemics, he re-opened his university and churches with devastating effect. His sexual scandals bothered some of his Christian followers in his mainstream churches, but his growing number of Patriot Churches weren't fazed. They liked the church aspect for its tax-exempt status and its focus on bigotry and conspiracies. He was removed from the umbrella organization from time to time, following his more lurid incidents, but that was just for show.

Karen Carli (KC) Rover. Rover was the only woman in the group, and, like black widow spiders, she epitomized the most dangerous side of her species. She was also the daughter of Carlton Rover, the former political operative who was instrumental in changing – or, as some would say, subverting – the arc of the Republican Party. She had tried and failed to capitalize on her father's name – never even considering what a bad idea that was – to break into politics. For some reason, however, she remained a power broker, and she was here to help restore some power to the brokers.

Semper Creud. The only child, fortunately, of the late senator from Florida, the young Creud was smart enough to know that he'd never be elected in Florida by an electorate that had become marginally smart enough to not vote for him. So, he moved to Alabama and was now the governor. He had dreams of becoming president, and most would say, "Dream on." Creud was there because … he'd been invited.

Grover Nerdkist II, the host. As indicated by the "II," Nerdkist was the namesake of his father, Grover Nerdkist, widely blamed – or credited – for putting his political party on a self-destructive path. Nerdkist and Rover shared that common heritage, and they both pursued the same goals with equal zeal, if not success. Both the junior Rover and Nerdkist had inherited sizeable fortunes from parents who didn't do anything productive except influence huge numbers of people to follow a particular path. Oh, and support the NRA.

What this gang of seven shared was the goal of regaining power to benefit themselves. They were all extremely wealthy, except for Creud, who hadn't figured out how to milk the system. They also shared the belief that the root cause of all their problems was the U.S. political system and, specifically, those people currently in power.

Before the discussion even began, PIS complained loudly and angrily, pointing unnecessarily at the only woman in the room. "Why is this woman not wearing something over her head?"

Failwell quickly came to her defense. "She's not that bad looking and she has a great body."

PIS responded even more forcefully, "Yes, her arms and legs are uncovered, too!"

Georgi growled, "Shut up, PIS. Her father was a genius and maybe she can help you and your fellow desert rats from starving to death."

Pouting, PIS said, "Well, I'm not staying then."

Georgi smiled menacingly, "Good, go eat sand."

Knowing that PIS was bluffing, Nerdkist decided to regain control. "Okay, everyone. Thanks for coming. Let's get started."

For the most part, these were not stupid people, and they knew that their quest would not be easy or quick. Nerdkist began, "Unfortunately our efforts over the past six years, despite some successes, have not proved sustainable. We may need to call on Georgi's connections again and start to consider Naresh's ideas more closely. I suggest that we continue, but substantially escalate our energy disruption program. I also have a strong belief that we need to develop a program that will keep us in power the next time we win, and that won't be for another four years."

Both Rover and Nerdkist knew the political landscape better than the others and doubted that the current Administration could be defeated in their second term bid, given the unfortunate effects of climate change.

Creud disagreed. "My margin of victory was the widest in Alabama history."

FINAL CHANCE

KC replied, "With respect, Sem, you won by a big margin because Alabama is extremely conservative, and you ran unopposed."

Volkov couldn't resist. "Yah, and you still only vin sixty percent of vote." He finished with an evil smile that withered Sem, shutting him up for the moment.

Grover gently explained. "We need to begin to educate people and change the message. And that takes time. My dad always said that you can't change a person's mind after they're twenty-one. Look at all the Millennials that flooded the electorate in the twenties. We need to start working on the 'Gen A's,' 'Gen Demic's' and the 'Domers'."

The oilmen had patience. With plenty of money and enough power from it, they could afford to wait it out, to an extent. Besides, all of them, except PIS, had diversified into financial services and other industries.

Volkov spoke. "Ve can vait for long term solution but ve need some relief soon. Oil don't spoil, but it take money to get and more to store it. Der's only so much plastic to make. And now, even roads not made vid asphalt.

"Ven your – " he paused, smiling and gesturing with his hands to include himself and the Americans – "our favorite president vus killed along vit da vimpy vice president, vaut job the voman dat become president had?"

Nerdkist had been trying to follow Georgi's unique take on English and replied, "That was the Speaker of the House."

Volkov asked, "So now if new president killed ... like black lady president?"

Nerdkist sadly laughed, "About a hundred people would have to die before we could take over."

That silenced the group, and they began discussing longer-term and less dramatic solutions. Grover put forth an idea that various oil interests in the U.S. could compete with SHARE for key managers, putting pressure on their doming plans.

Creud asked what these managers would do and Volkov said, "Send dem to Russia. I find verk for dem."

Nerdkist added that he had a number of friends who would also hire some.

Even if the Russian, Indian, and Saudi had a hard time fully understanding the details of all that was discussed, they did understand that their money would be needed.

Failwell had been thinking about Nerdkist's remark about not being able to change people's minds after twenty-one. "I'm not a politician and I'm not as rich as some of you, but I have an idea. I'd like to expand my educational reach and double, maybe triple, the number of private Patriot high schools so we can begin to guide our kids before it's too late. At the moment almost ten million students are attending my Christian and Patriot schools. With twenty million students, we can return our party to its winning ways. I also believe it can be profitable, but initially, it will take investment for land and buildings. We can start straight away with land that my brother and I own. We should be able to directly influence millions of kids a year and get them to influence others."

Rover weighed in. "I like that, Gerry. It will take time and money but let me know how we can help."

Failwell knew how she could help him, and it wasn't with his plan. The mere fact that she said something positive gave him hope, but just as he was about to move in, she changed the subject and shifted away from his idea, moving him to the sidelines … again.

"Presidents don't often come out of the blue. They enter the stage, sometimes in a modest way, such as giving a speech at a convention, or they become the champion of a high-profile cause. They become someone that their party will be watching and grooming, and we need to identify these people, too, and stop them. We can do it slowly and well in advance, gathering pictures, video clips, articles – even fabricating the facts and narratives so that when they're ready to ascend, we're ready to stop them."

Nerdkist might have kissed her if he hadn't been afraid of getting too close. He gushed. "I love it! They are also less protected earlier in their careers."

"Less protected" brought on one of Georgi's evil smiles, "But if ve can't stop dem before, ve know ve can do it after."

The ideas and discussion continued as the clock ticked toward 2053. Toasts and commitments were made. Volkov downed his vodkas, Argawal was drinking thirty-year whiskey, Rover and Nerdkist sipped their vintage champagne, while Creud chugged his beers. The Prince and Failwell, a recovered alcoholic, drank their fruit juices and stared at Rover for two entirely different reasons. Failwell was watching her to see if there was an opportunity to get her into bed, while the Prince was staring with disgust at her hair, arms, and legs.

Grover Nerdkist II was in good spirits as he raised his glass of champagne and exclaimed, "Happy New Year!"

***

Chapter 9 - The Inauguration - 2053

Washington, D.C., January 17th, 2053. The Beli-Tel team was ushered into a larger room at the same non-descript building in downtown D.C. There were the four chairs reserved for them as well as another fifteen set up around a large U-shaped group of draped tables. A man of about thirty approached and introduced himself as Tom Foster, the president-elect's chief of staff. He welcomed them and handed them lists of the attendees, listing the president-elect, vice-president-elect, the presumptive secretaries of SHARE, Health and Human Services, Homeland Security, and Housing and Urban Development, along with the CEO of SHARE, and several senior project managers from SHARE. He explained the agenda of the session, gulped, smiled, and said, "So, no pressure."

Including Foster, there were five nervous laughs and then the attendees started to arrive. Vijay and Alek had met some pretty important people, but not this important or this many, and they hoped that the 'kids' would be okay. They needn't have worried. Nadya and Jason confidently led the charge, meeting and greeting the new team as they arrived (who, truth be told, were more nervous than Nadya and Jason). This was "Day One-minus four" for them.

After the formal introductions, the president-elect, Rachel Metcalf, made sure that everyone was on the same page regarding the threat that the COVID viruses brought to dome environments and the objective that Beli-Tel had been charged with achieving. She briefly explained the success of the VT4 in identifying earlier COVID carriers, before turning the floor over to Vijay.

Vijay thanked the president-elect and her team and explained that they would present their work in two parts: the first would define what they would be looking for; the second, how they would find it and use it.

He briefly explained the similarities and differences between the past COVID strains, using a series of visuals on the large flat screen. He finished with a composite visual showing all the strains super-imposed on each other. It clearly showed how each strain mutated or morphed.

Vijay introduced Jason. "I'll turn the presentation over to Jason, my son, who is an excellent example of how something can morph into something much better."

The group laughed and Jason blushed. "Thanks, 'Dad'!" And they all chuckled.

Jason pointed out with a laser pointer how the strains mutated, and he explained that it wasn't sufficient to simply look for past strains; it was necessary to look for probable and possible mutations. He clicked on another slide showing additional areas that represented projected changes, based on percentage changes from the past.

He finished by explaining that they had added other non-COVID, but equally dangerous, diseases in their identification, such as polio, TB, hepatitis, HIV/Aids, Ebola, etc.

Jason handed over the presentation to Alek, who signaled that the cards he'd brought along be handed out to everyone.

Alek waited until everyone had a card and explained, "Attached to the card you're holding is an actual microchip that stores all the information printed on the card. Every field can be visible or suppressed for reading by a programmable reader. So, for example, my first name may be visible, or my first and last name, or my credit card number, phone number, etc. The capacity of the chip is almost infinite. The user decides what information to share, although if they decline information, they decline services. So, if I want to use my credit card information stored on the chip at restaurants, I authorize that, and a charge is made simply by okaying the amount, shown on a handheld device. But if I haven't authorized my card to be used, I must use my physical credit card.

"Equally, if I want to enter the Washington, D. C. Dome complex and I have declined some required information, I cannot enter without escalated human handling.

"Those are some simple examples of providing information, which our proposed chip will do. Now I'd like to introduce my daughter, Nadya, to explain the real reason we're here today."

Nadya pulled up Jason's last slide and said, "This is what we're looking for and the microchip has sensors that will help us do that."

She switched to a video of a person's head showing a pair of surgically gloved hands and a syringe-type instrument inserting a chip into the skin, just below and behind the ear. "This is an actual insertion, two minutes after applying a topical de-sensitizing liquid." What she didn't explain was that this a new chip being added to her father's head.

Nadya then went on to show how chip readers would download the data from the chip, including the required identification details and the medical parameters, giving an 'OK,' 'enhanced interview,' or even a 'high-alert' caution.

"This will help stop the importation of diseases into a dome. But if an infectious disease is present within the dome – possibly missed at the entry point or one that develops within the dome – the chip will send out alerts and identify every other chip it comes into proscribed proximities with. Alerts can then be automatically sent to each potential contact as well as health officials. Contact tracing on steroids."

She finished with, "We've been talking with SHARE and we can safely say that we will have enough chips and readers available two years before the first dome is completed. I thank you and now we'll turn it over to all of you for questions."

The presentation had lasted an hour. The questions, two hours, and it might have been longer, but everyone was getting hungry.

One of the questions posed to the presumptive Secretary of HHS was the potential problem of acceptance of the chip. The response was that people who refuse to get chipped will need to go through manual entry checks getting into a dome and at every business or building within the dome. She added, "We think they'll soon tire of that."

Everyone in the room was enthusiastic and the president-elect thanked them sincerely for their work. She told them that she and her team had already agreed to move forward if there weren't any major disagreements, so in the interest of time, consider it done; they would have paperwork completed within a week. She concluded, "Just because we're the federal government, doesn't mean we can't act quickly. I probably won't see you at the inaugural next week, but hopefully, I will at the ground-breaking."

And that was it. A two-plus billion-dollar contract including the chip readers and scanners!

***

Their deal called for a big celebration and, on Vijay's suggestion, they had made reservations to have dinner at RASA that evening, joined by Jennifer and Sophie. As good a chef as Vijay was, the others were confident that if he wanted to go to an Indian restaurant, it must be really good. First, however, Vijay and Jennifer wanted to walk a bit, so they set out ahead of the others, idly walking in the general direction of RASA.

Vijay had already discussed the new contract a bit with Jennifer, mentioning that he and the team would need to be in D.C. fairly often. This sparked a thought in Jennifer's mind. Perhaps, for everyone's comfort during their frequent trips to D.C., as well as for an investment. they should look at properties.

That's what she told everyone, but underlying reason was that she was convinced that Kari had a great career in politics. She'd seen what it takes to be good in the role and Kari had all of it, and a lot more. She was also on the right path. Both the Kennedys and Dukakis had served in the Brookline Town Meeting, and now she was in the Massachusetts House. Kari's next job would be in D.C.

As they ambled along, they passed a real estate office and Jennifer shared her idea – the comfort and investment part.

Vijay liked it and flashed his great grin. "That's a great idea! And D.C. will always be a good investment."

They continued on their way to dinner – which everyone loved – and six months later, Jennifer found and purchased a house on Voltas Place in Georgetown.

***

FINAL CHANCE

The Inauguration. January 21st, 2053. The inauguration was scheduled for the twenty-first, as January 20th was Martin Luther King Day. An estimated two million-plus people attended the inauguration of president-elect Rachel Metcalf and over fifty million watched on their TV or device screens, despite an almost thirty-minute power-outage blackout that affected dozens of larger cities. The large audiences were attributed, in part, because of the president herself – a single, mixed race, gay woman; and partly for the same reason that people had been drawn to high-wire acts at circuses. Something unplanned might happen.

Given the number of military personnel at the event, the civilian attendees were not the only ones who thought of that possibility. In addition, if one looked closely, there were many portable radar devices and other non-identifiable, but military-looking machines on the far peripheries of the event. There was a second ring in place another mile out. These were part of an advanced laser weapon system that could identify and destroy unwelcome UAVs.

Even less obvious to most attendees was a fleet of ten 'Drone Hunters' hovering silently around the perimeter of the Capitol and National Mall. They formed the other part of the laser weapon system. If a drone or manned aircraft entered the area, lasers could destroy it, or a 'Hunter' could catch it and carry it away. The lesson of 2046 had been heeded.

***

Mr. and Mrs. Vijay Patel, Mr. and Mrs. Alek Belikov, and the soon-to-be, Mr. and Mrs. Belikov-Patel stood in a special section, on the West Lawn of the U.S. Capitol, close to where the president-elect would become the president. It was a sunny, but very cold day, and it crossed the minds of every one of the three couples that this would probably be the last cold, undomed Inauguration.

The ceremony was inspiring, conjuring up the ideals of the country and the hopes of billions of people throughout the world, despite the sizable number of protestors on the fringe of the massive crowd. Oblivious to the protestors, Vijay was particularly moved. He briefly thought back to his childhood in a Mumbai slum, his meeting with the new American president, and his daughter as a promising member of the government. He blamed the tears in his eyes on the cold weather. And then it was over.

***

Washington, D.C. Dome Ground-Breaking. Like the New York model, the D.C. Dome would be a series of interconnecting domes and corridors. The largest dome and the first to be built would include the White House and Capitol Buildings. A major structural component would be built in the area of F Street and 20th Street NW, and that is where the ground-breaking would be celebrated. It is also where many hundreds, possibly thousands, of protestors had assembled.

They were a varied lot, and many carried signs that shouted their opposition to control, conformance, taking cars away, taking property away, losing rights, right to life, vaccinations, and government in general. There were also a lot of police and the same type of military vehicles and machines that had been at the Inauguration. So far, all was peaceful, if a bit noisy. Jason noticed, with a small measure of relief, that there were no anti-chip signs … yet.

The Belikovs and Patels had been given priority access so they had a good view of the "staged" set-up for the president and other officials, including an awful lot of beautiful new ceremonial shovels. There were also some very clean bulldozers and giant earth-moving equipment.

***

FINAL CHANCE

Farragut Square, Washington, D.C. Just a few miles away, an unmarked white van, similar to hundreds of identical vehicles in the District, pulled to the curb on 17th and K streets. Two men in blue boiler suits and baseball caps jumped out and carried a small black object behind some bushes. They quickly returned to the van and sped away. That would all be captured on surveillance cameras, but it would be of little help.

Less than a minute later, the small black object, which was now identifiable as a drone, slowly ascended, and headed southwest.

***

Back at the Dome Ground-Breaking, the chants from the protestors dramatically rose in volume, signaling the arrival of the president. About six big SUVs drove through the cordoned area, lined with police and Secret Service agents, into another large cordoned-off area containing the earthmoving equipment. The SUVs stopped, but no one emerged.

From just beyond the view of the gathering, hidden by buildings, four helicopters slowly appeared, and then, what appeared to be a very large bird came streaking into view toward another smaller, black, birdlike object. It was difficult to see from the ground, and it all happened very quickly, but a drone hunter had ensnared the black drone launched from Farragut Square in netting and whisked it away toward the Potomac. A long fifteen minutes later, President Rachel Metcalf emerged from one of the SUVs along with five other people from the other SUVs. They were greeted with loud cheers, that partially drowned out the protestors, at least briefly.

At the ground-breaking site, the small group donned hard hats and were handed the gleaming shovels that would grace a few important rooms in the years to come. And then, after the requisite speeches, they were in their SUVs departing the area.

The news that evening would lead off with its main story about a foiled assassination. No other details were known or, at least, offered, except for the speeches. A repeat of the 2046 assassination had been averted. But they were still completely in the dark over who was behind it and if they were the same people from 2046.

***

Chapter 10 – Dates & States

Cambridge, Massachusetts. The four Beli-Tel principals were in their new Cambridge offices and Jason commented, "It was only last week that we were in D.C., rubbing shoulders with the president and her team, but it seems like ages ago."

Alek replied, "Yes, and that was the fun part of this job. Now, reality meets the road."

Vijay chimed in. "Let's keep the pressure on ourselves so we can celebrate the wedding. March fourteenth, right?"

"It's the fifteenth, Dad," corrected Jason.

Alek joked, "Your father is getting old, Jason. At least he was close!"

They laughed.

Nadya said, "The White House has kept their promise to respond quickly. Here is their list of changes for the chip content. Nothing major," as she passed out copies.

They reviewed the revisions and Jason commented, "They like the general identification profile – with just a few minor adjustments – and they accepted our disease identification parameters."

Vijay interjected, "I'm relieved about that. Anything more restrictive and we would risk missing new diseases, but any less restrictive and we'd be catching too many people to assess. So now our biggest challenge is designing the software that will read the chips, and get clarity and sign-offs for what data will be required and which agencies, establishments, and entities get what data. Simply entering a dome shouldn't flash the user's credit cards or other sensitive information. And getting a haircut doesn't require a driver's license or Social Security card. Who's your contact for that, Nadya?"

"Janet Hoffman, from the Attorney General's office. They didn't want the FBI involved with sensitive data."

Vijay looked at Alek and blushed, as he recalled his night in jail for sharing information with the FBI. He said, "Good idea," getting a laugh from everyone.

Alek added, "Jason and Nadya have recruited a few hotshot programmers who can help get the framework written. So as soon as we get the details from Janet, we can populate the software detail. Are we set with the chip reading equipment?"

Jason replied, "We are. Based on the dome building schedule and roll-out, ABM Corp has confirmed their ability to meet it."

They finished discussing the remaining chip issues and Nadya asked, "I appreciate that it's only been about two weeks since we agreed on the program, but has anyone heard about how they are going to sell it?"

Vijay told them that Kari had mentioned to Jennifer that there would be a fierce battle, but that the Party had control of the House and Senate, so they were going to do it. The dome won't be finished for quite some time, and they will quietly use incentives and a PR campaign to build awareness, understanding, and trust.

Jason commented on the anti-chip efforts that he'd seen and heard. "There's a lot of pushback and scaremongering going on about chips. Privacy issues and even cancer."

Alek scoffed, "Privacy concerns are real, but I've always felt that if you have nothing to hide, who cares who sees it, as long as it doesn't compromise your finances. As for cancer, that's just fear-mongering. Do you know where this coming from?"

Jason replied, "Kari said it was coming from the ultra-conservative wing of the Republicans. There was a guy and a woman who were quoted. I can't remember their names. … Wait, the guy was named after the Sesame Street puppet, Grover." He smiled as childhood memories flooded in. "Can't remember his last name, though."

And then he remembered the woman's first name. "The woman's name was Karen." He laughed about his memory recall and thought to himself about reading the article. "I remembered Grover because I liked him, and then Karen because it's often derogatory."

***

Boston, Massachusetts. First-year House Representative Karima Patel was loving her new role in the Massachusetts State House and she had quickly begun to make a name for herself. Energetic and curious, Kari served on four committees, including Global Warming, Technology, and Intergovernmental Affairs, Healthcare, and Education. She was also one of the youngest members in the House, but she knew how to handle herself around people who had been "in the game" for a while. She could thank her parents for that, and she could thank her mom for the very quick acceptance extended to her. Jennifer was well respected by most of the members.

Despite the workload and committee meetings, she also seemed to find time for a social life, particularly one involving Laurence Donald, the Member from the twentieth district in Middlesex.

Laurence had narrowly escaped losing his seat to a member of Kari's party, a fate that had affected five other incumbents. That hadn't stopped him from admiring the freshman representative who was a fellow member on "TIG," the Technology and Intergovernmental Affairs committee. After a typical late-night committee meeting focused on doming the cities and towns of the state, Laurence asked her if she'd like to have a quick drink.

Kari looked at the tall and quite handsome committee colleague and accepted. She knew he was from the "other side," but she had an open mind and was pretty independent; besides, maybe she could change him.

They stopped at an up-market bar frequented by legislators, but they weren't hiding anything, so it didn't matter who saw them.

Their conversation was casual, and Laurence congratulated her on her election, dropping a compliment that she had some big shoes to fill. He had known and worked with Jennifer.

Kari congratulated him on his victory, magnifying the feat, given what had happened to a number of his party colleagues. She asked how long he'd been in the House and his answer surprised her.

FINAL CHANCE

"This is my fifth term," he said.

Kari replied, only half-jokingly, "Did you run right after school?" She assumed he'd gone to college, but her question could have meant high school. He looked very young.

Laurence laughed. "You're not far off. I graduated from high school at seventeen, got my bachelor's at twenty, and a law degree at twenty-three. Spent a year and a half in my father's law firm and stood for election."

Kari then realized who she was talking with. Donald, Thomas, and Franklin, LLC was a heavy-hitting law firm in Cambridge. They were known as a conservative ally and much of their practice was well-paid party work.

Laurence asked about her interest in "TIG" and Kari explained, "My father and brother are involved with dome technology, so I thought this would be a good idea to get involved from another angle."

Laurence asked specifics and she explained that she didn't know the details, only that they were involved in some type of electronic access system.

"Of course. Your father invented the ..." – he started to say death watch but caught himself – "watch that predicted dying and also recognized COVID symptoms. Duh! Not sure how I'd forgotten that, given that you're Jennifer Patel's daughter."

He shook his head and they both laughed at his mental lapse. Laurence realized that this young woman was mesmerizing and that he'd found himself losing concentration.

They spent the next hour talking about domes and it was clear that they had opposing views on how to handle the costs and loss of freedoms. Still, it was a pleasant and constructive conversation and they both enjoyed it. And Kari made a mental note to find out more about the Beli-Tel dome project.

After a while, Kari said that she needed to get home and Laurence asked her if she'd like to have dinner one night. She said that she would and explained that a couple of planned social events and the other three committee meetings would put a firm date back at least ten days.

Laurence accepted a date twelve days out, February twenty-second, and waited with her until her Uber arrived.

Sitting quietly and alone in a dark corner of the bar, Senator Joseph Fitzhugh watched the young couple leave and he sent a text.

***

Edinburg, Pennsylvania. Grover Nerdkist read the text and smiled.

***

The State of Washington D.C. President Rachel Metcalf announced that she had just signed the Congressional bill making the District of Columbia the fifty-first state. It would be called "The State of Washington D.C." That would add two Senate seats and an amendment to the 1941 Apportionment Act would allow an additional seat in the House.

The president also had some less jubilant news. "Researchers from the University of Edinburgh have confirmed that their prediction of twenty years ago has materialized and that the warmer average temperatures are triggering the release of an increasing amount of planet-warming carbon dioxide from the soil. If we cannot reduce our carbon footprint quickly, the amount of additional carbon emission released would be like adding a new country the size of the United States to the world.

"I have asked SHARE to come up with an accelerated doming plan as quickly as possible, and I've asked the relevant committees in both the House and Senate to coordinate an action plan."

***

Chapter 11 - Fast Track

SHARE Headquarters, Pasadena, California. Aziz Khan shared the president's concern about the threat posed by additional carbon emissions from the soil, especially from the once-frozen Arctic tundra, Antarctica, and Siberia, but he didn't see how it was possible to meet her proposed timeframe for dome completion. He'd had doubts about meeting the original plan dates, largely because of the significant delays caused by protestors and the shortage of available workers.

Aziz almost thought it was funny that he was struggling to find workers at good pay rates while thousands of people had nothing better to do than protest ... for free. He was puzzled, too, that the oil and gas industry seemed to be competing aggressively for the type of project managers he desperately needed, causing delays and driving up his salary and overtime costs.

SHARE currently had over a hundred thousand employees and direct contractors, plus close to a million more through partnered construction and technology companies.

One of his senior project managers, Eddie Wong, who was coordinating training for SHARE's Chinese partner, had just called, and his news was much better than Aziz could have hoped for.

FINAL CHANCE

Wong had told him that the Chinese could supply almost five-hundred-thousand more skilled laborers to replace internationally-based U.S. workers, who would return home to fill the U.S. vacancies. Aziz smiled as he realized that this Chinese largesse would also help China maintain and grow its influence in global markets. But he needed people now to meet the president's schedule.

His cell phone chirped with a VIP tone. It was the Secretary for SHARE, Emma Steadman. A highly respected multi-specialist engineer, Steadman had been recruited to conceive, plan, and execute the most ambitious infrastructure project ever undertaken. She was indefatigable, collaborative, and possessed an ability to see both the big picture and little details at the same time. And as smart and competent as Aziz was, he was in awe of her abilities as well as her calm, almost relaxed disposition.

Steadman was calling to get an update on the manpower constraint and to impart some news.

Aziz relayed the information he'd just received about China's willingness to help.

Aziz could almost see Steadman's smile as she quickly arrived at the same thought he'd had. "What won't they do to peddle their influence?"

And then she quickly added, "But how did they find a half-million spare workers?"

Aziz explained the other news from Eddie Wong. "The Chinese just announced that they would build fewer domes than anticipated, strongly encouraging people to migrate to the major cities."

"But we're doing that, too."

Aziz chuckled, "Their definition of 'strongly encouraging' is different than ours. They also have different views about protesting."

Steadman replied, "That was the other thing I wanted to talk about. It appears that the protests are being organized by Conservative operatives. That's not illegal but the Attorney General wants to monitor the protests in case they develop into more serious actions. I want you to broaden our surveillance camera coverage and alert all your project managers to report any situations that even get close to out of control."

***

Cambridge, Massachusetts. Kari suggested meeting Laurence at Oleana, a smart neighborhood Turkish/ Mediterranean restaurant. She arrived first and the staff greeted her warmly, suggesting a table on their small patio. The weather was unseasonably warm and there were heaters, so she opted for that. A few minutes later, Laurence arrived, escorted by the restaurant owner. She could tell they knew each other well.

Laurence apologized for being late and complimented her choice of tables, adding, "It's even more charming in the spring and summer with leaves on the trees.

They hadn't seen each other since the last TIG committee meeting, so they warmed up with current events, 'what have you been doing lately' banter, and several small hot meze plates. Kari selected a couple of vegetarian ones and Laurence chose one with quail and one with fish.

FINAL CHANCE

Laurence had done his research and asked, "How are your brother's wedding plans going? Will they have time to get away or will the dome project keep them close to home?"

Kari had spoken with Jason about the project after her last conversation with Laurence, so she would be more knowledgeable. "The wedding plans are well under control, thanks to my mother and Jason's fiancé's mother. The future bride and groom will just have to show up, and at the moment it's even money that they will."

"Or even money that they won't?" retorted Laurence.

Kari laughed. "They're making good progress on their work, even if the overall dome project has some hiccups."

"By hiccups, are you referring to the chipping protests?"

"Yes. The Beli-Tel part of the project just needs to be ready for the first dome. It's already being trialed at the agricultural zones and there hasn't been much said about it. Workers in various industries have been chipped for some time so it really isn't news."

Laurence retorted, "The chips used in tech and finance are pretty benign compared with the new chips, from what I understand. Plus workers in agriculture are less likely to push back."

Kari replied, smiling, "Actually there was some pushback and fortunately, there're no viruses out there right now, so for the moment, a chip is just a chip."

"So, the chips function as ID and a biological virus checker?"

Kari laughed and said, "That's the plan, and they'd like it to replace cell phones, too," and then she changed the subject.

"I'm guessing that you might have some misgivings about the Chinese assistance that was just announced?"

"Good guess. We continue to give the Chinese more ways to dominate us. And I don't buy that tired line that they can't find workers."

"Why is that a line? What would SHARE gain by lying about that? We do have pretty full employment at the moment."

Laurence smiled but a shadow across his face prevented Kari from deciphering whether it was a warm or condescending smile. It was his turn to change the subject and his words and tone were warm, as he asked, "How long have you known your brother's fiancé?"

"I was three when both Nadya and Jason were born. My parents and Nadya's parents are good friends so we saw each other a lot until our teen years."

"Like that time when kids don't want to be seen with their parents?" Laurence quipped.

Kari laughed, "Something like that."

"So, did they have a crush on each other the whole time?"

Kari replied, "They did have a crush when they were younger but drifted apart as we got older. Then years later, they ran into each other again and it all re-kindled."

Laurence asked, "Who were your big crushes?"

Kari blushed but flatly stated, "I've never had one. I was a geek, interested in science and the law. I preferred working with my father on experiments to going out with boys. That changed over time, but I'm always so busy. No time for crushes."

FINAL CHANCE

"Are you seeing anyone right now?"

Kari deadpanned, "As a matter of fact, I am."

Laurence missed her irony, "Is it serious?"

Kari was having fun. "Oh, it's still pretty early. And from a legal perspective, the jury's still out."

Realizing that Kari had been teasing him, Laurence blushed. "Well, based on the numbness of the guy you're currently seeing, the jury may be out for some time."

They both laughed and Laurence took her hand. "When can I see you again?"

Kari decided, "How'd you like to be a 'plus-one' at the wedding on March fifteenth?"

"I'd love to, but that's three weeks from now!"

Kari teased, "I'll see you at TIG next week, and perhaps we can have a drink afterward."

Laurence teased back, "I see you haven't completely bought into your party's fondness for fast-tracking."

They left the restaurant as Kari's Uber arrived and Kari accepted Laurence's kiss, giving her something to think about during her ride home. She arrived home before arriving on a verdict.

***

Chapter 12 – Wedding Derailing?

Monday, March 10, 2053. There wasn't a newspaper or news station that didn't carry the story that the nation woke up to: Massive strikes had shut down over fifty agricultural domes producing vegetables, poultry, and beef. By 9:00 AM in all time zones, shelves of meat and frozen vegetables had been stripped bare in every store across the country. And as more "agri-domes" were shut down, the situation would get even worse.

The cause of the strike, as reported by union officials, related to the microchips that the workers had been forced to accept as a condition of employment. Many of the workers didn't like the idea but they wanted and needed the work. They'd been told that the chips were benign and carried information that was safe and secure. That was true as was the statement that chipping was a common practice amongst highly paid financial and tech company employees.

But then, a large number of identity thefts occurred involving the newly chipped workers. Their bank accounts had been cleaned out and their credit cards maxed out. There were even rumors about the chips causing cancer, but those reports were unconfirmed.

A spokesperson from SHARE advised that throughout all the testing, the integrity of the data held on the chips had withstood rigorous hack tests. They were actively investigating the problem.

FINAL CHANCE

The following day, the shelf stripping continued and almost twenty trucks carrying meat and vegetables had been attacked and their contents were stolen. Two truckers were shot.

***

Beli-Tel offices, Cambridge, Massachusetts. Nadya and Jason had seen the news flash very late on Sunday. It was too late to call Alek and Vijay, but they left messages to check out the news and that they would be in very early.

They arrived at their offices before 5:00 AM, wide awake and needing to get better information than simply what they'd heard on the news. It was just after 2:00 AM in California when their phone rang. It was Jeff Hepple, their main contact at SHARE. He didn't have a lot of details, but he told them that the thefts targeted about fifty people at twelve 'agri-zones.'

Nadya asked, "How many agriculture zones are there, and how many have been chipped?"

Jeff clicked some keys and said, "One-hundred-fifty-one zones and ninety-seven of them chipped."

Jason asked what details of the thefts were available and Jeff advised that there were twelve zones where the data breaches had occurred. No other information was available yet, but he'd send the locations of the twelve affected sites immediately and any other information as received.

Jason and Nadya had just begun verbalizing their thoughts about what could have happened when first Vijay and then Alek rushed in.

Jason began to tell them about their conversation with Hepple when Nadya interrupted. "Jeff's list just came through. I'll print out copies."

They all looked at the shortlist of twelve 'ag zones' that had been hit with identity theft and nothing jumped out to help their thinking. The zones encompassed beef, corn, onions, potatoes, poultry, and soybeans across nine states.

Alek appeared to be the most upset. "It's impossible!" Speaking to Nadya and Jason he asked, "Have you looked at the database?"

Jason replied, "Not yet. Jeff didn't have any details of the people affected."

Alek clarified, "No, I want to see if there's anything structural in the database that would have made it vulnerable since we handed it off. We do have access, don't we?"

Nadya had begun clicking keys and a few seconds later she said, "Yes. I'm in."

Alek wheeled his chair over and Nadya moved out of his way.

Vijay asked, "Are you checking the access files?"

Alek mumbled, "Yes. I need to identify and validate the access types and filter them out. A breach could have occurred anytime between yesterday and two weeks ago."

The office phone rang, and it was the FBI. They were sending someone out to gather data.

While Alek clicked away, the others brainstormed, coming up with a sizeable list of questions including who the fifty people were, when the breach could have happened, and how did it play out? Did it all happen at once? What was the timing and how did the breach discoveries morph into the theory that it was chip-related?

FINAL CHANCE

Nadya and Jason had another question that was only asked of each other and only by their eyes – will this affect the wedding?

Alek continued to verify approved accesses and then filter out others of the same type. With over eight thousand people chipped, their comings and goings along with various machine and computer accesses numbered in the millions. His quest was interrupted by the arrival of the FBI.

Agents Madison Porter and Bonnie Sloane seemed too young to Vijay and Alek, but they were immediately identified by Nadya and Jason as fellow "Gen Alphas." The agents were from the cyber-crime division and they had some questions but also some additional information.

Alek asked to more closely inspect their identification. He then asked for their business cards and who they reported to. Nadya and Jason were still staring at him as he excused himself to another office and shut the door. They looked at Vijay who simply smiled.

Agent Sloane explained that they had just received a list of the people whose accounts had been hacked and they had been authorized to share it with Beli-Tel to understand what happened. First and foremost, however, they wanted to determine if the hack could have been initiated through Beli-Tel's staff or systems.

Nadya and Jason were a little offended, but Alek and Vijay understood the logic of looking at all possibilities. All four of them, plus their staff, had been vetted by the FBI as a routine procedure to proceed with their part of the program. Alek returned, and he explained that only the four of them had access to the database and that he had been working on verifying and eliminating all authorized accesses.

Agent Porter replied that they had already vetted the accesses and that all were authorized. She asked if Beli-Tel held or had access to any information that included the personal details of the people who had been hacked.

Vijay answered. "None. We only worked on developing the system architecture and until today, we've never had access nor cause to even look at the live database."

Nadya asked a question they'd discussed earlier about who the fifty people were and how did the whole hack and discovery play out?

Agent Sloane handed Nadya the list of affected people. It listed forty-nine names. She then explained what they knew. The affected employees began to see credit card and bank account issues beginning on Thursday. The zones operate 24/7 so by the weekend it became known what was going on and that the chips were the common thread.

Nadya looked at the list and said, "Based on this, some of the sites have only one or two affected people, and there are hundreds of people working in each of them, in unrelated companies across nine states. How could that develop so quickly into a comprehensive story for a strike?"

She handed the list to Jason, who looked at it quickly and asked, "Are any of these sites connected in any way?"

The agents pulled some additional documents from their cases and looked through them. Agent Sloane said, "Two of them are owned by the same company. The others are not connected."

Nadya interjected, "That was where I was going with my question. How plausible is it that these disconnected instances became a broad movement so quickly?"

Vijay added, "So you're suggesting that this story, along with the complete fairytale about cancer, is the result of a propaganda movement against the doming?"

Her mind swirling, Nadya simply nodded.

Alek took the list of names and began typing away as the others continued the discussion. The agents agreed that it seemed far-fetched that the disparate hacks could coalesce that quickly into strike action.

Jason picked up the list that Jeff had sent, scanned it, and smiled. "I was talking with my sister, Kari, the other day. She's a representative in the Massachusetts House and she told me that the dome strike action was being supported by Conservatives. Look at this list. Twelve sites, all in nine Conservative states. Out of a hundred-fifty-one zones in forty-two states."

Alek almost shouted, "Bingo. Two of these hacked people haven't been chipped yet."

Agent Porter asked, "Are you sure?"

Alek replied, "Well, they may have been physically chipped but since they aren't in the database yet, the chip contains no information."

Agent Porter asked Alek for the names of the two victims and asked, "Are you suggesting that the information for forty-nine employees was provided by their employers for the purpose of hacking and inciting a strike?"

The four Beli-Tel principals looked at each other and Vijay answered for them, "That appears to be the most likely scenario." The others nodded.

The agents collected additional information and printouts, but they left with a very different view about what had happened.

Nadya immediately asked her father why he was being such a jerk about their IDs and who they reported to.

Alek smiled, "Experience."

Vijay was smiling broadly when he said, "Your father didn't ask that once before, a long time ago, and it didn't turn out well; but more importantly, it looks like the wedding is still on!"

***

Chapter 13 – Vows

Holy Epiphany Russian Orthodox Church, Boston, Massachusetts. Nadya Anastasia Belikov and Jason Krishna Patel were married at the picturesque onion-domed church in a simple ceremony, or as simple as a ceremony in a Russian Orthodox church could be. There was a small handful of family and close friends attending. Nadya had first seen the church as a young girl and although she attended infrequently, it fulfilled a lifelong dream.

Afterward, the newlyweds and attendees returned to Jennifer and Vijay's Chestnut Hill home for a reception. Vijay and Jennifer had convinced Sophie and Alek to let them host the reception at their home and Vijay had engaged the owner of his favorite Indian restaurant to cater the event.

Among the guests were Kari and her "plus one," Laurence Donald. Vijay was quite taken with Laurence, possibly on account of his manners and height. Vijay could look him straight in the eye. Jennifer had reservations, although she kept them to herself. She knew Laurence from her time in the Massachusetts House and she had a hard time squaring his arguments and voting record with that of a caring human being.

Kari was pleased that Donald seemed to enjoy the conversation with her brother and Nadya as they discussed the dome development and their involvement. The newlyweds were enjoying it too until Donald asked them if the strikes at the agri-zones had caused them any problems. Nadya answered that there were a couple of small hiccups, but Jason seemed to shift gears. The "a-ha" session with the FBI and the follow-up that pointed the finger to a Conservative plan had prompted him to look up the story about his 'friend' Grover and Karen.

Bordering on belligerent, Jason asked, "Do you know Grover Nerdkist and Karen Rover?"

Laurence dropped his smile and stiffened, either from Jason's attitude shift or the actual question. "I know who they are," he answered a little shakily.

Kari and Nadya looked on curiously as Jason continued. "You can ask them if they enjoyed their game and if they plan on reimbursing the forty-nine people who lost money because of them." Jason turned and walked away, chased by Nadya who hadn't fully realized where Jason was coming from.

Laurence recovered and asked Kari, "What was that about?"

She apologized and fobbed it off to the stress of the event, but she was puzzled, too.

***

Chestnut Hill, Massachusetts. Nadya followed Jason to the bar and confronted him. "What was that about?"

"Remember when I told the story about the Conservatives behind the dome protests?"

"Yes."

"Well, I'm sure that they also caused the strikes, and Grover Nerdkist and Karen Rover seem to be the big wheels orchestrating the diversions. Laurence is the same kind of Conservative. He seemed nice at first but then I remembered something my mom said about him and when he asked about the strikes, it hit a nerve. I wish Kari wouldn't hang out with him."

"I don't think she's that serious. It'll fade."

"Not soon enough for me."

Nadya smiled and said, "We're off to Cabo tomorrow morning so we can forget about everything for a week. And tonight, as your new bride, I'll try to take your mind off of everything, even sooner."

Jason smiled, relaxed, and pulled Nadya to him. "I'm looking forward to both those things so much I've already forgotten about everything else."

Their kiss brought smiles to all the onlookers.

***

Alek came over to refresh his drink and Nadya asked, "Are you going to reveal your advanced FBI interrogation tactics with us?"

Alek tried to escape but Jason joined the fun. "Yeah, com'on, Alek, we're going to Mexico and it might come in handy."

Relenting, Alek told them about a time when FBI agents had come to his office demanding access to his computer. The building security guard had told him that he'd checked their ID, but it turned out they weren't FBI. They hacked the company's database, setting off a chain of events that led to Alek being kidnapped. He drifted off to a lot of detail, including his first head chip, until Sophie rescued them.

"You two have a flight at the crack of dawn so you better get moving."

***

While everyone else was smiling at the newlywed's kiss, Laurence's smile may not have been as sincere, but he took Kari's hands and asked, "Will you have dinner with me tonight? With your schedule, I may not see you again until someone else gets married."

Kari laughed, "Sure. I guess Indian food isn't everyone's favorite. But don't tell my father I said that!"

They had a very nice meal in a small bistro-type restaurant and both, for different reasons, kept politics out of the conversation. Kari felt a little guilty for her brother's borderline rudeness, and Laurence wanted to maintain the romantic glow that he knew often accompanied a wedding. It was still early, so Laurence invited Kari back to his flat to continue their conversation.

Kari liked Laurence and found him interesting, if for no other reason than his different view of life. They were both from wealthy families, although hers was "new money" and she was pretty sure that there was never a time that any Donald was as poor as her father's family.

Laurence's flat was on the twenty-second floor of a stunning new high-rise. It was very tastefully modern with a good number of original paintings. Bright colors jumped up from rugs on polished wood floors and tasteful accents adorned walls, nooks, and shelves. Expensive, comfortable furniture and cushions afforded views through large windows, framing a dusky Boston skyline.

Kari was taken by the look and feel and frankly, she was surprised. She assumed that Laurence, being a Conservative, from old money and a storied Boston-area family, would live in an older building with more conservative décor. She complimented him. "I like your place. It's different than I'd imagined."

"Did you think I was an old fuddy-duddy? Early American furniture with doilies on the arms and backs?"

She laughed when she realized that actually would be closer to her expectations, but she simply said, "No. Not old." And they both laughed.

They talked, listened to soft music, and allowed the romantic glow from the wedding to do its work. It worked on Kari by clearing her brain from her overloaded to-do lists and responsibilities, focusing instead on her emotional and physical needs. And it worked on Laurence ... actually it wasn't necessary for anything other than Kari's presence to motivate his physical needs.

It had been a long time since Kari's last physical encounter, so when Laurence leaned over and kissed her, he released in her a passion that frankly surprised him. That passion was still smoldering in the morning when they awoke, and it wasn't until well into lunchtime that, physically exhausted, sexually satiated, and biologically starving, they went out in search of food.

After satisfying their ravenous appetites, the two lovers took disparate emotional paths. Actually, Kari took a very non-emotional path and re-focused on her professional role and responsibilities for the start of the week. There was also a nagging question that she couldn't quite articulate about the interaction between her brother and Laurence. But that would need to wait until Jason and Nadya returned.

For his part, Laurence was feeling head-over-heels in love, or certainly 'in lust,' and he suggested going back to his place. Kari was slightly impressed with his stamina and desire, but she was now back in control.

Laurence reluctantly accepted her departure and said he would take her home. He was surprised, not that she agreed to the ride, but when she told him that she lived at her parents' house. It gave them something neutral to talk about on the ten-minute Sunday drive. Kari explained that after winning the House seat, she gave up the flat she'd had since university. At school and during her brief law career, she only used it to sleep in and it was pretty basic, at best. She enjoyed her parents and they had always given her plenty of independence. Plus, she wanted to benefit from her mother's time in the House. Still, Laurence couldn't get over a thirty-something (thirty-three, actually) year old woman living at home.

They arrived and she leaned over and gave him a brief kiss as she opened the door and jumped out. Laurence felt as though he'd just had a cold, but dry shower.

***

Jennifer heard Kari come in and greeted her with a knowing smile. Kari wanted to say, "See, I'm straight!" But she just said, "Hi Mom. Great party yesterday! Did Jason and Nadya get off okay?"

Jennifer confirmed their successful departure and Kari said she wanted to change and freshen up. When Kari returned, she made some tea and she and her mom sat on kitchen barstools, an act that had been repeated many times for almost thirty years.

Jennifer asked, "Did you and Laurence have fun?"

Kari smiled and retorted innocently, "At the reception?"

Jennifer laughed and said, "Of course, what did you think I meant?"

Smiling, Kari answered, "Yes we did, and to anticipate your next question, we did afterward as well."

"Good!" Jennifer answered sincerely. But then she turned more serious and asked, "I didn't hear the conversation, but it seemed that Jason was upset about something."

Kari and her mom had no secrets. She explained her concern about the interaction, and while she could sort of understand why Jason would be upset about the false attack on the chip project, she was unclear why he'd go after Laurence over it. The nagging question re-appeared in a recess of her mind, but she ended the conversation by saying, "I think he was just in high emotional gear. He had a lot going on."

Jennifer teased, "Did yesterday give you any ideas?"

Kari teased back, "Mother, please! You're not asking for details of my sex life, are you?"

Vijay entered the kitchen and asked, "What are you two laughing about?"

***

Cambridge, Massachusetts. Back in his apartment, Laurence picked up the call without looking at the caller ID. Grover Nerdkist II's slimy voice came through all too clear. "Well, you really are a lover boy. Hope you enjoyed the evening as much as we enjoyed the pictures."

"What the fuck are you talking about?"

"Oh, I think you can figure it out," taunted the other.

Laurence began screaming profanities and it was almost a minute later that he realized that Nerdkist had disconnected.

***

Chapter 14 – An Interesting Favor

Beli-Tel HQ, Cambridge, Massachusetts. Mr. and Mrs. Belikov-Patel returned from their honeymoon in Baja, refreshed and ready to begin their new life. They were also very tan, especially Jason, despite their religiously applied SPF-90 sunscreen and their heightened pursuit of more indoor pleasures. During their short trip, as they looked out at the sparkling blue ocean and walked along the warmer-than-expected water's edge – they experienced the sad realization that this might be the last time they would ever be able to touch the sea.

Vijay welcomed them back and invited them all to his home on Saturday for a welcome back dinner. Just the Belikovs and Patels. Kari, of course, would also be there. Jason growled, "I hope she's not bringing her 'plus-one' again."

Vijay was surprised. "She isn't, but what's wrong with him?"

Jason just said "Good. We'll be there."

Nadya deflected the tension. "So, what's happening with the chip program, and are there any developments regarding the fake identity theft strikes." The answer to that last question was, "No," so Nadya asked what happened to the forty-nine victims. No one knew.

Alek shrugged and jokingly said that since half the team was gone, they were too busy to ask.

Shaking her head and rolling her eyes at her father's poor joke, Nadya went to her desk and pulled out the card from the FBI Agent, Bonnie Sloane, and called her.

Agent Sloane answered and gave her a high-level update. The FBI had contacted the union heads who had called the strikes, trying to get an understanding of what had prompted the actions at twelve agri-zones. In all cases, the union heads had been tipped off by anonymous sources that a small number of people had been victims of identity theft as a result of the chips, and that these people represented the tip of the iceberg. The victims were real so the story carried credibility, which also helped to reinforce the second unfounded rumor from the anonymous sources – that widespread cancer would result from being chipped.

The tip-off also referenced the other unions that were taking action and so, when the unions approached the companies' management and were summarily rebuffed, the strikes were called.

Not surprisingly, no one at the affected companies admitted to the unauthorized leaking of employee information. They had received statements from all the companies' CEOs, and they were finishing the process of interviewing the companies' HR staff. Jason had suggested that the FBI should talk with Grover Nerdkist II and Karen Rover since they were the ones making the accusations. Sloane confirmed that they had, but Nerdkist and Rover claimed to know nothing about it.

Nadya asked if the victims could recover their losses, as their information had been given out by their companies.

Sloane replied, "The only way they could get their money back, or some of it, was if their companies admitted wrongdoing. The employees were too afraid to ask or push legally, and the companies didn't want to expose themselves."

Nadya lashed out, "So because these people were used by the corporations, they get screwed."

Nadya's retort prompted Agent Sloane to share some additional news and she cautioned Nadya that it was still unconfirmed. An HR employee at one of the sites had been fired and she had called Sloane. The HR staffer was aware that someone had accessed the file of one of the victims at the time of the strike. She didn't know the purpose of the action, but she thought it unusual at the time. Agent Sloane said that's all they knew right now but they'd keep her in the loop.

Angrily, Nadya shared Sloane's recap with Jason, Alek, and Vijay. Both SHARE and Beli-Tel had been shaken by the accusations and, despite their pressing the FBI to pursue the case more aggressively, all they got was a vow that they would.

Alek suggested that everyone just forget it and move on. He stated what they all knew, or felt. "A very comprehensive review of the chip database held at SHARE showed that there hadn't been a breach, pointing the finger at the companies' records as the source. We've done nothing wrong, so let's keep moving forward."

Vijay agreed and opened the door to discuss what Beli-Tel should pursue next. "The chip program is running under SHARE's management now. We have an ongoing commitment to monitor potential infectious disease developments and continually upgrade the chip's content, but that's not enough to keep us busy, so where should we focus our energy?"

Vijay's question went unanswered as both Jason and Nadya couldn't let go of the false data breach. Alek suggested that they pursue the telephony capability of the chip with an interface to a VT5. Vijay agreed, and the younger partners unenthusiastically nodded their okays. But they weren't done with the chip incident yet.

***

Nadya called a good friend of hers who worked for the Boston Globe, Susie Harper. Before she hung up, Nadya's final words were, "I can't thank you enough, Susie. And remember, you cannot ever reveal where you got the list of names."

***

At the welcome back dinner, Kari cut Jason out of the herd for a one on one. They had a very candid relationship, so she asked, "Jace, can you explain your reaction to Laurence at the reception?"

Jason quipped, "Did you want to say 'over' reaction?"

Kari was sincere. "No! There was something in your mind that made you upset, and I'd like to know what it was. No judgment, but you're my brother whom I love and respect."

Jason and Kari had always been close, and Jason knew she had no agenda other than her question. He smiled and awkwardly admitted, "Maybe it was an over-reaction. I'm pretty certain that the strike action and rumors were started by the same people that have been organizing the dome protests, namely Grover Nerdkist and Karen Rover. Conservative operatives. And perhaps I was imagining it, but there was something about the way Laurence asked me about the incident that seemed smug and perhaps even complicit."

Kari replied, "Well, that's the way his Party feels about the domes so maybe he was smug. But complicit?"

Jason searched for the right words, "I don't know. Has he ever fished for information from you about our project?"

Kari said, "No." But as the word came out, she recalled Laurence's reaction to her comment about chips in agri-domes. Was it surprise or ... recognition of "valuable information?"

Jason picked up her hesitation. "What?"

Kari explained the exchange but added that it hadn't exactly been a secret. But then she remembered that Laurence didn't appear to know that the chip functioned for both identification and disease detection. And that she'd blabbed about it being used for phones.

Jason began by agreeing that knowledge about the agri-domes had been in the public domain and that their existence had been very low profile and below the radar. But then he continued, "Not many people give much thought about those involved with the food supply chain, and if they think about them at all, especially the Laurence Donalds of the world, it's as a less important, lower-income group."

And then, a little embarrassed at having made his sister feel guilty, he tried to make an excuse. "It was probably just my imagination and an overload of things going on."

Kari laughed and said, "Yeah! Like your wedding! Let's put it to rest. I was just worried that you had an instinct that he was an ax murderer!"

Jason put his arm around her shoulder to rejoin the group, saying, "I don't know that he isn't!"

***

Over dinner, Nadya and Jason regaled the group with their stories of Cabo: Disappointing attempts at whale watching and snorkeling – but wonderful swimming in the large kidney-shaped pool with its palm-shaded swim-up bar, and the luxury of living in shorts and swimsuits in March. They also mentioned their realization about how long people would be able to enjoy the outdoors. They had gone through more than a dozen bottles of "SPF-90" sunscreen lotion.

Jason added a thought directed to their parents. "Nadya, Kari, and I are in our thirties, and very shortly we will lose the natural world that you and we have known. The outdoors, the rain, the snow, the rivers, lakes, oceans – all of it will be beyond our reach. Behind the glass. They'll join the extinct animals and become the dinosaurs we only read about or see in a museum. And if we have children, they won't even have what we had. It's so sad. So incredibly sad. Sometimes I wonder..." He trailed off, knowing that he was among those creating this new world.

This time it was Kari's turn to console Jason. "And that is why what you are doing, what SHARE is doing, and what much of the world is doing is critically important," she said. "We shouldn't see it as the end. We, at least I, see it as a new beginning to allow all of us to experience once again, the beauty of the world."

The conversation stopped for a few moments while everyone absorbed the enormity of the two statements.

Vijay was the first to break the silence. "Kari's right, and while it's not a short-term fix, the combination of doming and elimination of fossil fuel will keep everyone safe and allow the environment to heal. We can't give up."

There was more silence and the conversation slowly veered to a more positive level.

Nadya mentioned the good PR the chips were getting, thanks to Susie Harper's exposé in The Boston Globe. The true story about the identity thefts had spread like wildfire across news channels, magazines, and newspapers, and chips were once again seen as safe ... even though the identity thieves were still at large

Sophie asked Kari how she was enjoying government and Jennifer quipped, "Enjoying is probably not the word I would use."

But Kari enthusiastically replied, "Actually I do enjoy it. I really do. We are making changes – smaller and slower than I'd like – that help people and make life better for them."

Sophie asked, with a coy smile, "So, are you meeting any interesting people?"

Kari feigned an angry glare at Jennifer, "Did my mother set you up to ask that?" They all laughed, and Kari had successfully avoided answering Sophie's question.

***

Kari hadn't actively been avoiding Laurence, but you could have fooled him. He'd called, emailed, texted, tried to bump into her (as a benign form of stalking) and even sent flowers. If you asked her, she was busy. She was serving on four committees, and she took her work seriously. That included a great deal of research and preparation. She liked him, but he was simply not a top priority.

Out of guilt, she agreed to meet with him for a drink after a TIG committee meeting. He'd tried to have her come to his place, but she rebuffed him.

As usual, they warmed up with "shop talk" about the TIG meeting and politics in general. He even asked how Jason and Nadya's honeymoon had gone, possibly with the hope that it might rekindle feelings from the post-reception evening. It didn't.

Laurence poured more tea for Kari and ordered himself another whiskey as he steeled himself and asked, "Kari, have I done anything to offend you?"

Kari answered honestly, "No."

"I thought we had a very special evening after the reception and I'd hoped it was the start of a relationship."

Kari drew a deep breath. "I'll admit that the combination of the wedding, reception, and you, enabled me to escape my reality and just be me. I had a great time and I thank you for it. But I am driven. Some might say very ambitious, even overly so." And then smiling, she added, "I know that is not a flattering label for a woman. That night was fun for me, and hopefully you, but there are millions of people out there, billions actually, who either aren't having fun or soon won't, unless we solve our pressing problems."

Laurence asked, "And do you need to solve those problems for the world on your own?"

Kari sensed a reproach and pushed back. "Of course not. But if I wanted a personal partner, you and I wouldn't work. Our views of the world are too different."

"We could agree to avoid politics."

Kari burst out laughing. "You can't be serious. Look, I'm just not ready for a relationship. If I was, then anything could be possible. I like you and I'm not saying that I never want to see you. Can we just leave it at that?"

Laurence was resigned. "Okay. Still friends?"

"Yes," Kari said as she expertly keyed in an Uber request.

Laurence offered to take her home, but the evening was over.

***

Boston, Massachusetts. Susie Harper had been working late again, as usual. What had started as a favor to her friend Nadya had just become much more interesting. And her editor agreed.

Her FBI contact wouldn't give her details, but it appeared that the unauthorized credit card usage and bank account withdrawals were centered in Philadelphia. They had identified a suspect, even though he couldn't "hack his way out of a paper bag." Her contact indicated that the suspect claimed to have received the information from an unidentified source for a twenty-five percent cut of whatever he got. When his premises were searched, they found a stack of documents with the victims' details, including one that included a section of an employment file — information that was definitely not contained on a chip.

Susie had spoken with many of the victims and seven had indicated that they'd been threatened with losing their jobs if they made any comments to anyone. But it was her conversation with five others that spiced things up even more. They had already lost their jobs and Susie was digging into the whys. So far, the digging led to a dead-end. They had no idea about how they had been victimized or why it happened.

***

Chapter 15 – Valued Employees

Cambridge, Massachusetts. Jason had received a weighty document covering the telephony objectives for all domes. For the first time, all cell phone providers would need to adhere to common system architecture, both within each dome and across all domes. This was considered critical because of spatial limitations within a dome. It also improved carrier efficiencies. The document included details of the various tests that had been conducted as they experimented with 7G, 8G, and a few other hybrid network technologies. The importance of getting it right was apparent, given the detailed testing that had been carried out. They'd even recorded calls made and received in the domes and used both human and artificial intelligence to compare audio quality.

One of the charts listed the existing domes, which were, at the time, confined to agri-zones and a few private domes. One, in particular, caught his attention. It was the domed estate of Grover Nerdkist II. Jason looked at the dome detail and was disgusted by the extravagance of the private doming project which included stables, an oversized garage – more like a good-sized warehouse – and separate staff housing.

He'd already "tried and convicted" both Nerdkist and Rover for inciting the dome protests and the agri-dome strike action. It rankled him that someone with funds sufficient to build his own dome would be able to use people to protest against domes where they could safely live their lives. There was nothing he could do about that … yet.

The State of Washington, D.C. The FBI was making little progress in their investigation of the faked chip hacking of employee data.

Using the unintentionally included employment information they found at the suspect's house, they did interview the CEO of the business. He was a hired executive and not part of the corporate group. He confirmed that he should have been made aware of any employee information that was shared outside the business, but certainly, that had not happened in this case. He suggested that they speak with his VP of HR.

The VP of HR, Margie Buskirk, seemed nervous and a little defensive, but she insisted that no requests had been made of her nor was she aware of any information being leaked.

With the two instances where the victims had not been chipped, the information was almost certainly from the company. The FBI used that leverage to play a more aggressive game, but still, nothing surfaced.

***

Boston, Massachusetts. Good timing, an FBI connection, and excellent investigative journalism moved Susie Harper closer to solving the story. Susie called Margie Buskirk the evening following the FBI's attempt to find out who leaked the details.

At first, Margie tried to rebuff Susie by saying that she'd already told the FBI all she knew. Susie appeared to accept and understand that, and she asked Margie if she knew Gloria Gomez, one of the victims. Margie confirmed that she did. Susie commented, "She seems like a nice person."

Margie replied, "She is. I feel really sorry that this has happened to her."

Susie agreed. "It must be very difficult for her to deal with that, on top of her husband splitting and leaving her and two young children to fend for themselves. They'll need to move now, too."

Margie was slow to respond, and Susie thought she heard a sob, so she pressed on. "I know you told the FBI that you don't know how that information got out, and I appreciate that you have to be very careful about what you say to them, especially if you only have a suspicion. You can talk with me though, as I can withhold information about where it came from. This case involves nine different zones so I can make it impossible for you to be identified. And it could help Gloria … and her kids, if we have proof and force the company to reimburse her."

Another delay in responding before Margie said, "You guarantee that I won't be identified?"

Susie responded confidently. "Yes, Margie. What would you like to tell me?"

"Mr. Rhine warned me not to speak with anyone about this."

Susie asked, "When did he warn you, recently or when he first asked for a file?"

Margie thought and said, "He warned me just the other day. I'd almost forgotten about it."

Susie reassured her that her identity would be protected, and Margie proceeded to detail the first call she got from the group's Chief Financial Officer, Charles Rhine. He wanted a copy of a file of a "deserving employee." Someone well-liked. He needed it ASAP and he told Margie to select it and send it to him, using a personal email address. He also told her it was very confidential.

Margie explained that she had carried out his request and although it seemed unusual, she had been happy to help Gloria. So, when the union leaders broke the news about the hacks and that Gloria was one of them, she was confused. She had been expecting something good to happen to Gloria and she began to worry that the request for her file was related.

Susie asked about the union rep's announcement. Margie told her that when the union rep called her, she had asked if there were others. He said, "Yes," but he didn't know any names, other than Gloria's.

Susie asked Margie if she would send her a copy of what she sent Rhine. Margie hesitated but then agreed.

Susie sat back and thought, "Do I need to give up so much to use this lead?" She knew that an unnamed source was not evidence. As she looked at her computer screen, her hopes rose when she saw that Rhine's group owned another agri-zone business where an employee had been "hacked. And this was also the company who had recently fired their HR Director."

A half-hour later her hopes were well-founded. The HR Director at the other company, Lonnie Burns, had been recently sacked. Susie was able to get Lonnie's cell phone number and Lonnie defiantly told a similar story about Rhine, but when her employee was "hacked," Lonnie had called Rhine, demanding to know if the hack had anything to do with his request. Rhine told her to keep her mouth shut or else, but Lonnie persisted, and she was fired, with a further warning to keep quiet.

Susie used the information from both Margie and Lonnie to bluff and coerce two more HR execs, and then she got a bonus. The last HR Director she spoke with, who was based in Alabama, told a similar story about one of her senior execs asking her for a valued employee. But the exec had added another piece of information – the request came from the governor of the state, the not so honorable Semper Creud. That's when Susie decided to involve the FBI, in exchange for a head start ongoing public.

Creud was able to successfully deny his way out of it when the company executive admitted that he hadn't spoken directly with the governor; but for Susie, Nadya and Jason, Creud was added to their list of bad guys, along with Nerdkist and Rover.

As a result of all this – and the U.S. justice system being what it is – the suspect in Philadelphia was convicted and sentenced for several crimes; Charles Rhine and a few other executives lost their jobs; but otherwise, the saga died a pretty swift death. Susie's story covering the faked hacks and the severe financial pressure it put on the victims prompted most of the companies to reimburse the victims for their losses. "Go Fund Me" sites covered the others. And, finally, the food strike came to an end.

***

SHARE HQ, Pasadena, CA. As the year progressed, so did climate change. But this year, man had been able to level the playing field with nature, at least concerning fires. Wildfires had been a growing phenomenon in California, Oregon, and Washington since the 1990s. And each year thereafter seemed to set a new record.

So, in 2046, one of the first stated objectives of SHARE was to deal with the fires. Under a public-private partnership (PPP), research began in earnest to develop effective solar-powered desalinization plants, connected to what could be called massive sprinkler systems. Research was also carried out to ensure that the sprinklers were delivering just enough water to maintain the ecosystem that had been the norm before climate change. The goal was to keep the vegetation at optimum levels to prevent the raging fires that consumed thousands of square miles of forests and fields. It was thought that if the long periods of drought could be eliminated, much of the specialized Pacific Coast vegetation might survive the environment's onslaught.

In late 2052, the first systems were installed, covering thousands of square miles around towns and cities. Now, with limitless seawater to convert, and limitless sunshine for solar power, the coastal areas would be closely monitored for environmental threats. Plans were at the ready to protect large areas – even under domes – if necessary.

All things considered, SHARE was pleased with their progress, despite the protests. Dome construction had begun at all fifty-one state capitals and over one-hundred other major cities. By year-end, it was expected to have over two hundred completed agri-domes and significant progress and some completions on almost one-hundred revitalization domes. 2054 would mark the first transitions into domed living.

***

Cambridge, Massachusetts. Laurence looked at his ringing phone and groaned. He reluctantly pressed "Accept" and said, as enthusiastically as he could, "Hello Grover."

"Hello, Laurence. How's the budding romance?"

Laurence quickly struggled for a good answer, and to keep his composure at the same time. He'd scoured his apartment after his last call with Nerdkist and found a camera with wi-fi capability. "We've both been pretty busy lately and haven't been able to connect. I'll be seeing her soon."

Sarcastically, Grover replied, "Maybe your assessment of your girlfriend's feeling about you was a bit overblown."

Laurence fought to stay calm, and he was still pissed off at himself for giving Nerdkist details of his night with Kari. He took a deep breath as he realized that without Nerdkist's help, he wouldn't win another term. "Don't worry, I'll be able to stay close. The agri-dome intel was certainly helpful. Right?"

"It was, but this is a long game. We need to keep the pressure on and if we can't, we'll need to use those very titillating photos. In the meantime, get close and give us areas to exploit. Otherwise helping you out with your next election may not be as interesting for us as the last time. That took a pretty significant effort."

Laurence looked at his phone and saw that Nerdkist had disconnected. He'd just been reminded of the significant help – more like significant bribes – to lose enough of his opponent's ballots so Laurence could win his seat. He wasn't afraid of Grover as much as he was of his father, and if he didn't make Grover happier soon, it would be his father's scorn he'd be facing. He was also pretty sure that Nerdkist would not only withdraw assistance but also expose the election fraud, laying the blame on Laurence. Sometimes, Laurence wished that he'd just become a lawyer. But that would mean working for his father!

But what could he do? He was pretty sure that Kari was firm with her brush-off. Could a girl like Kari really enjoy sex as much as she had, and treat it as a one-night stand? Did she actually enjoy it as much as he thought she had? Self-doubt welled up and Laurence was at a loss for answers.

***

Chapter 16 – Failures

Cambridge, Massachusetts. Just before the August recess, Laurence and Kari met unexpectedly at a party thrown by a long-time House member. The unexpected part was Kari's reaction. Laurence knew she would be there. As it happened, they were two of the very few people who were there on their own.

They talked about safe topics that would be appropriate for complete strangers. Laurence had lost all his confidence and swagger, but he needed to get something for Grover. So, he asked, "How is your family and Team Beli-Tel doing? Cooking up some more sci-fi surprises?"

Kari looked at him, smiled, and took a sip of her iced tea, alerted by the question. Still smiling, she said, "They sure are. They each have amazing imaginations and when they put them together, it's like a super-power. Their current one is … well, I'm sworn to secrecy. Sorry, but you'll hear about it soon and I expect that many of your fellow party members will be pretty upset."

Laurence was trembling with excitement and tried to tease additional information, but Kari just said, "Sorry, I shouldn't have said anything. I need to go find our hostess," and she walked away.

***

Laurence went to his car and punched in a speed-dial number. Grover answered sarcastically, "Hello Lover Boy. Hope you have something for me."

Laurence explained, "Kari caught herself before she told me what they're working on. Seems big and she said that we, meaning the Party, won't like it."

Angrily Grover replied, "That's it? That's all your silver tongue could get out of her?"

As angrily as he dared, Laurence taunted back, "You're the one with all the connections. Why don't you work them to connect the dots?"

The line went dead.

***

Kari wasn't looking for the hostess. She just needed to walk away. As she did, she thought to herself, what was I thinking that night? Was I that horny? She laughed out loud, causing a couple of curious glances at seeing someone alone, laughing to herself. And then she laughed again as she thought about Laurence's failure to see through her completely made-up story about the secret project.

***

The White House. President Rachel Metcalf needed a vacation. Being single and driven, she hadn't had a day off since … she couldn't remember. She knew she hadn't taken a day off since her inauguration in January and she certainly couldn't remember taking any time off during her year-long campaign slog. She desperately needed to unwind, enjoy the peace and quiet, and a lot more of what she hadn't had in a long time.

Metcalf had locked everything away for over a year. She hadn't hidden her gayness and that hadn't stopped people from voting for her. But being gay was a concept. Photographs and stories were visceral and could be manipulated and exploited. She didn't need or want those distractions. And so, she had eschewed inviting anyone to stay at the White House because she knew the result.

Metcalf was a longtime friend of Artie and Etta Branson Andrews, the twin children of Holly Branson and her husband, Freddie Andrews. Holly was the daughter of Sir Richard Branson, the British business magnate, who purchased Necker Island in 1978. Artie and Etta understood the privacy and security that their very high-profile friend would need, and they invited her to Necker.

They decided to give President Metcalf a group of villas overlooking a private cove and beach. One villa would be used exclusively by the president and the other villas for her security detail and a small White House staff. They hired a manager to oversee the overall hospitality aspects two months in advance of the president's arrival. Her name was Naomi Wyatt. Originally from Jamaica, she had worked for some of the most prestigious hotel groups in the world.

Several very fortunate Secret Service staff made a number of trips to Necker and they were pleased with the villas' physical layout and the high degree of isolation and protectability from unwanted intruders. Anti-aircraft/UAV protection was set up and plans for a fleet of drone hunters were drawn up.

The Secret Service obtained the list of the service staff that would be assigned to the villas and they all checked out. Naomi Wyatt's vetting had a few minor flags and inconsistencies, mostly concerning her prior contacts and coincident proximity to the president. When briefed, President Metcalf recalled that she had met Wyatt very briefly while at an event at a Los Angeles area hotel where Wyatt was working. Wyatt, on the other hand, didn't recall the meeting. There were also several coincidental proximities between the two at various U.S. cities, although no meetings between them had taken place. Artie and Etta explained that they had recruited Wyatt through a high-end agency and the story held up. So, in the end, the Secret Service signed off on Wyatt's role during the president's stay.

***

Necker Island, British Virgin Islands. President Rachel Metcalf was looking forward to this break ... and she was determined to enjoy every minute. She arrived mid-afternoon and, within an hour, was on the pristine white beach caressed by the gentle lapping waves of the Caribbean, covered in the requisite high SPF suntan lotion as well as a light T-shirt over her swimsuit. The palm trees fluttered, the water was awesome, warm, and deceivingly clear, and the anti-UAV equipment was effectively camouflaged. She swam, snorkeled among the few remaining fish, read a "Welcome to the Islands" magazine, and simply relaxed in the shade of her beach umbrella for almost four uninterrupted hours. She had told her White House team that unless an emergency arose, she would be ready for a briefing at 6:00 PM.

Her briefing was routine. After all, she had a very capable vice president handling matters back in D.C. And then it was time for a quiet, fresh seafood dinner. Under the watchful and fairly inconspicuous eyes of the Secret Service detail, Naomi Wyatt arrived to welcome the president, double-check her food requests and timing, and introduce the staff that would be taking care of her during her stay.

FINAL CHANCE

Valerie Blair, who headed up the Secret Service team, was paying very close attention to Ms. Wyatt and, so far, saw no problems. She had studied the vetting dossier of Wyatt and had signed off.

The president enjoyed her meal in a way that she could almost not remember doing before. There was only the sound of gentle waves lapping nearby, silver utensils clinking on fine china, and the internal sounds of swallowing delicious food. The irony of the enjoyable outdoor dinner wasn't lost on her, and she struggled momentarily between her role as Domer in Chief and the loss of nature's beauty. Her struggle was one-sided, however. There were no immediate options to living life under domes, and her dinner that night, accompanied by nature's beauty, might be one of the last she'd enjoy.

After dinner, with a half-moon reflecting the sun's light, the president walked down to the water. The soft, still-warm sand enveloped her bare feet, and the water offered a refreshing change. She strolled along, the small waves lapping at her feet when suddenly, a dark figure rose from the water and purposefully strode toward her. The beach was immediately bathed in high-powered searchlight beams, focused on the president and the dark figure moving toward her. A half-dozen agents raced toward the pair from various directions with a warning – "Freeze!" – coming from one of them. The dark figure stopped, but Metcalf continued the few yards between them and took her hand.

She turned around and, still holding the hand of the dark figure, walked toward the beach and her protection detail. Agent Blair was closest to her and the president said, "It's okay. Please tell them to turn off the lights."

Blair relayed the command and Metcalf said, "Agent Blair, I think you've met Naomi Wyatt?"

Metcalf spoke with Blair for a few minutes and suddenly, the beach was as it had been just moments before. Calm, quiet, pristine, and heavenly. Metcalf and Wyatt, who was wearing a black one-piece bathing suit, stood there for a while longer before returning to the villa. They disappeared into Metcalf's room and emerged in the early morning for a pre-breakfast swim.

Blair had briefed her team that Wyatt would remain as the president's guest for the duration of the visit, and she had promised the president that it would remain private. She even assured the president that the drone hunters would guarantee that paparazzi-controlled UAVs would not get within range. Metcalf's heaven on Necker Island just got even more heavenly.

The days floated by, each one even better than the last, as the two women grew into spaces that had been empty for both of them for a long time. And, by all reports, there was nothing in the news regarding their relationship. It seemed that at that moment, all was good in the world.

***

Anegada Island. The trawler flying the Panamanian flag was unremarkable as it lay just off the southeast coast of Anegada Island. Its Liberian flag and the transceiver associated with it were now safely stored away. The captain of the vessel had reported his arrival and, in return, received his detailed instructions. At 2:45 AM, the crew lowered a large cylindrical-shaped object into the water and watched as it increasingly picked up speed and disappeared, heading in a southwesterly direction. The modified torpedo would reach a speed of forty miles per hour as it covered the thirteen miles to its target. The GPS-guided weapon could detect and avoid rocks and other vessels while never losing sight of its ultimate target. And it packed enough explosive power to level buildings, even those on land.

FINAL CHANCE

Nineteen minutes after the launch, the crew on the trawler could see a fireball on the near horizon and a second or two later, they heard the explosion. A perfectly timed commercial satellite visual being viewed at an unmarked location near Moscow confirmed the damage. That confirmation prompted a phone call and an order. The order was executed within a minute as the trawler exploded, leaving almost nothing and certainly no one to offer any clues about their mission. Another call went to Edinburg, Pennsylvania, and there were only two words spoken. "It's done."

***

Edinburg, Pennsylvania. Grover Nerdkist II woke up earlier than normal because he couldn't wait to see and hear the news. He made a quick cup of cappuccino and settled into his favorite chair to watch Faux News. The morning-show host was talking with someone he didn't recognize, and he didn't hear what they were saying because he was transfixed by the banner below the two speakers. "President escapes near-miss assassination attempt."

He then managed to focus on what was being said between the two speakers, which was that a type of torpedo had emerged from the Caribbean, hurtling up the beach toward the villa where the president was vacationing. The villa was leveled, killing three Secret Service agents and two resort staff. The president was not in the villa when the attack took place, and she was shaken but uninjured.

There were no videos or photos available, but the president had made a statement. "I thank everyone who has offered their love and support, but I especially thank and grieve for the remarkable men and women of the Secret Service whose lives were lost early this morning. I also grieve for the resort staff who have also lost their lives and for the families of everyone who died.

"Very importantly, and I emphasize that, we will find those responsible for this vicious attack and they will be brought to justice. I will be returning to the White House later this morning."

Nerdkist sat there for a moment and thought, "What the f***!" Then he pulled out his cell phone and typed and sent that same message.

***

Chapter 17 - Righting Wrongs

The White House. President Metcalf had called for a meeting with the Joint Chiefs of Staff, her National Security Advisor, Homeland Security Advisor, and the heads of the CIA and FBI at 7:00 AM the day after her return from her shortened vacation.

The information regarding the attack on Necker Island was scant. Satellite records showed that a projectile had originated from a ship, just off the coast of Anegada. The projectile traveled thirteen miles to Necker Island where it detonated at the villa where the president was staying. One of the surviving Secret Service agents saw a torpedo-like object emerge from the surf, traveling at a high speed, and proceed up the beach where it exploded after hitting the villa. The torpedo left tracks in the sand that would indicate it had rollers or wheels to facilitate its terrestrial journey.

Recordings from the satellites showed the ship's course — arriving at Anegada from its origin at the Yamal Peninsula in Russia. Its Automatic Identification System (AIS) showed it as registered in Liberia. The international Vessel Tracking Services (VTS) system then showed it disappearing from its system, possibly because the ship's crew had turned off their AIS. Another ship, with Panamanian registry, then appeared in the same place, broadcasting its identity via AIS. Thirty-two minutes later neither the satellites nor the VTS system showed any vessel in that spot. Satellite imagery did record what appeared to be an explosion at those coordinates.

The Chairperson of the Joint Chiefs finished her briefing simply, "So, we know how it happened but not why or who."

Metcalf said, "I know of the Yamal Peninsula as a major environmental threat because of the huge amount of methane gas escaping through the thinning permafrost. Any other claims to fame?"

Heidi Butler, CIA Director, replied. "Yes, Yamal holds Russia's biggest natural gas reserves. But of more relevance, Georgi Volkov owns the major gas company at Yamal, GazProd, which is under sanctions right now. Actually 'right now' isn't accurate. The company has been operating under sanctions for almost three decades. GazProd has violated laws across the board. Hacking, sponsoring terrorism, murder, money laundering. You name it, GazProd has done it."

Metcalf asked, "I don't suppose we'd get very far talking with him?"

Butler replied. "No, and he's been banned from the U.S., UK, Europe, and most other countries with laws and morals."

She turned to General Chavez. "General, do you have any feeling about whether the attack was civilian, or might there be government involvement?"

Chavez smiled and said, "When you use the words Russia and gas or oil in the same sentence, it becomes hard to separate. While most of what happened could be entirely civilian, the weapon wasn't. How they obtained it would answer your question."

Ollie Barth, the president's National Security Advisor, added, "Based on the web chatter we've seen – and there hasn't been much, or any of significance – I'd say it was private, although getting a favor, or a torpedo, from the Russian military, would not be a first-time event."

Metcalf mused. "We never did find whoever carried out the 2046 assassination nor the earlier attempt on me. All three were sophisticated and possibly had some connection to military weapons.

"How can we get to him?" Metcalf continued, "Shamalov and I get along fairly well … as well as Russian autocrats and U.S. Presidents can, but I doubt he'd agree to extradition. And I'm guessing Georgi doesn't come to Florida in the winter?"

Butler chuckled. "We could invite him. Seriously, we could keep the sanctions but drop his banning. I don't think there's much more we can do in addition to the sanctions in place unless we had more evidence. If we could prove it, we could try to grab him somewhere."

Metcalf asked, "Could we drop the ban, or would he see right through it?"

Barth said, "I think he would, especially right now. Maybe when things cool down, in a year or two."

Metcalf shook her head, "There is a very real possibility that the three assassination efforts are related. I don't want a fourth, whether it's on my watch or someone else's. Let's keep our options open but let's also consider Volkov as a prime suspect. So, make sure we are doing everything we can to tighten the noose. Thanks, everyone."

***

Back in the Oval Office, President Metcalf began her calls to the families of the three murdered Secret Service agents. The hardest one was to Valerie Blair's mother. Valerie was a single mom. Her husband had been killed in a Marine training exercise and Valerie's mother had picked up the role of surrogate for their three-year-old son during Valerie's extended postings. Now she would have to take it on permanently.

In their short time together at Necker Island, Valerie and Rachel had bonded. She'd immediately understood the president's desire for discretion, and she made sure that her team respected it.

The president knew that the Secret Service would make sure that Tyler Blair, Valerie's son, would be taken care of to a certain degree, but she added, "Mrs. Roberts, I only knew your daughter a short while, but we connected. She told me about Tyler, and I could tell by the love that came out through her words what he meant to her. I could also tell how much comfort your caring for Tyler gave her. I won't be president forever, but I will make myself available to you and Tyler as long as I'm alive. If you ever need anything, please call me. And when you think that Tyler might appreciate a visit to the White House, please let me know. Don't wait too long, though. Politics is a fickle business."

Rachel Metcalf wiped away a tear, took a deep breath, and went back to being the President of the United States.

***

Cambridge, Massachusetts. Alek arrived at the Beli-Tel office. The door was slightly ajar, but it was dark inside, so he knew he was the first to arrive. Still standing outside the door, off to the side, he called in, "Anyone there?"

After listening for movement, he reached inside and switched on all the lights. Still nothing, so he cautiously entered. As he surveyed the open-plan space, he could see that the computers had been removed and the file drawers open.

FINAL CHANCE

Before he did anything else, he removed his laptop from his backpack and sat down at a table in the reception area, taking care not to touch anything. He typed away at his keyboard and then pulled out his cellphone and called the police.

Vijay was the next to arrive, followed by Jason and Nadya five minutes later. Alek explained what he'd found and that he'd only been in for about fifteen minutes. He told them that the police were on their way and that he'd triggered the general kill switch that would wipe the desktops if they were connected to the internet. He'd also initiated a search for the machines but, so far, found nothing. That meant they hadn't been switched on and connected.

Whatever was on the desktops wasn't a concern because to access data, assuming they could get by the initial password, required a secondary server-generated passkey. Alek had programmed a trap, asking the user to request a passkey that required a phone or internet connection that could help identify the computer's location while also triggering a "kill switch" that would wipe the machine.

Anything taken from the files residing on the desktops was of no value – simply labels and fields that would be populated with data, once connected to a cloud-based server. No, it was the why and who that were the concerns. They'd have to report the break-in to SHARE, but those two questions would be the only ones they'd care about, too.

A pair of detectives arrived, and again, they looked like kids to Alek and Vijay. And their own kids watched with curious amusement as Alek held their IDs and seemed to read every word on them. He even laid them on the table and photographed them. Alek finished his vetting and explained what he'd found and what he'd done. He looked at his laptop and said, "If any of the missing machines are turned on and connected to the internet, I'll get a message with the location."

One of the detectives remarked that if the thieves were pros, they'd disguise their location so you may not get a good location fix, but he was impressed by the trap Alek had set. He added that there was an equal chance they were in it for the hardware.

Jason asked if that was common in the area and the detectives confirmed that it wasn't unheard of. Questions were asked and answered, lists of missing items made, and a technical person did the fingerprint searching with what Jason thought was a cool-looking camera device.

When they were alone again, the four principals discussed the puzzling theft. The why's and who's dominated the conversation but most likely, they mostly agreed, it was simple computer theft. The odd one out that made it mostly instead of unanimous was Jason. He had a hunch. Actually, it was stronger than that.

Stepping into the conference room and closing the door, he said, "Gaya. Call Kari." The Beli-Tel proprietary virtual assistant App did as she was asked, and Kari answered.

"Hey, Bro," she parodied. "What's happenin'?"

Jason parodied back in a Brooklyn accent. "Hey, Sis. How ya doin'?"

They both laughed and Kari asked, "To what do I have the honor to speak with my esteemed brother?"

"When was the last time you spoke with Laurence?"

That brought Kari down to a more serious level. "A couple weeks ago. Why?"

FINAL CHANCE

"Did he ask any questions about us or Beli-Tel?"

Kari laughed, but it was fraught with some concern. "Yes, he did. And I hope I haven't caused a problem."

Jason replied quickly. "What do you mean?"

Kari explained the 'secret project' jest she'd made and laughed, but Jason came back hard. "Why the hell did you do that?"

"I'm sorry. I don't know. He seemed interested and I thought it'd be funny to allude to something and then close the door."

"Well, it probably led to our offices being broken into and our computers taken."

Kari started to say, "Why would you think that?" But as she did, she remembered the coincidence with the chip reference, so she continued. "You think he was behind both the chip incident and now this?"

Jason calmed down a bit and was thinking. "I doubt he had anything to do with it directly, but I wouldn't be surprised if he'd shared your little joke with someone else who was responsible. Would it cause you a problem if I mentioned this to the police? It would at least make me feel good to know he was being interrogated."

Now Kari was angry. "Leave the interrogation to me. He will wish it were the police after I get through with him."

Jason had rarely seen this side of Kari. She was generally calm and ruffle-proof, and just hearing her anger and imagining her going at Donald brought a smile to his face. "Okay, Sis. He's all yours."

***

Cambridge, Massachusetts. Laurence grimaced when he saw the caller ID. Before he could even get a half-hearted mumble out, Grover attacked.

"Based on your information, which was a piss-poor excuse for real information, we had to take some big risks to find out what Beli-Tel was working on."

Alarmed, Laurence asked, "What do you mean by big risks?"

"We had to get the information held in their computers."

"So, you hacked them?"

"No, we tried but couldn't get in, so we took them."

"You broke into their office?"

"No, asshole! We waited until they looked away and then quietly took them out. How else would we get them?"

"I can't believe this," but he was also pleased that his help assisted their efforts. "So, are you happy with what you got?"

"NO! They wiped the data. We got nothing!"

Laurence was panicked. "Well, I want nothing more to do with this!" And he disconnected.

His brain was muddled, and he couldn't think clearly. His phone rang and he panicked, thinking it was Nerdkist again."

***

FINAL CHANCE

Kari had debated whether she wanted a phone or in-person confrontation with Laurence. She decided on the latter. Laurence answered her call, "What?"

Kari was surprised but she didn't give a damn about why he answered that way. "Is this a bad time?"

"Oh, hi Kari. Sorry. This is a surprise."

Kari tried to be friendly and polite, but it was difficult. "Hi. I wondered if you'd like to meet for a drink sometime?"

Laurence was torn between the stress of his call with Nerdkist, his excitement of Kari calling, and his fear over the situation he'd created. "Sure. I'm free this evening. Just a drink or dinner as well?"

"Let's start with a drink. I'll meet you at The Twenty-First Amendment. The place we went to before, say 6:30?"

"Perfect." And that was all because the line went dead. He was puzzled. What's this about? His conscience had found a small need for morality, so he wondered if she had found out what he'd done. But then his ego convinced him that she possibly realized what she was missing by avoiding him, so he began to look forward to the evening, hoping for a replay of the night that seemed years ago.

***

The Twenty-First Amendment, Cambridge, MA. Kari arrived twenty-five minutes late, deliberately, and she didn't apologize. She even ordered a glass of wine – red wine – that she knew she wouldn't drink. She pretended to go along with his usual warm-up about neutral political issues and how are you and what have you been doing bullshit. When he finished his awkward monologue, with him asking rambling questions and Kari giving him one or two-word replies, Kari got down to her planned business by asking him, "Why didn't you ask about what Beli-Tel is up to, or are you afraid another break-in and theft might give you away?"

Laurence was so startled that he blurted out, "I ... I didn't have anything ..." before he caught himself.

Kari pounced. "Oh, so you knew?"

Laurence tried to recover. "Yes. I heard about it."

Kari parried back, "From who?"

Of course, Laurence feigned not remembering because he certainly wasn't going to give up Nerdkist.

Kari gave him a withering look. "Fortunately for you, the only damage to Beli-Tel was an inconvenience. They're too smart for dumb shits like you to leave valuable information vulnerable to break-ins. And although part of me wants to dig to find a connection between you and the break-in, I'm prepared to chalk it up to experience, a bad experience, as long as you never speak to me again. Is that a deal?"

On one hand, Laurence wanted that deal, 'cut his losses and walk away.' But Nerdkist had the photos. Laurence tried to deny any knowledge of the break-in, but Kari cut him off.

"Do. You. Agree?"

Laurence realized that he had two options. Come clean with Kari and tell her about the photos – after all, he hadn't known about the camera, or he could take her deal and not face the music ... tonight.

FINAL CHANCE

For some reason that Laurence could never understand, he decided to face the music. "Kari, I'll accept your terms, but first I have something very important to tell you."

"I'm not sure I want to hear anything you have to say."

Laurence was as scared as he was when his father was angry with him. "You, you need to hear this and then I'll never speak to you again."

Kari nodded and issued a terse, "Okay."

Laurence signaled for another drink and they both sat silently until it arrived. He took a big gulp and set it down. Looking downward to avoid her eyes, he said, "I recently found out that someone had planted a camera in my apartment." He paused and looked at her for a reaction, but there was none.

He continued, this time looking at her, "In my bedroom."

He watched the anger quickly build and explode as she picked up her drink and thrust the red wine at his face.

Very calmly with a sufficient degree of menace, she said, "Tell me right now who put the camera there and who broke into Beli-Tel's offices or the wine will be the least of your problems."

The bravery he exhibited a few moments ago vanished and eyes downward, he mumbled, "Grover Nerdkist."

Kari got up and left The Twenty-First Amendment, a sick feeling in her stomach.

Laurence sat alone with his drink and thoughts. The server came over to clear Kari's glass and jumped when she saw Laurence's condition. She hurried back with a clean towel. He cleaned himself up as best he could and as he wiped away the wine, his next steps became clearer.

***

Chapter 18 – The 2050s

Cambridge, Massachusetts. On the night that Kari left The Twenty-First Amendment after she met with Laurence, she'd immediately discussed the situation with her mother. Jennifer was sympathetic but she understood that the presence of the photos could cause political harm, even though public perception of scandals had changed. She made two suggestions. One was that she should call her lawyer for advice; the second was that Kari needed to be upfront with anyone who might consider or appoint her to a position. Elections were different, but Jennifer hoped there was a way to head off problems in any eventuality.

As a result, a pre-emptive cease-and-desist order was issued that was tied to an agreement that Nerdkist destroy the photos, and that if any of them were ever released, charges would be pressed for the breaking, entering, and theft at Beli-Tel's office. The cease-and-desist order stated that they had a credible witness who would testify to Nerdkist's guilt.

***

While in Kari's second term in the Massachusetts State House, a U.S. senator from Massachusetts died in office. Governor Sally Rhydes, partly because of her admiration for Jennifer, but mainly based on Karima's outstanding work and reputation in the Massachusetts House, decided to appoint Karima to the vacant post.

During what was planned to be a perfunctory interview with Governor Rhydes to discuss the appointment, Kari summoned up her nerve and drew from the advice that her mother had given her two years earlier.

Kari brought up the possibility of compromising photos. Rhydes laughed and said, "I doubt you were doing anything that the voters haven't done themselves. Besides, this appointment will allow you to see if they're going to honor the cease-and-desist. Is that all?"

Kari won the special election held five months later, and a year after that, she retained her U.S. Senate seat at the regular election.

Kari was fortunate in many respects. In addition to her inherited intelligence, she was following numerous trail-blazing women, many of color, who had made being a woman candidate for high office quite normal. She was also fiercely independent, and her father's wealth, which he generously shared with her, allowed her to eschew contributions from special interest groups. Thirdly, her education and training in science, combined with her practical pro-bono experience working with ordinary people from diverse backgrounds, positioned her to bring exceptional and timely wisdom and authority to her work in the Senate.

The mid-2050s was a watershed period for science and progress on many fronts. By 2056, all but a handful of state capitals had been domed and dozens of major cities were completed or nearly there. The agri-dome projects were finished, solar energy was effortlessly producing eighty-five percent of the country's energy needs, and wind and hydro energy easily picked up the rest.

FINAL CHANCE

The reality and necessity of domes – as well as their immediate benefit of pleasant weather – had convinced the vast majority of people to embrace the program, and the protests slowed to a trickle. Political opposition was minimal, and the country raced forward, without the usual back-stepping that normally eroded progress. Kari was able to initiate several successful Senate bills that effectively addressed the most pressing issues of the environment, as well as healthcare, education, and income inequality. People were taking notice ... including Grover Nerdkist II.

***

Cambridge, Massachusetts and The State of Washington, D.C. The year 2058 would considerably change the lives of two members of the Patel-Belikov family. Nadya Belikov-Patel was pregnant for the first time, and the future parents and future grandparents were over the moon. The Massachusetts team swung into action to trade in Nadya and Jason's apartment for a home and to get it ready for their new arrival. It was relatively easy, as all they had to do was find a place and hire decorators. None of the six adults had any do-it-yourself or decorating skills.

2058 would also be remembered as the year Kari met Otis Graham.

***

The State of Washington, D.C. Kari had always been a high-energy over-achiever, but since arriving in the Senate, she had somehow upped her game. Early in the year, she attended a seminar, "Learning for Tomorrow's Business," sponsored by SHARE to highlight its work in education. The premise was to prepare the future generation with skill sets relevant to their new world. The keynote speaker was Otis Graham, President of George Washington University.

The Secretary of SHARE, Emma Steadman, introduced Graham, citing a long list of accomplishments – including the fact that Graham had been a star football player at Stanford who had turned down a professional football career to attend Oxford as a Rhodes Scholar.

As Graham spoke, his passion for the power of education was obvious. He was a strong proponent of broad access to education, advocating affordability of higher education, and openness to foreign students. He saw this latter area as critical to maintaining a vibrant worldview, both through the injection of diverse input as well as exporting American thought and values back to visiting students' countries.

Not surprisingly, Graham was a firm believer that education should not just keep up with industry but stay one or two steps ahead to ensure relevancy and lead the way for businesses through science, innovation, and analysis.

As he outlined his vision, his audience was glued to every word. And while his message was profound and thought-provoking, his delivery style was entertaining, as he intertwined his ideas and passion with humor and self-deprecating asides about football.

Kari didn't know much about football, but she was definitely attracted to his mind, sense of humor, and passion for education. Of course, his physique didn't go entirely unappreciated. He was upbeat and possessed a big, sincere grin that contrasted well against his dark brown skin. Kari was mesmerized.

After the session, Kari was determined to meet Graham, as she patiently waited for the clutch of people surrounding him to thin out and give her the opportunity. And then he was holding out his hand, glancing at her name tag, and she heard the voice she'd been listening to a short while ago say, "Senator Patel. Thank you for attending the session. I hope you heard enough tonight to enlist your support for the Administration's desire to transform our education system."

For the first time in her life, Kari was momentarily tongue-tied. Fortunately, another attendee introduced himself to Graham, affording her a moment to recover. And when she did, there was no going back. They talked about education, they talked about themselves. They discovered that Graham and Jennifer had both attended Stanford and were both athletes. And when Graham divined that Kari's father was Vijay Patel, he shook his sleeve down to reveal his VT4 watch.

They only stopped talking when the facilities team at the hotel apologetically told them that they needed to re-set the room. Graham asked Kari if she'd have dinner with him one night and Kari was disappointed that it couldn't be that night, or the next, or even the next.

***

Mr. Braxton Bar & Kitchen, The State of Washington, D.C. Given the combined incompatibility of their diaries, it was a full week later that Otis Graham and Senator Kari Patel met at the trendy establishment. It seemed like a full month for Kari, and she was excited and, yes ... nervous. Proof of that was when − not long after they'd arrived − a friend of Kari's recognized her and stopped at their table to say hello. Kari introduced Otis as Otto, and as she said the name, his smile alerted her of the error, but it was too late. He good-naturedly teased her for almost two years, leaving voicemails and even signing emails with "Otto."

After a long dinner, more focused on conversation than courses, Kari and Otis took an Uber to her Voltas Place home that Jennifer had purchased a few years ago. Otis had booked the car to drop Kari off and continue to his apartment, but she asked him in. The Uber to Otis' apartment was not booked again until late the next morning. And even then, it was moved back to mid-afternoon.

Kari had found her man and Otis had met his match. They made an attractive couple benefitting from earlier racial trailblazers in this very cosmopolitan city-state. Most people didn't give a second thought to the budding relationship between the Indian American senator and the president of a prominent university who was a descendent of African slaves. On the contrary, they were immediately on the "A-List" of the movers and shakers in a city that thrived on connections.

***

As the year progressed, so did Kari's and Otis's relationship and careers. While Kari accumulated political capital and made a name for herself in the Senate, Otis was similarly creating a brand for himself and his vision in the field of education along with a demand for his time.

Reaction to his speech at the SHARE conference in January had kindled a spark in the imaginations of both educators and business leaders, and they all wanted more from Otis. Kari shared his beliefs, especially his popular vision of an evolving curriculum to ensure that education was always a step or two ahead of tomorrow's requirements.

As happy as they both were, their professional time commitments were keeping them apart, far more than either of them wanted.

***

Chapter 19 - "Meet the Family"

Cambridge, Massachusetts. A few months before Thanksgiving, 2057, Nadya gave birth to Adam, a healthy eight-plus pounder. He was immediately in grave danger of being irreversibly spoiled by any one of the six adults in the Belikov-Patel family, especially those now known as grandparents.

Adam's birth defined a developing plan of Kari's to bring Otis up to Chestnut Hill to meet the family over the long Thanksgiving weekend. She knew that he'd know what that meant, and she was nervous about his reaction.

For his part, when Otis heard those words, "meet the family," he felt a little spike in anxiety, but at the same time, he knew what it meant, and he did his best to remain cool as he very enthusiastically agreed.

Any concerns that either Kari or Otis had about meeting the growing Massachusetts clan were immediately dismissed when everyone embraced Otis as though they had known him forever. Kari was thrilled as the two most important people in her life, welcomed the newest member of that club, not just to their home, but to their family.

It was a very special Thanksgiving in so many ways. In addition to the arrival of a new child along with the hope and dreams for the future, both Jennifer and Vijay were comforted to know that Kari had finally found her partner. Otis's intelligent and curious mind was on full display through his insightful questions about the mostly scientific work involving the Beli-Tel team and SHARE. He and Jennifer also found a lot to talk about through their Stanford connection as well as their shared love and interest in Kari.

***

Cambridge, Massachusetts. Vijay and Alek were both in their seventies and, by their standards at least, they were slowing down. The "kids" were completely in control of the operation and they'd brought a few more "youngsters" in. That aside, they were in most days because Nadya and Jason brought Adam to the office. Little Adam was a bit too young for pre-school and bringing him to the office created a symbiotic situation that everyone enjoyed. The granddads got to see their children and grandson and Nadya and Jason got to hang out with their dads and get free child-minding services.

Then, with the 2060 elections less than two years away, President Metcalf's staff called with a new business opportunity.

After close to five decades, the Russians were still doing their best to interfere in the U.S. elections. For what purpose, no one could tell you, including the Russians. Perhaps it was now just part of their DNA and they had taken election hacking to Olympic sport levels. With almost fifty years of practice, they were indisputably the world champs. But they were about to be taken down by a couple of "kids" and a tiny microchip.

The staffer asked Beli-Tel for a proposal that would fundamentally change the election process. There were two objectives: Stop the hacking and make it even easier for people to vote.

FINAL CHANCE

Nadya and Jason, with just a little help from their dads, decided to take on the Russians by squeezing more utility from the embedded chips. The kids were driven and wanted to wrap it up as soon as possible because Nadya was pregnant again. They had time, but they wanted to have everything finished well before her due date.

What they created was sheer genius. Their system was both non-hackable and so easy to use that voter turnout would reach the low ninety percentiles. Of course, a voting tax incentive helped as well. Using hyper-encrypted alerts sent directly to everyone's implanted chip, eligible voters received a unique encoded ID. Using their computers, they would make their ballot choices, and then upload those choices to their chip. The chip would validate the authenticity and send it to a single processing center. No hanging chads, long lines, post office glitches, ballot box removals, or credible reports of fraud. And thanks to a constitutional change, no Electoral College. The one person, one vote system had arrived, and the Russian "Olympians" would either have to retire or play in another country.

***

New Years' Eve 2057, Edinburg, Pennsylvania. The gang was were all there to celebrate and plot, but perhaps not in that order. Unsurprisingly, Georgi Volkov reminded everyone that there wasn't much to celebrate.

"I try big plans. Bad luck. I votched like hawk. Vot anyone else do? Neeshtoh! Mean nothing. Nada. Zip."

Their perennial host, Grover Nerdkist II, tried to flatter and mollify Georgi. Nerdkist likened having Georgi in his home to having a barely sated saber-toothed tiger roaming free, and ready to pounce.

"Georgi, we greatly appreciate your efforts and financial support. We just need to wait for the right time. The presidential elections begin this year, and we will be watching closely to see if we can eliminate the frontrunner for the Democrats."

Georgi roared back, confirming Nerdkist's analogy. "Dat's yur plan? Kill dere best vun so less best vins?

Carefully and weakly, Nerdkist answered, "We don't have a chance to win this next election."

Before he could continue, Volkov jumped up and shouted, "Vy I spend money and take chance come here? Ven you do something good. I come back!"

Volkov stormed out of the room.

Nobody said a word until Semper Creud said, "K.C. Why don't you get him to stay? He won't hit a woman."

Naresh Argawal, the Prince, and Jerry Failwell remained silent and shaken. The four men waited. They heard the front door slam and K.C. returned.

"I asked him to stay and tried to compliment him, but he just spouted a few sentences in – probably Russian – and stormed out.

The rest of New Year's Eve at Grover's dome was more like a wake.

***

Chapter 20 - A Big Decision

The State of Washington, D.C. You could call it the "stamp of approval" aftereffect or simply a sigh of relief that it had gone well, but Kari's and Otis's relationship changed after their Thanksgiving at Chestnut Hill. It grew and established an even greater sense of permanency. Otis never got around to completely moving in with Kari, although as time rolled on, there was not much left of Otis at his flat. You could count the number of nights he spent there on one hand, and that was usually when Kari was away.

During frequent discussions – rather than proposals – Otis gently pressed Kari to marry him. She loved him but possibly because of their insanely busy schedules, there was simply not enough time for it – or was there something else?

***

There was nothing special or auspicious about 2058, but even then, with two years to go, you could already feel the early buzz of the presidential election. Official campaigning would not start until January 1st, 2060, as a result of the election reforms recently passed, however, unofficial campaigning was already widespread.

The number of parties, often confused with lobbying, steadily grew, adding even more weight to Kari's and Otis's already heavy social schedules.

Conversations at these gatherings often required a post-mortem as the participants searched for hidden meanings buried within the rhetoric. Kari was constantly asking herself, "Were seeds being planted?" Otis wondered, "Was I being sounded out or assessed?"

Some conversations were less obtuse with prospective candidates, lobbyists, and lawmakers outright asking for support. As a result, invitations were evaluated as to their level of sincerity or the recipients' possible willingness to accept the possible request for support. In a city not known for sincerity, the bar was being lowered.

Kari's and Otis's takes on the phenomenon were very different. Otis wasn't a politician, and he would grab almost any opportunity to advance his passion, even if it didn't involve him. But that didn't mean he was blind to vacuous or misguided plans.

Kari, on the other hand, had quickly honed her political instincts, which, to her credit, she used less for personal gain than for sniffing out bullshit or even more nefarious schemes. As a sitting senator, who was not up for election in 2060, she was frequently approached for assistance or endorsements, especially from U.S. House and State congressional members.

***

Chestnut Hill, Massachusetts. Just before Thanksgiving, Nadya had given birth to Vijay Jr., and both Kari and Otis were looking forward to the holiday break and seeing the growing family again.

Kari had been secretly hoping that Nadya's child production would divert her mother's overt encouragement for her to join in the fun. It didn't, and Kari found herself holding either Adam or Vijay Jr. almost without stop. She truly believed that her mother had told everyone else to drop a baby in her arms every chance they could.

She was holding Vijay Jr. who was wide awake and staring at her through his big dark eyes – the kind of stare that makes you uncomfortable as you wonder what they're thinking. She smiled, seeing the resemblance to her father and she drifted away to another place, hypnotized by the infant's gaze. Then she returned to being present and brought the baby over to his mother while she went to look for hers.

Finding her mom and dad in the kitchen, she said, "Mom, can I see you a minute?"

They went into a bedroom and Kari shut the door and pulled her mom down to sit next to her on the bed. She held her mom's hands in her own and looked directly into her gray eyes through a pair just like them and said, "Mom, I've always wanted to make you and dad happy, and I know how happy you'd be for me to have a child … but I can't. I can't rationalize bringing a child into this uncertain world. A world where we can't exist outside our domes. Instead, I'm going to do everything I can to make the world a place that is good for children. Safe for children. And … I'm sorry."

The two pair of gray eyes welled up and Jennifer sniffed and said, "Kari, you've always made us happy, and we are so incredibly proud of you. I understand and I'm behind you all the way. What needs to be done is huge, but if anyone can do it, it will be you. I love you."

The two women embraced, and the welling eyes turned into fountains. They were crying all out when the door opened and a rattled Vijay said, "How did you know I burned the string beans?"

**

The next morning Jennifer took Kari aside and asked her to take a walk. Kari's pledge to save the world had dredged up some thoughts in Jennifer's mind, and not from the deep recesses. She'd been in politics, and although she started late in life, she'd met many very successful politicians, giving her the ability to assess and compare their strengths with Kari's.

Jennifer got right to the point. "If you're going to change the world, there's only one job that will make that possible."

Kari hadn't made any comments about the upcoming elections so her retort surprised Jennifer.

"I know and I've been giving it a lot of thought."

Jennifer wasn't sure if Kari had understood. "I'm talking about the presidency. It's the only job with the leverage to change this country and the world."

"I know, Mom, and at the moment my choices are next year or in eight years. Bo Sanders is the presumptive nominee, and he's the frontrunner after serving as vice president for eight years. However, quite a few influential members of the Party have spoken with me about entering the race. To be honest, I think they want to boost my chances to be selected as vice president."

"That's not a bad place to end up."

"No, but running for second place doesn't feel good. I want to discuss it with Otis when we go home. And you will definitely be the second person to know."

"Speaking of Otis, any discussion about marriage?"

"He wants to – and I would, too – but I need to decide what I'm going to do first. You'll also be the second person to know that when we decide … or actually, when I decide."

***

Georgetown, State of Washington, D.C. Back at Voltas Place after their enjoyable Thanksgiving, Kari filled Otis in on her discussion with her mother. She gently eased into the part about having thought about running, and this time she was surprised.

Otis had been thinking about it for some time and he was convinced that she could win the primary and the White House. Part of that was because he loved her, and part because he wasn't political. He voted for her Party because the alternative was unthinkable, but he viewed her Party as a herd of cats … virtually impossible to manage or coalesce around the details of a single issue.

She remembered him saying, "Yes, when you win, but I expect there will be a large field, including some far-out lunatics. When I studied in the UK, candidates like that belonged to their own parties, like the Official Monster Raving Loony Party."

She loved Otis dearly, on many levels, and that included his logic and his tactical skills.

So, on that fateful night, when they were discussing her candidacy, he said, "Look, a presidential campaign is unlike anything either one of us has ever experienced and I want to be with you, every day and every night. If for no other reason than you'll have someone to confide in. But even more importantly, a campaign will seem like a part-time gig once you're elected, and then we, actually you, really will be too busy. You've told the Party that you'll give them an answer next month, so ..."

Abruptly, Otis got up and disappeared in the direction of their bedroom. Moments later he returned and went down on one knee. He held up a small, open jewelry box containing his mother's engagement ring, and looking up at Kari, he said, "I love you, Karima Patel. Will you marry me ... while we have the time?"

They married one week later, in Atlanta, at the church Otis had attended while growing up. It was a simple ceremony, with his sister, Samantha, Kari's parents, and her brother, Jason. Nadya stayed home with Adam and Vijay Jr. Sadly, Otis's parents had died in a car accident two years earlier.

***

Edinburg, Pennsylvania. Grover's New Year's Eve party was called off when the main attraction said "Nyet."

***

Two weeks after Otis's proposal, Karima Patel-Graham and her husband returned from their Christmas mini-moon – four days at a secluded, domed villa near Dorado Beach in Puerto Rico, the fifty-second state. She was ready for the fray.

FINAL CHANCE

Kari called Isabelle Martin, the chairperson of her Party's nominating committee. Martin was already an institution unto herself and had been chairing the Committee for over fifteen years. She was an intimidating figure and during their earlier conversations, Kari had a hard time calling her Isabelle; but now she had good news. News she was certain that Martin would like.

"Good morning, Isabelle," bubbled Kari.

A few seconds passed before Martin coolly replied, "Are you calling to ask for my congratulations."

Kari didn't expect her unannounced marriage and very brief honeymoon to be a surprise to anyone, but Martin's extreme coolness unnerved her. "No, I just wanted to tell you that I am formally announcing my candidacy."

With the same coolness, Martin replied. "Thank you for at least sharing that."

Kari had recovered. "Do we have a problem?"

Martin answered. "Problems, as in more than one would be more accurate."

Kari readied for a fight. "Well, spit them out."

Martin was quick this time. "Number one, Otis will need to be vetted and then there's the issue of optics and public opinion. We've never had a racially mixed couple in the White House."

Kari got the easy one out the way first. "Otis has nothing to hide. I know him pretty damn well. We know everything about each other, including every embarrassing thing that's ever happened to us."

Martin interrupted and tried to de-escalate this point because both she and Kari knew that it was the second concern that would be more contentious. "I don't doubt that, but it will take time. But before we discuss the second problem, why did you sneak off and get married? You're not pregnant, are you?"

That stung Kari, but it wasn't Martin's fault. Kari had made a decision and despite her mother's rebuff of being disappointed, Kari knew the truth, so the mere mention of pregnancy brought back one of the biggest regrets of her life. Automatically, excuses raced through her mind. At first, there was never enough time, and of course, she hadn't found the right man. But even before she'd met Otis, who was the right man, there were grave doubts that the earth would survive the environmental free-fall it found itself in. Why would she bring a child into a world like that?

Martin's, "Kari, are you there?" brought her back to the present.

"I just wanted to get married, have a short honeymoon, and start making plans to win the nomination and the White House. And sneaking off? Seriously, is that even possible? And no, I'm not pregnant."

Not helping Kari's state of mind, Martin replied, "Well that's good."

Kari's temper flared. "As for your optics and public opinion, have you not noticed that Bo Sanders is black, and his wife, Molly, is white. And I mean really white, as in blonde. I'm willing to bet that there are a hell of a lot of people, probably in states that we won't win anyway, who wouldn't call me white. Besides, it's not like we never had a black president or a black woman president or a black couple or a female president in the White House."

FINAL CHANCE

Martin sighed, "I'll be frank with you, Karima. Bo Sanders is the presumptive favorite. He's been the VP for eight years and he and his wife are part of the furniture. Nobody sees their color. You're a new face and a lot of us here are pulling for you. What's done is done but we just felt that you were a stronger candidate before you married Otis. We're not going to bet the ranch on you until we have a better view of your electability. You're getting a late start insofar as infrastructure and there are a dozen candidates already out there, including the vice president."

Undeterred, Kari retorted, sincerely. "I'm used to winning elections with healthy competition. I'm ready for it and, married to Otis, I'm stronger for it. But is the Party ready for me?"

Isabelle Martin paused to ensure she used the right words. She liked Kari but her only objective was to win the election. "You'll get the help and support you need but you need to show us that you have the heart for it ... and the brains."

Kari smiled for the first time and simply said, "Game on."

***

Chapter 21 – The 2060 Election

The State of Washington, D.C. With President Metcalf finishing her second term, the Party fielded a very diverse and good-sized group of candidates. Bo Sanders, the popular, two-term vice president would be the presumptive favorite; however, many saw him as being too progressive. Both parties were already months into planning their primary races and the opposition party's field still numbered in the twenties.

***

Kari threw herself into the campaign with incredible energy and incisive messaging. She visited the early voting states: Iowa, New Hampshire, Nevada, South Carolina, California, Colorado, Maine, Massachusetts, Minnesota, North Carolina, and Texas, returning home, when possible. She was off to a very good start, connecting with voters with a genuine sincerity often missing in politicians. Thanks to Otis, she received the backing of the Teacher's Union along with other moderates from her party.

Her parents were over-the-top proud, and their front lawn showed it with dozens of Kari signs sprouting up all over.

***

Vijay had a meeting at Johns Hopkins Hospital in Baltimore and wasted no time using the opportunity to grab a night and dinner with Kari and Otis. Kari was excited and even planned a big Indian meal.

FINAL CHANCE

After dinner, Vijay casually mentioned that he had cancer. He explained that, about a year ago, he had been doing some experiments with the VT5 watch focused on the identification of cancer cells, using his own blood. During that process, he picked up some blood analysis anomalies and shared the outputs with a research scientist at Johns Hopkins whom he had known for some time. The scientist was skeptical at first because he couldn't detect any signs of cancer using the medical tools currently available to him. But Vijay knew what his sophisticated algorithms were showing, and over six months, his cancer finally became detectable through available tools.

Kari was extremely shaken to hear his story, even before Vijay told them that he had been undergoing treatment at Sloan Kettering in New York for the past six months.

"What? You have cancer and are undergoing treatments and I'm just hearing about it?"

Vijay tried to reassure her. "Kari, it is nothing. We caught it so early that it's not much more dangerous than a headache. Just a little more complicated. And this is why I didn't tell you. It's nothing to worry about."

"Does Mom know?"

"Of course. And she's not worried. I have two more sessions at Sloan, and then the watch," pointing at his VT5, "and I will monitor it. 'Uncle Alek' and I are working to get the VT5 platform to perform a similar set of diagnostics to what I used to find the pre-cancer. It's an exciting breakthrough and could be a game-changing interim step in the fight against cancer."

***

The Primary Circuit. Despite her late start, Kari came in second in the Iowa Caucus, and she won in New Hampshire. Depending on which poll you followed, she was a close second or third; and Super Tuesday and the Tuesday after that were still to come. With twenty states voting, including Massachusetts, the "Ides of March" would be more than just a Shakespearean line.

***

Chestnut Hill, Massachusetts. Kari decided to be in Massachusetts on Super Tuesday and her campaign was confident that she would be celebrating the win of her home state. She planned to have an early dinner with her mom, dad, and Otis before they all decamped to her Boston campaign headquarters for what she hoped would be a rousing victory. Vijay was in New York at Sloan Kettering for his final treatment and would be home in time for dinner. It would be an exciting, and hopefully victorious evening.

Kari and Otis arrived at her parents' home in the early afternoon. Otis worked on his e-mails in Vijay's office while Kari helped Jennifer in the kitchen. The mother-daughter politicians chatted away. Their nervous energy caused them to giggle as they chopped and stirred.

At 4:05 PM, both Kari's and Jennifer's phones rang almost simultaneously, and Otis received a message at the same time. He looked at his phone. It was a newsflash. "Breaking News: A Northeast Shuttle plane had crashed on take-off from LaGuardia. There were no survivors."

A chill ran through him. He didn't know Vijay's travel details, only that he was flying from New York to Boston and would be home by dinner.

FINAL CHANCE

Quietly, unaware that his wife's and mother-in-law's phones had rung, he slowly descended the stairs and headed to the kitchen. Even before he got there, he heard the crying and knew that they knew.

***

If Kari even heard the outcomes of Super Tuesday, she couldn't have absorbed them. "Win" was a word that would be most incongruous on this Tuesday in February.

After talking with the officials at LaGuardia, they realized that nothing could be accomplished there. The next morning, Otis drove Kari and Jennifer to Logan Airport in Boston to receive Vijay's remains. Upon returning home from the funeral parlor, Kari and Otis went to their room where she told him that she was dropping out of the race. Her heart was broken and unfit for the task. Neither Otis nor Jennifer tried to change her mind. And even the following day, when Kari was able to focus on Tuesday's results and see that she and Bo Sanders were in a virtual tie, she remained steadfast in her decision.

Dealing with Vijay's funeral was the hardest thing she had ever done. His death came out of the blue. There was no Final Notice and no time to react or prepare. The day of the funeral was a date on their calendars that she and her mother could only look at with dread.

That day arrived and to say that Vijay's funeral was well-attended would be a gross understatement. The entire Patel and Belikov families were there and Vijay's brother, Sanjay, and his wife, Leela, flew over from India. There were dozens of Vijay's ex-colleagues from VitalTech, including J. Edward Konig, whose private equity firm launched Vijay and the VT2 into the big time, along with every member of Vijay's two management teams ... many of Jennifer's political and charitable friends, including the governor ... and Kari's and Otis's political and personal friends. President Metcalf even sent her secretary of SHARE to attend and honor someone who they considered to be one of the program's vital architects.

Four former law enforcement officials also attended: FBI Director, Eric Hawke, FBI Special Agent, Zoe Brouet, FBI Technical Director, Ninad Gupte, and Secret Service Agent, Demi Magret. They had all worked with Vijay to stop Russian agents from interfering in a presidential election in the twenties.

All in all, if one was counting, over five hundred came to honor and say goodbye to the brilliant Indian kid from a slum in Mumbai.

***

Edinburg, Pennsylvania. On Wednesday, after the announcement that Kari had dropped out from the race, Nerdkist sent a very short text. "Abort the attack."

***

Sanders won the nomination and the Presidency. Kari had endorsed him when she withdrew and he, in turn, offered her the vice president role, but Kari wasn't ready yet. She planned to finish her term in the Senate and then see how she felt.

Sanders appointed Otis as his U.S. Secretary of Education. It was the position of his dreams, giving Otis the power to shape education on a broad scale.

***

The State of Washington, D.C. The nation and the world that Bo Sanders inherited in 2061 were, by most measures, in the best shape in modern history. There were no wars, no great famines, no pandemics, and on the surface, everything was running the way it was planned. Yet the very big elephant was still in the domes – a fragile and inhospitable environment.

***

Edinburg, Pennsylvania, New Year's Eve 2060. Grover Nerdkist held his annual event, and despite the previous acrimony, sanctions, and embargo against Georgi, he was there, and eager to cause trouble.

As soon as Nerdkist called their meeting to order, Georgi took control. "Ve have ben meeting for fifteen years and only ting has happened vus black lady president killed to help good party be president. And dat vus all by me." Gesturing to the others he asked, "Vot you all do?"

Naresh Argawal was thinking about the failed torpedo attack again. "I have an idea to make your weapons more effective."

Georgi scoffed, "Vot you know about vepons?"

Argawal smiled, "Explosions are not guaranteed. The range is limited, and objects can shield targets. Explosions and gaseous poison are a more lethal combination."
There was something about this combination of explosives and poison that actually crossed a line for the Americans. Killing presidents with explosives seemed okay with them. Poison was a step too far.

Nerdkist objected, "Whoa! Poison gas? That's illegal!"

Argawal, Georgi, and Prince Ibrahim broke out laughing. Argawal's English was the best of the three and as he stifled his laugh he asked, "And killing a president isn't?"

Nerdkist replied, "But the Geneva Convention bans the use of poison gas."

The Prince had been quiet – preoccupied by the presence of an uncovered woman – and careful to avoid Georgi's taunts. Breaking his silence, he replied, "If they not know who do it, they can do nothing."

Flashing Argawal and the Prince a quick smile, Georgi said, "Okay. Ve not talk about poison gas in front of American sissies." He laughed, "Ya, sissy same word in Russian."

Semper Creud wanted to show everyone that he was involved, but he really didn't know how, nor could he, even if he'd known. He also wanted to stay beneath the radar after his botched attempt to help with the agri-dome strikes.

Karen Rover wanted to keep Georgi motivated. "Georgi. First of all, we appreciate your efforts, and we thank you. Our system is a bit convoluted." Karen realized she better speak simply. "Complicated. This new president is very liberal, and we think that many people will not be happy with his approach. That gives us a chance to change parts of our government to make his plans difficult to achieve and it may even help elect a president who is sympathetic to us. So, it would be very good if something were to happen to this president."

Rover was right. Bo Sanders had chosen Doug Johnson as his VP only because his Party had insisted on it. They felt it was important as a counter to Sanders' very progressive views.

FINAL CHANCE

Nerdkist wanted to keep Georgi engaged without endorsing the heinous plan that he was sure Georgi was planning. "Karen's right, Georgi. You've done all we could ask for and without the bad luck, it might have changed things faster."

He added, "We had a plan in place to eliminate a likely presidential candidate, but she withdrew, so we stopped it. We have some other plans in place."

Rover broached an idea of decreasing the price of oil still further to entice people to consider oil-powered backup to counter power outages. Nerdkist reminded her that the U.S. had banned carbon emissions, but perhaps other countries might consider it.

He added, "Besides, there have been surprisingly few outages."

"Ve can change dat," was Georgi's enthusiastic response.

Argawal cautioned, "We can't just play on the edges of disrupting power. We need to create significant and newsworthy articles – so bad the whole world hears about them."

Nerdkist added, "You're right. They do have to be very significant to make any impact. We need to cripple big essential industries, hospitals, and infrastructure. And not just cause inconveniences. People must die to make an impact."

Rover chimed in. "I can help to amplify the impact. Loop me in on the plan so I can get ahead of the news cycles and be ready to capture the negative reactions and get them out to the media to create vocal outrage about being totally reliant on solar and wind power."

Nerdkist suggested that if the outages are significant, they will make the news automatically, and then, "We can field experts who comment on the fact that solar and wind power are not reliable, and that secure – oil or gas – backup power is required. We start to sow bigger and bigger seeds."

Creud asked, "How hard would that be to do? Create big outages."

Georgi responded. "Easy. Da grids computer-control. I make big impact. Tell me ver and ven."

That idea prompted a discussion between Georgi and the Prince. Creud was out of his element intellectually so he remained silent, and Gerry Failwell had nothing to add. He was still looking for an opening to get Karen into bed.

Shortly after midnight, Argawal pulled Georgi aside and confided, "I have an idea." And they adjourned to another room.

***

Chapter 22 – The State of the States – 2061

The state of the states. The United States was home to over 10,000 domes or dome clusters. There were just over 9,000 city, town, and suburban dome clusters. Not surprisingly, there were still those individuals – and even a few small communities – who refused to live within a dome. They struggled, either eking out meager and barely sustainable lives raising animals and growing some crops or commuting to industrial domes. Over time they either died from cancer or eye and respiratory ailments, or they moved into a town or city dome for treatment and lived out their lives safely, out of the carcinogenic sun and toxic air.

Overall, the ambitious plans of the United States and most of the world were showing promise concerning the environment. The deterioration of the ozone layer had slowed, but it was still early days, very early, and the patience of some people and countries was worryingly thin.

Outside the domes, wildfires continued to lay waste to millions of acres of uninhabited and unprotected land around the world. More and more areas were turning hotter and more arid, creating limitless fuel for fires. The United States was something of an exception. The well-watered Revitalization Domes, as well as the extensive Pacific Coast sprinklers, were working.

Flooding, however, was a global issue, either from rising seas as the polar caps melted, or severe and irregular precipitation. Outsized storms, such as hurricanes or tornados, were increasingly regular occurrences, ignoring seasonal and geographic patterns. The domes had been constructed to handle the most powerful storms on record, but there was concern that if the storms continued to worsen, catastrophic death and destruction could result.

The melting polar ice brought with it two additional concerns. One was the release of huge quantities of methane gas. Already, thawing permafrost land areas were contributing significant quantities of methane. So, while the human race had almost eliminated its carbon footprint, nature was busy producing its own.

The other problem from melting ice caps and permafrost was the potential to unleash anthrax-like diseases, flu, viruses, and even dangerous ticks and mosquitos.

Hopefully, the implanted chips and detection devices in use at the domes would help in the event of an outbreak. So far, they had quickly identified new disease threats and enabled actions to isolate and contain them before they were able to grow to pandemic stature. But how well would they work with diseases that might be very different than those already known?

***

Industrial change. Well before the first dome was even complete, the United States had declared itself carbon emission-free, putting natural gas and coal producers virtually out of business. Crude oil extraction and refining continued, but solely to make jet fuel, plastics, and a myriad of other products. Other countries soon followed suit as a condition of the assistance that the U.S. was providing.

FINAL CHANCE

Manufacturers making fossil-fuel-burning machines –
including cars, trucks, or other vehicles – had to quickly get
with the program, which required electricity from solar, wind,
or hydropower.

And get with the program they did. Companies adapted,
reinvented themselves, and started up whole new industries.
The major problem remained: finding enough workers. The
whole world needed them.

This massive transformation, especially when combined
with the SHARE program's need for workers, practically
eliminated unemployment for those mentally and physically
able to work.

***

The human threat. As well as everything was going, the
biggest threat of all came from human beings – both at home
and abroad. There were businesses affected by the changes
that were too slow to adapt and lost out to other, more nimble
companies. Their owners, managers, and employees were
angry.

Others made mistakes and blamed everyone else. Still,
others didn't want to adapt, but that wasn't an option. And
then some just wanted to burn a little fossil fuel for old times'
sake and profit.

Perhaps the largest aligned opposition group came from
the politicians of the conservative party and their "news"
outlets. These politicians watched as all the things they had
historically railed against were starting to pay off handsomely
for their constituents. As the conservative news outlets lost
advertisers, the special interest groups became less likely to
support candidates that had very steep climbs to get elected.
They were losing both constituents and financial supporters.

Another group that was angry, but didn't have much power, were those once referred to as "deplorables." For the most part, they had lost their military-grade automatic weapons and their gun cheering NRA. On top of that, they remembered how quickly and efficiently the military had cleared them away when they tried to revolt. Embarrassingly so. They still had guns sufficient for hunting and keeping away the odd burglar. But the Proud Boys weren't so proud, and the Klansmen were keeping their sheets in the linen closet.

And then there were the religious fundamentalists or evangelicals. They objected to the 'smaller family' incentives, birth control, women's rights, gay rights, and pretty much rights to anyone unlike themselves. Jesus would not have been impressed.

Many of these groups didn't dislike domes as much as they didn't like to see so many people being helped to get better healthcare, education, and jobs. Proof of that was made clear by the sheer number of private domed estates, many even bigger than Grover Nerdkist II's.

***

The political climate. Climate change may have been on the tip of most people's tongues, but political change wasn't. In part, that was because so much change had already taken place, and it was working.

Congress was operating more efficiently than ever with fixed-term limits. Even though one party had been dominating election outcomes, new, enthusiastic candidates entered the system at a faster rate, allowing the electorate more choice than ever before. And the last of the Supreme Court's lifetime appointees had passed away or retired, replaced with ten-year term judges whose terms would expire at the rate of one appointee per four-year presidential term.

***

The geo-political climate. As in the U.S., most of the world was fully occupied with protecting themselves from the ravages of climate change. Ensuring food supplies, building domes, improving or replacing infrastructure to withstand the severity of floods and wind, were the all-consuming subjects and goals. And most of the world was, to a greater or lesser extent, dependent upon the U.S. for technology and assistance in achieving that protection.

Certain industries around the world were damaged or rendered obsolete by the harsh restrictions on carbon emissions. Some of those industries, such as oil, gas, and coal, were nationalized industries in some countries that substantially funded their governments.

The American attitude toward the global carbon emission agreement was absolute. Countries that deviated from this standard, either directly or complicitly, were subject to severe sanctions, and not only from the U.S. Everyone knew that they all must comply if the earth was to recover. Not following the agreement was not a smart option.

President Bo Sanders was inheriting the perfect economy for a progressive. The treasury was solid, thanks to an almost fully employed populace, booming businesses, income from overseas programs, and scaled back military spending. Most everyone had a job, good healthcare, and their kids had access to education.

***

Chapter 23 - Moving Day Wrinkles

The State of Washington, D.C. Kari and Otis had just settled into their married relationship, but Kari was still adjusting to the reality of life without her father. Not surprisingly, Otis's appointment to the Secretary of Education position was a huge morale boost for both of them, and it seemed to help rescue Kari from her doldrums. Otis's enthusiasm and optimism were highly contagious.

One of Kari's first reactions to her reborn optimism was to finally get a dog. They had talked about it a lot but never seemed to have the time. Otis never had a dog, but Kari grew up with a furry "brother," Fritz. Fritz was a shepadoodle (half German shepherd, half poodle), and Kari was definitely a doodle fan, but she was concerned that another shepadoodle might not be able to match her feelings and memories of Fritz. So, they decided on a goldendoodle (half golden retriever) and named him, Yogi.

The cuteness, vitality, and innocence of a puppy lifted the Patel-Grahams' happiness to higher levels. Yogi's playfulness and desire to please seemed to be just what was needed at Voltas Place.

***

The inauguration, January 20th, 2061. Kari and Otis had front row seats for the inauguration, and it was a high point in Otis's life. Kari was thrilled for him, but the event brought her back down to reality, compared with the past three weeks of frolicking with Yogi while the Senate limped along in "lame duck" fashion. They'd had a lot of time to enjoy each other and their furry addition to the family, but now, it was back to business as usual.

As he watched Bo Sanders' inauguration, Otis looked at Kari and asked, "Are you alright?"

"Do you mean am I sad about being at Bo's inauguration instead of my own?"

"Yes."

Kari wasn't feeling sorry for herself for not being the person sworn in, but the event did conjure up Vijay's recent death. Many things still did.

She squeezed his hand and said, "No. I do miss my father though, but as long as I have this big hand to squeeze, I'll be just fine."

It was a beautiful day and although most everyone was aware that it was bitterly cold outside, inside the dome it was a very pleasant seventy degrees.

Bo Sanders was an impressive figure: tall, handsome, and articulate, with a bearing that came from eight years as the number two executive in the Administration. His speech was extremely complimentary of Rachel Metcalf's accomplishments during her two terms, as any true account would have to agree. She was a giant. A one-of-a-kind in every respect, including escaping two assassination attempts.

It was an emotional day in Washington, as it always was for public officials on inauguration day – people entering new roles and moving in, and an equal number leaving their positions and moving out. Even outside of the business of government, Washington sees twenty to twenty-five percent of renters and homeowners change in the months following an election, if the Party in power changes. Today's changes, of course, would not be as dramatic, but the air was still charged with excitement.

***

After a quiet stroll home, Kari and Otis let Yogi out and, despite his playing tight end in college, Otis took on the role of quarterback, throwing a ball to the appreciative puppy. Once the appreciative aspect turned to tired, Kari and Otis had a light lunch and relaxed, watching the Inaugural Parade on TV along with some talking heads and replays of the inauguration ceremony.

They were chilling out, with nothing to do except get ready for an inaugural ball or two when suddenly the station announced that the White House had been evacuated, adding that the president and family were safe. No other details were available. Automatically, both Otis and Kari pulled out their phones and made calls, each retreating to a different corner of the room.

It took a couple of tries for each of them, but Otis hung up and said, "I got the story."

Kari hung up and Otis explained what he'd learned. "When Bo and his family got to the White House after the parade, a White House staff member asked Molly where she wanted a specific piece of furniture, kinda like a safe, that hadn't been marked for placement. When Molly said it wasn't theirs, the

Secret Service scrambled into action and evacuated the building. It's now been taken away in a bomb disposal unit and everyone is returning."

Kari was surprised. "They were already moved in, and Rachel moved out, by the time they returned from lunch?"

Otis smiled and shook his head. "Yep. That's one busy place on January twentieth! The White House staff and movers have five hours to get it all done."

Kari added, "Five hours? Rachel out of the White House and the Sanders out of the Naval Observatory and into the White House! So, how does that work? I guess the Sanders tagged everything that was being moved with a specific location at the White House, days in advance. But then wouldn't the movers have noticed a missing tag?"

"Hmm, you're right. So, they either missed it or the item was already on the truck or was added during the transfer."

Kari thought and said, "But then the mover could just put it anywhere. Why even ask?"

Otis responded. "The movers that bring the Sanders' things are not allowed into the White House. So, when the White House staff were placing things, they asked the question."

"Sounds like a logistical nightmare, but then they're only moving personal stuff. Not furniture, refrigerators, and washing machines."

Otis smiled again. "Not like we mere mortals do!"

***

As they prepared for the evening, Otis got a call and, after a couple of minutes of serious conversation, he somberly related the contents of the call to Kari.

"That was Erika Ruiz, Bo's chief of staff. It was a bomb and not just that. There was poison gas. It could have taken down half the White House and killed hundreds of people with the explosion and poison gas."

Kari looked at Otis, her grey eyes wide with horror. "How did they know it was poison gas?" she asked.

Otis said, "Apparently when they detonated the bomb, they used a gas-tight containment chamber that could assess the gas. Miraculously, nobody got hurt.

"Who would try to pull that off? And why?"

Otis reminded Kari, "There have now been three assassination attempts and one assassination. After the attempts on Rachel, signs were pointing to a rogue Russian, possibly with connections to the Russian government. Anyhow, Erika has put the full cabinet on alert and reminded us not to accept any congratulatory gifts."

Kari nodded briefly. "That's right, I remember. They were talking about an oil guy in Siberia, weren't they?"

"Yeah. Wouldn't surprise me that it won't just be talking now. This will raise the stakes."

***

One would think that after an assassination attempt on the president, the District would be quiet and subdued. But that would be very wrong. Lucky attendees had spent thousands, tens of thousands, and even hundreds of thousands to attend the ball of their choice, with seating companions that made it worthwhile. The most famous actors, musicians, sports stars, and politicians were the draws for each one of the two-dozen official and unofficial balls. And of course, no one could attend wearing last year's gown, so add several thousand to that.

Both Kari and Otis wanted to attend the Neighborhood Ball and the Emily's List Ball. There were a few additional ones that they would try to get to, mainly because of the entertainment line-up, but these two were on their "must attend" list. They were going for the atmosphere, fun, and hopefully, the dancing. Otis had once made the mistake of telling Kari that she had a little Bollywood in her moves and that just egged her on.

The nighttime sixty-eight-degree temperature under the dome was more than thirty degrees warmer than outside the dome, so they didn't need coats as they entered a driverless Uber to the Washington Convention Center for the fourteenth Neighborhood Ball. The event was started by President Barack Obama in 2009 to encourage residents of the District to attend by offering ticket prices that were either free or at very modest prices. There were three differences between then and now – the District had become a State, there were no free tickets, and the modest prices were twenty times higher. The Ball was also digitally connected to satellite Neighborhood Balls in over fifty cities. President Bo Sanders and the First Lady, Molly, would begin their long night of parties here, addressing both the local and remote venues and then leading off the dancing. Large screens and the latest technology would help keep all the parties and excitement connected at full throttle.

Despite arriving early, the party was in full swing when they arrived and the well-known couple was quickly engaged in a long succession of short and convivial conversations, including a warm conversation with the new president and his wife. Kari was acquainted with Bo Sanders through her brief campaign run, but Otis and Sanders had known each other for quite a few years, mainly through football. Sanders played college ball at USC and they had met on opposing sides many times. When Sanders announced Otis as his Education secretary, he'd commented that in the past they'd only met as members of the opposite team. He was now very happy that they were going to be teammates.

The seriousness of the afternoon's near-disaster at the White House was put on hold. This was an evening to have fun.

They bumped into a few more acquaintances and then pulled themselves away to "get down and boogie" on the crowded dance floor.

About an hour later, the music stopped, and Bo Sanders addressed the attendees at the Convention Center as well as those at the satellite Neighborhood Balls around the country. He kept it short and upbeat and then he and Molly walked onto the dance floor, encouraging the many neighborhoods across the five time zones to join in.

Kari and Otis decided to walk the domed one-mile distance to the National Gallery for the Emily's List Ball. Emily's List had been a powerful force in helping women, including Kari, achieve political office since 1985. Originally their goal was even more specific – helping female candidates who favored abortion rights. The name "Emily" was an acronym for "Early Money Is Like Yeast," and the founder, Ellen Malcolm, explained that "it makes the dough rise."

Although the District was alive and happening, it was relatively quiet as Kari and Otis held hands and idly chatted as they made their way up Seventh Street.

Just outside the security barrier at the Gallery, they encountered a small and peaceful all-male protest that could only be described as extremely bizarre. The protest seemed to be made up of three small groups. The most identifiable was a group of Hasidic or Haredi Jews, carrying placards that were mostly in Hebrew; but a couple of signs in English voiced their protest against women working and, God forbid, making laws.

The second sub-group that seemed to have some congruity was a small group of Muslims, with pretty much the same argument. They too had signs written in Arabic and English.

The last sub-group could only be called that because they were different than the others. Their signs were all in English, of a sort, and the men were white Christians. Their signs were pro-life except for one that read, "Vote 4 wimmen in kitchens!"

Kari and Otis walked by slowly, looking at the group and then each other, both thinking, "Is this real?" It was only when they reached the entrance and a police officer asked for their invitations and scanned their chips that they stopped laughing.

The Emily's List Ball was a smaller event and Kari, in particular, knew many of the attendees. But it was one that Otis knew who got their rapt attention: Erika Ruiz, the new president's chief of staff.

The discovery of a bomb in the White House earlier that day appeared to have had a much bigger effect on Erika than

Bo, but that was not surprising. Bo was a seasoned politician and not present when the bomb was discovered, while Erika had actually seen the bomb and had stood right next to it. She hadn't been able to erase that vision, nor would she for some time. Otis and Kari's heartfelt concern for her melted Erika's resolve and the three of them hugged until she regained her composure. Kari then took her arm and led her off to the Ladies' Room.

Otis accepted a glass of champagne from a server, silently wishing it was a cold beer. As he took a sip, he heard, "Good evening, Otis." He turned to see an attractive, older woman standing before him with a matching glass of champagne. She looked familiar and his puzzled look gave away his need for help with her name. She said, "Isabelle Martin."

They hadn't met before, as the Chairs of the political parties generally operated in the background (or as some would say, in the shadows).

Kari had told Otis about her phone conversation with Martin before her earlier presidential campaign, so Otis was not pre-disposed to fondness; however, his natural inclination for warmth and kindness overcame any ill feelings.

"Good evening, Ms. Martin."

"Isabelle, please. Where's Karima?"

Otis smiled. "She'll be back in a moment. Congratulations, by the way, on another blue wave. I'm truly amazed at how you do it."

Martin asked, "Do what?"

Without hesitation, Otis answered, "Herd cats."

FINAL CHANCE

They were both full-out laughing when Kari returned with a quizzical look on her face. "That must have been a good one."

Martin replied, "You've got a good one here. When you've been around as long as I have, you realize that a sense of humor is possibly the best trait a partner can have."

Kari linked Otis's arm with hers and said, "You got that right!"

Isabelle held up her glass and said, "Best wishes in your new post, Otis. I have a feeling that your tenure in Education will change a lot of things. And Kari, I hope I'm still alive to toast you at another inaugural in eight years."

Kari smiled, "We'll see," as Isabelle glided away.

Kari updated Otis on Erika. "She'll be alright, but she decided to go home. Why don't we do the same? We both have big days tomorrow, so let's make sure we have time to finish this night off properly."

Otis smiled and gave her a knowing look out of the corner of his eye, "Or improperly."

Kari returned the look and ripped her phone from her purse to hail an Uber.

***

Chapter 24 - Situations

The Situation Room. Everyone was assembled in the Situation Room when Bo Sanders arrived. Although it was his first time attending as POTUS, he'd been here many times as VPOTUS and he was familiar with all the people in the room. The only new face in the room was Erika Ruiz, who Sanders had brought over from her role as his chief of staff when he was VP. He hadn't made any changes to the positions of National Security Advisor, Homeland Security Advisor, or heads of the CIA and FBI. He had worked with them under President Metcalf, and he respected their abilities.

Sanders opened the session. "Welcome to my first Situation Room session. I've requested this smaller meeting for two reasons. First, I'd like to ask this group that when we have these smaller sessions, we converse on a first-name basis. We can revert to the Mr. President stuff when others are attending. Okay? I need your candid input and I don't want the charade of hierarchy to get in the way of that."

The group returned his question with big smiles and, "Sure, Bo." "Okay, Bo." "Right on, Bo," and a "Yes Sir, Bo," from General Chavez, which for a moment, lightened the upcoming seriousness of the meeting.

Sanders shifted his smile into neutral. "What do we know so far about the bomb?"

FINAL CHANCE

The group was aware of the latest developments, so FBI Director Joe Strickland led off. "We have the moving company's worker, Dar Leaf, in custody. He confessed pretty quickly but we don't think he really understood what he was handling. He had been given a thousand dollars to put the package on the truck. He did that at the company's warehouse and had hidden it behind some hanging padded blankets. He'd been contacted by a guy he knew who'd done some contract moving work."

Strickland then emphasized his next sentence. "This 'guy' was a Russian immigrant, Maksim Antonov. Based on the details the moving company had on Antonov, we went to his last known address and found him dead – shot in the head. We found nothing helpful in his apartment, but Leaf had said he'd received a call from Antonov, so we checked and found that Antonov did have a phone account. The phone was probably taken when he was killed. The records showed the call to Leaf and ..." Strickland looked directly at Sanders, "there were several calls from Russia. We're trying to trace them. That's it."

Heidi Butler, the Director of the CIA reminded the group about whom they were probably dealing with. "Some of you may recall that after the attack on President Metcalf on Necker Island, we discussed Georgi Volkov as a suspect. We could never get Shamalov's cooperation to question Volkov."

Sanders jumped in. "I'm pretty sure I'll be getting a standard congratulatory call from Shamalov today and I'll raise the question again. But in the meantime, I'd like other options. And understanding that Volkov is barred from coming here, that includes grabbing him somewhere else, including Russia. So, Joe, keep the pressure on the tracing. Heidi and General Chavez ... whoops, Lydia, can you start to think about what an extraction would look like? I'll talk with the

Attorney General today and let her know what I'm thinking."

***

Lyndon Baines Johnson Building, The State of Washington, D.C. Secretary of Education, Otis B. Graham was on day one of his dream job. And he would readily admit that sitting at the top of a five-thousand-person strong department with close to a hundred-million-dollar budget was just a bit intimidating. Otis was pragmatic, but the excitement of what he and his team could accomplish burned far brighter than the daunting administrative challenges ahead. He smiled to himself, realizing that he probably had more problems than Bo Sanders, although Sanders' were more immediately life-threatening.

Otis had decided that his initial focus was on college affordability and effectiveness. The pushbacks here would mostly spring from funding issues at the state level. But one important ally in this regard was business, and next week he would chair another "Learning for Tomorrow's Business" session.

Otis realized that he had a job – actually a mission – that could keep him at his desk twenty-four hours a day. So, he made a vow to himself that he would, unless something unusual occurred, leave his office by six every day. He loved the possibilities that his new job offered, but he also loved his wife. He sensed that despite Kari's protestation that she wasn't bothered by the fact that it was Bo, and not herself, being inaugurated, she just might need a psychological boost. So, he packed up his briefcase, convinced that all the problems and opportunities would be safe until he tackled them again the next day, and walked home.

***

FINAL CHANCE

The White House. The president received his anticipated call from President Shamalov. After the brief, well-rehearsed, and pre-scripted congratulations, Sanders asked about interviewing Volkov.

In a most charming voice, which fooled only himself, Shamalov said, "Ahh yes. The very popular Mr. Volkov. President Metcalf asked too." And then, turning off the charm, he said with less polish, "I give you same answer. Call him. If he wants talk, okay with me. But I not force him to talk or arrest him. So, answer is same as with lady. Nyet. Good luck in new job."

Erika had been in the Oval Office during the call. She asked if he wanted the next congratulatory call and Bo told her instead to get Sue at Justice for him.

Bo had known Sue Cappiello since she had been Attorney General of Massachusetts. Her ever-present good nature and great sense of humor often hid her deep understanding of the law as well as her compassion.

"Hey, Sue. How are you?"

"I'm just fine, Mister President. What can the Department of Justice do for the leader of the free world?"

"Cut the crap, Ms. Attorney General. I do need your help or, at least, advice."

"What's the situation?"

"Does the name Georgi Volkov mean anything to you?"

"Do you mean apart from his big boat, sanctions, and banning?"

"Rachel Metcalf believed that Volkov was behind the attack or attacks on her, but Shamalov wouldn't help. I just tried with him and got another 'Nyet.' What happens if we grab Volkov and bring him in for questioning?"

"Do you mean other than a world war? Seriously, Mr. President. Tell me you're not contemplating that?"

"Of course not. I was just curious. ... That bad, huh?"

"What do we have on him?"

"Nothing, really. But if we got phone records of him contacting the people who planted the bomb the other day?"

"Hmm. Better, but still pretty thin. Perhaps there're some crumbs in the Metcalf investigation. I'll look."

"Okay. Let's see what Heidi and Joe dig up. Despite dealing with a vengeful president, how's your first day?"

"So far, so good. Making sure my team is the right one."

***

Georgetown. Kari was startled when she heard the front door open. Cautiously, she peaked around the corner and let out a sigh of relief as she watched Otis try to juggle his briefcase and a bouquet of flowers while fending off a leaping goldendoodle. He put the case down and Kari rescued the flowers as he accepted the leaps and kisses from Yogi.

Otis laughed, "Well I'm glad someone's happy to see me!"

Kari moved in, trying to outmaneuver Yogi and hug Otis. "I'm thrilled to see you, too, but I thought you'd be working late. You didn't get fired already, did you?"

"No. Not yet."

"I haven't even thought about starting dinner."

"Good. I've booked us a table at the French restaurant in …," looking at his watch, "forty-five minutes. We can walk over, so get crackin'. What's Yogi's situation?"

"He's been fed but he'd love a few minutes outside with his dad. What's the occasion? Did you fix the world's education problems already?"

"Just get ready."

***

Chapter 25 - Botox, Anyone?

The Situation Room. The same small team that met yesterday was back again.

Sanders walked in. "Good morning."

FBI Director, Joe Strickland began, "Good morning Mr. ahh ... Bo. We've traced the number that called Antonov, and it is a type of unregistered pay-as-you-go phone. It was issued from a phone shop in St. Petersburg, which happens to be the home of GazProd, Georgi Volkov's company. We were also able to get a transcript of the call."

Sanders interrupted. "How did you get that?"

"The dome telephony architecture captures all calls within it. Leaf is under arrest for a felony and Antonov would have been if he was alive. That might have been enough but the fact that Antonov is dead pushed the judge over the line, and he allowed it."

Sanders nodded understanding, but you could tell his mind was thinking about what Strickland had just said.

Strickland continued. "The call from Antonov to Leaf was simply an offer, but the one that Antonov received was more interesting. First of all, it was in Russian. Secondly, it included a threat to Antonov's family in Russia if he didn't successfully follow through with the request. And thirdly, it tied that threat to his brother's job at GazProd."

Sanders asked, "How do we know that?"

"The threat was that his brother might suffer a serious accident on his job, and we know from correspondence found at Antonov's apartment that his brother worked at GazProd."

Sanders said, "That tightens the noose a little bit but not nearly enough."

The CIA Director, Heidi Butler jumped in. "When we were investigating the Necker Island attack, we traced the ship that launched the torpedo as having originated its voyage to the Yamal Peninsula."

Sanders replied cautiously. "Hmm. You're looking for a match to or from the Russian number sometime before the Necker Island attack and immediately afterward, across the entire country?"

Everyone looked at Butler as he said, "Yep."

Strickland asked, "Heidi, so you're thinking that there may have been some type of coordination from the U.S.?"

Butler confirmed and Strickland said it seemed reasonable and he'd run it by the Department of Justice.

Sanders had another thought. "Is this search as simple as entering the Russian phone number and some date parameters?"

Strickland confirmed, "Yes. Pretty much."

Sanders said, "Let's run that sucker back as early as we can. We might find more calls between Antonov and Russia, or even pick something up on the earlier Metcalf attack. Anything else?"

Strickland added a cautionary note. "Let's not get our hopes up. These phones are typically used for short periods, one job at a time, but we can try it."

Ollie Barth, the president's National Security Advisor, quickly stuck his hand up. "We've analyzed the gas. Really nasty stuff. A form of botulinum neurotoxin. You've all heard of one of its formulations – Botox. But this version is scarily deadly. We haven't seen it used as a weapon before so there's no history to trace it to a possible enemy."

"Except the U.S. Army," added General Chavez." That got everyone's attention and she continued, "At the outbreak of World War II, the Army investigated the possibility of weaponizing the toxin at Ft. Detrick in Maryland. That was the genesis of the U.S. biological weapons center at the site until 1969. Now it's become the center for our biological defense program."

Sanders asked, "Are you saying that this could be a domestic attack?"

Chavez replied, "I doubt it, given the evidence we've uncovered, but it's possible that if some toxin is stored there, it could be where it came from. I've asked some questions and will let you know."

Barth added, "The toxin itself isn't difficult to make and since it's used as the source for Botox, it's available from many companies. I did some research and, in the 1990s, a Japanese cult sprayed the stuff around in subways and nobody died.

The gas we found, however, is much more complex and it turned the normally slow-acting botulinum neurotoxin into an extremely aggressive nerve agent. The bomb was powerful but pretty straightforward. The gas was sophisticated."

Sanders asked if anyone had anything else and there was nothing, so he summed up. "Joe. Looks like you've got the action items. Get a sign-off from Justice on the expanded phone trawl and if it's a go, run that telephone number through the system. See ya all tomorrow."

They met again the next day and the next – all week, in fact – but the news was … well, there was no news. The search for additional calls from the Russian number turned up nothing. So, they were back to square one.

As had happened with President Metcalf, the all-consuming job of the presidency meant that the focus was always on the next pressing problem at hand, and there were always plenty of those to keep the bomb attempt investigation relegated to the back burner.

***

The State of Washington, D.C. The most pressing issue at the moment had become the frequent and lethal power outages. At first, they were inconveniences. But then they intensified, as hospitals, transportation, and industries were shut down for hours at a time. The outages were often coupled with power storage drainages and blocks so that backup power wasn't available when needed.

The outrages that popped up around the country seemed to be as much about the inability to provide backup power generated from fossil fuel as the outages themselves. The growing calls for reliable fossil fuel power backup had been rebuffed until people died as hospitals and supply chains (especially food-related) were affected. Now, the strict policy of using only renewable energy was in jeopardy.

As a result, Sanders' Situation Room guests this morning included the Secretary of SHARE, Emma Steadman ... the Administrator of the Environmental Protection Agency, Noelle Warren ... the Secretary of Homeland Security, Althea Crawford ... and the Secretary of Energy, Carolyn Woodson, in addition to Joe Strickland and the Vice President, Doug Johnson.

Sanders arrived a few minutes late, said his hellos on the run, and, as he took his seat, said, "I've asked Joe to join us because these outages aren't coincidences, especially when they're coupled with power backup drains and blocks. But first, Carolyn, what's the latest on last night's LA outage?"

"It was similar to the others except for the duration – over four hours. No obvious cause. And although the backup power banks were fully charged, they showed to be less than ten percent available. That forced the monitoring system to ration out only a small amount of power. Tragically, that prolonged the outage at UCLA Med Center and two deaths occurred."

Sanders replied, "We're getting serious grief all around the country from a much wider group than the usual oil/gas nutters – if it were up to them, we'd all have money to burn. But now, clinicians, transportation, agri-business, and millions of disgruntled citizens are clamoring for action. We're one hundred percent dependent on electricity and it's getting to the point where we can't depend on it. There are two issues I want to focus on this morning, and they're interdependent. The first is understanding why this is happening. Althea, what's your assessment?"

FINAL CHANCE

"Structurally, there is nothing wrong with our generation, transmission, and storage systems," said the Secretary of Homeland Security. "It's the power management system that's failing and, from all the analysis and troubleshooting we've done, we believe it's being hacked. The power goes off and then comes back on without any inputs from us, making it very difficult to find the cause. Last night's four-hour duration gave us much more time to investigate, but it's still unclear what the cause is. We asked the FBI to assist."

Sanders looked at Joe Strickland, "Joe. Any ideas?"

"We were in the system when it switched back on early this morning and there were a couple of things that seemed unusual but nothing conclusive. We're running simulations on a replay of the outage, start to finish. I hope we'll have more information later today."

Sanders asked, "Okay. Let me ask this? What if this goes unchecked, even if it's just today? What are our options?"

Secretary Woodson spoke first. "Mr. President ... Bo. When the doming program was planned along with the move to renewable energy, we agreed to have a disaster backup system in place that would be able to provide power to the industrial domes, agri-domes, and city domes. In those early days, we maintained the existing power stations to be in a constant state of readiness, connected to the grids at all times. Over the years, a combination of never needing the backup and the big demand for labor slowly eroded the readiness levels of the power plants. Most of these plants are essentially mothballed and it would take weeks – if not longer – to get them up and running."

Sanders visibly slumped and asked, "Althea, any thoughts?"

"It wouldn't be pretty, but the Army and National Guards have mobile power plants that could deliver power directly to hospitals and other critical facilities."

Given even a little hope, Sanders perked up. "How many units are out there?"

"Of the size we would need, a few thousand. But how many would be immediately operable, I couldn't say."

Noelle Warren interjected, "I'm not objecting to that plan but if we do that, how does that sit with our international agreements on carbon emissions?"

Sanders acknowledged the problem. "It will cost us, but we can't sustain the damage the outages are inflicting."

Woodson injected some hope. "We're working on establishing a manual override of the power management system that will let us fully utilize the power in the storage banks. That's enough for twenty-four hours of power for each dome unit, and if we ration it out to critical facilities, we can probably extend that to thirty-six hours. That might at least give us time to position the mobile units."

That gave Sanders an idea. "Carolyn, how long does it take to fully charge the power banks?"

"Not sure, as there are many variables. I think I know where you're going though, and I think that with a manual override on the power management system, along with some rationing, we should be able to keep all critical activities up and running, barring some extraordinarily bad weather."

"How much disruption would persist for non-critical use?"

"It should be minimal and confined to nights."

Sanders asked, hopefully, "When do you expect to have the override in place?"

Woodson looked at her silenced phone, tapped it, smiled, and said, "It's done."

Sanders smiled, "Great. Now, Emma, Carolyn, what about doubling up storage capacity at critical sites?" What are the issues, timeframes, costs?

Emma Steadman was pretty confident that there was a decent inventory of storage banks available and that the costs weren't prohibitive. She'd have a list of critical sites and priorities drawn up and move on it.

Sanders was pleased and adjourned the meeting with a plea to Joe. "Okay. We got our band-aid, but we need to find out who's doing this, ASAP."

The meeting ended and as Sanders watched his VP, Doug Johnson leave, he felt bad as he realized that he hadn't asked Doug for his thoughts.

***

Edinburg, Pennsylvania. Nerdkist looked at the caller ID on his phone and said cheerily, "Good morning. What kind of interesting tidbits do you have today?"

He listened for a while and hung up, not nearly as happy as he'd been moments earlier.

***

Chapter 26 - The Year of the Storage Battery

The State of Washington, D.C. The best the FBI could do was to trace the power hacks to Russia, and none of the other agencies could do better than that. It could be government or civilian, and the odds were even, despite Moscow disavowing any knowledge.

The band-aid on the system using a manual override worked ... to the extent that critical industries were kept functioning. That silenced the loudest and most organized critics, but the brownouts and occasional blackouts for domestic users were beginning to get worrisome. Conservative political groups, funded mostly by the almost dormant fossil fuel industry, fanned the flames using exaggerations and lies in attempts to whip up anti-government sentiment.

Sanders refused to buckle and violate the U.S.'s global environmental agreements. Science and the chaotic climate were on his side: the environment was still too fragile.

Pretty much ignoring the anti-government propaganda, the more practical general population stayed out of the debates and simply bought household storage batteries. The demand was incredible, pushing the industry to new levels. Other countries, fearing that what was happening in the U.S. might spread, jumped on the bandwagon, buying batteries that most would never need.

On the political front, however, many in Sanders' party were worried, especially those coming up for re-election in 2062. Karima Patel-Graham would be one of those – if she decided to run – but she stood firmly with Sanders on the issue and made no secret about it.

***

Voltas Place, The State of Washington, D.C. Other than brownouts and the rare blackout, the rest of 2061 rolled on uneventfully, both within the U.S. and around the world. Otis was loving his new role, loving Kari and loving Yogi. For her part, each passing day, week, and month moved her father's death further into the past. The sudden realizations that he wasn't there – accompanied by feeling like the air was being sucked out of reach – were becoming fewer and a little less intense.

Jennifer was spending Thanksgiving in D.C., and the Thursday holiday gave Kari and Otis more time to spend with her. Jennifer came down when she could, always by train, and both Kari and Otis looked forward to her visits almost as much as Yogi did. "Grandma," as Kari and Otis called Jennifer when talking with Yogi, loved spending the days walking around the domed state with her furry "grandchild." Her visits weren't as often as the D.C. family would have liked, but Jennifer also had two human grandchildren in Cambridge to spoil now.

After the traditional Thanksgiving dinner that the three humans had contributed their various skills to prepare – and Yogi had shown his appreciation for – Jennifer casually asked Kari if she'd given any more thought about running again for the Senate next year. Otis looked on, intently, as he had been avoiding asking that question.

Kari let a few seconds go by, long enough to create additional interest, before saying, "I have."

There was an even longer silence before Jennifer finally asked, "And?"

Quickly, this time, Kari smiled and said, "Yes."

There were big grins and happy exclamations, so much so that it roused Yogi from his turkey-induced nap, his tail wagging furiously.

Jennifer's interest in politics had never waned, but her other priorities had pushed it lower on her list. Now, in the presence of two politicians – Otis would argue that he wasn't one – she enjoyed re-immersing herself. She asked Kari what had helped her make that decision.

Kari referred to their conversation a few years ago and expressed her desire to be a part of the important work going on, especially with the president's controversial aid to dozens of countries around the world in helping them dome.

Kari stated the obvious, that these countries could not afford to adequately dome and convert to clean energy, leaving millions to suffer or die, while allowing carbon emissions to hamper the earth's recovery. "What choice do we have? China, Russia, and Europe are also assisting the poorer countries. For the first time, the world is fighting the same fight against the same enemy. And I want to be on the frontlines."

Otis added, "It's amazing that people who have everything they want, object when we help others in need. Especially when all our needs are the same."

Jennifer smiled. "It's not amazing, it's just business as usual for the lobbyists and publicists doing their jobs for those few greedy people. Vijay used to be surprised about the obvious wrongs of our political and economic system. He was so refreshingly naïve when it came to people's behavior. He could never understand why some would purposefully hurt others."

Kari quipped, "You're talking about a guy who would try to catch flies alive and move them outside. I remember getting a disapproving look once for squashing a big ugly spider on the wall after being so proud of my bravery. But going back to my decision to run, I'm ready for the fight. Besides, what else could I do?"

Her rhetorical question was met with two broad grins. Both Jennifer and Otis were happy with her first answer.

***

Chestnut Hill, Massachusetts. One month later, the combined Patel, Belikov, Graham clan had all gathered at Jennifer's to celebrate New Year's Eve – seeing out 2061 and welcoming in 2062. Kari, Otis, and Yogi had been up for Christmas and would return to D.C. the following week. They had all spent a full year without Vijay's physical presence, but the memories remained vivid.

Nadya and Jason's two children – Adam, and Vijay Jr. – had formed a boisterous threesome with Yogi. They played soccer with him for hours, trying to see if their budding passing skills could thwart Yogi's quick and effective reflexes. Often in the afternoons, the adults were treated to the quiet and moving scene of the three of them asleep on the sofa in the TV room, prompting both Nadya and Jason to begin thinking that maybe it was time for a puppy of their own.

Jennifer was seventy-three and still ran three to five miles every morning, but she'd traded in her martial arts gear for a yoga mat. She loved minding her grandchildren and she still spent a lot of time with her charity interests.

Alek was officially retired but he kept up with developments at Beli-Tel and was always tinkering with something. He and Sophie had made it their goal to visit all of the hundred-twenty-five – and growing – re-vitalization domes. They had notched up sixty-seven so far.

Kari and Otis fielded the constant questions about the world of "inner-politics" and everyone was thrilled that Kari was running for the Senate again. Alek, Nadya, and Jason, the three techies, peppered Kari with dozens of questions and theories about the power grid hacking, and Jason exposed his lingering suspicion of Laurence Donald, Grover Nerdkist, and Karen Rover.

Kari confirmed only what was reported in the press, that the hacking appeared to come from Russia but that no further information was known. Alek wondered if they were looking at it from the right perspective, but he kept his thoughts to himself.

They all had high-capacity home power batteries that were fully topped up, and they all knew they had a lot to be thankful for.

***

Edinburg, Pennsylvania. The gang was back and despite the White House bomb failure, and the fairly mild effects of the power hacks, their spirits were surprisingly high. This was due, in part, because Volkov was happy. He had once again eluded his ban against entering the country; and as he and Argawal talked in hushed tones in the hallway, their smiles were reminiscent of Cheshire cats.

FINAL CHANCE

While Volkov's cheery mood was welcomed, it also prompted concern – especially with Nerdkist, who must have had a shred of morality as he wondered what heinous plan was being considered. He even asked Volkov why he was so upbeat. With a wink and a finger to lips, Volkov replied that they would all find out soon enough. Chills ran down Nerdkist's spine.

***

Chapter 27 - Blast from the Past?

Somewhere high above the Arctic Circle. The international team of archaeologists and scientists from the U.S., Russia, Finland, Germany, Italy, and Greece had just finished their two-month investigation of the oldest and northern-most known civilization in the Arctic. A number of them were flying out immediately to the U.S. to present their astonishing findings to the annual Archaeological Institute of America (AIA) Conference, findings that could affect the current measures in place to deal with climate change.

***

The State of Washington, D.C. The AIA was the world's oldest and largest archaeological organization, founded in 1879. The 2062 annual meeting was being held at the Marquis Hotel and boasted over three thousand attendees. The record crowd size was due, in part, to the presentation by the Arctic Team.

One of the Team's major objectives was to find, study and assess the risks of ancient pathogens or other disease causes that might be released from the melting glaciers. They were examining a five-thousand-year-old civilization that had become partially exposed by the melting ice. Russian oil explorers had come across the area and alerted the scientific and archaeological communities of its existence.

FINAL CHANCE

The eight-member presenting team was first on the program, and the Washington Convention Center was packed – the audience on the edges of their seats. Their material was mesmerizing, at least to fellow archaeologists and scientists, especially as it was fresh – literally less than a week old – and was being seen and reported for the first time.

Dr. Toni Fauci was the lead presenter. She covered their findings in an extremely detailed yet understandable way, ensuring that the many journalists present would be able to clearly and accurately communicate with their audiences. The methodology and conclusions were scientifically sound, and the bottom line – which drew a major sigh of relief – was that the risks from ancient pathogens were extremely low. Headlines throughout the world quickly trumpeted the removal of this potential nightmare scenario from the long list of theoretical climate change dangers.

***

Early the next morning, a Marquis hotel operator rang the bellman's desk to request that a staff member knock at the door of room forty-two-twelve, as the occupant was not answering her wake-up call.

Frankie Norton, the young bellman, knocked. He then knocked louder, calling out, "Wake-up call!" And then banging, he tried one last time. As per the hotel's procedure, he used his pass key to open the door, calling out loudly, "Good morning, wake-up call!"

There was no reply and the black-out curtains covering the windows made it impossible to see, so he switched on the light. There were a lot of pillows on the bed, and he wasn't immediately sure if anyone was in it. Seeing that the bathroom door was open, he slowly walked toward the bed, moving to the side so he could see over and around the pillows.

As he came within arm's length of the bed, Frankie Norton gasped and screamed as he looked down at the dead woman, her eyes and mouth both wide open and her face contorted and frozen in a permanent look of anguish and pain. He stood staring, numb with fear, until he finally picked up the bedside phone and called the front desk.

Returning to the lobby he was surprised to see that the medics and police had responded so quickly. The night manager was still there, and Frankie commented, "That was fast. I just called it in."

The manager seemed distracted and said, "Called what in?"

"A dead woman in forty-two twelve."

"Forty-two-twelve? They're here for fifty-two-eleven."

***

Even one death in an eleven-hundred room hotel was unusual, and two was enough to bring out a detective from the D.C. Police – but by the time Detective Snodgrass arrived, there were three dead, and by noon, all eight members of the Arctic Team had been found dead in their rooms.

Snodgrass called for police and medical back-up. The police ascertained that of the two-thousand-plus guests staying in the hotel, all except the eight were alive. Doctors from D.C. hospitals as well as Walter Reed and Johns Hopkins were examining the bodies and discussing their opinions. None of them could offer anything but speculation, except for the inescapable logic that they contracted something on their Arctic field trip.

FINAL CHANCE

Members of the CDC arrived, and, with the help of the AIA, they began contacting the other members of the recent Arctic trip who had not come to D.C. It was difficult to contact any of them, but of the ones who were located, they were all dead.

Over the next few hours, ambulances were seen leaving the Marquis, carrying the bodies to various hospitals in the area for further examination.

***

The White House. President Sanders was briefed on the deaths and emerging information and views of the medical experts. So far, the consensus of the experts' opinions was that the deaths at the Marquis were the result of mycotic aneurysms brought on by septic embolisms. The condition is extremely rare and is typically caused by bacterial infection. That was of little help to the president.

***

The CDC had finally located all of the Arctic Team members, and all were dead except for one Russian. The symptoms appeared to be the same.

***

Johns Hopkins University Hospital. A scientist at the hospital, Dr. Marco Rigoni, had isolated a bacterium in one of the victims that could have been responsible for the infection that led to the aneurysm. Scientists conducting their tests on the other victims were alerted of the possibility. Dr. Rigoni's comments included his description of the bacteria. "It matches no other bacteria in our data-base, and its unique attributes made it difficult to identify."

Over the course of another couple of days, all the medical scientists involved with the other victims, both in the U.S. and elsewhere, had confirmed the presence of Rigoni's bacterial discovery.

***

A few days later all hell broke loose. Dozens of people who had attended the AIA conference, plus people who had been at the Marquis hotel, died suddenly and mysteriously, with the same symptoms that the Artic Team had shown. Frankie Norton was among them. This was a communicable disease and the CDC swung into action.

Working closely with the scientists who had been working with the victims, they quickly came to the conclusion that the disease was transmitted through contaminated surfaces. That was about all they knew. The disease appeared extremely aggressive – under five days from contact to death – but up to this point, nobody knew what the progressive preliminary symptoms were.

Utilizing the sophisticated contact tracing that Beli-Tel had uploaded into the embedded chips, the CDC immediately began to contact and talk with – in person or by phone – those potential victims who had been in contact with the deceased.

The following day, close to a hundred people, all over the country died, and the word from Europe and Russia was almost as bad.

The embedded chips alerted the CDC that over two thousand attendees at the conference had left the D.C. dome to travel onwards to their home domes or elsewhere. The geometric progression over five days was staggering – tens of thousands of contacts were likely, and the progression characteristics were still unknown. The president was apprised of the potential disaster and he decided to "talk to the people."

In his national TV address, President Sanders urged everyone to follow the CDC guidelines, explaining what they should do to minimize their chance of becoming infected. He also shared many of the actions taken by the CDC.

Feedback on the address and Sanders' handling of the situation was mainly positive, but there was still significant pushback, especially as it related to the continued "incarceration" within the domes.

***

Dr. Rigoni had made the most progress with understanding the bacteria's characteristics and he became the point person interfacing with the CDC and a number of pharmaceutical companies to develop a vaccine.

***

The CDC had requested a blood sample from the Russian survivor from the Arctic expedition, Ivan Petrovitch. They were told that he had died, although they were unsure about his cause of death. Dr. Rigoni was advised, and through private channels, he contacted a Russian friend from his medical school days who now worked for the Russian Ministry of Health, or Minzdrav. It took a few days, but his friend was able to send Rigoni an extremely detailed, electronic analysis from a blood sample immediately following Petrovitch's death.

Rigoni observed the presence of "memory" T-lymphocytes, as well as B-lymphocytes that were specific to the bacteria he had found in the victims. These cells were indicative of a successful defense and cleansing of infected blood cells. Exactly what a vaccine would do.

He contacted his Russian friend again and asked if there might be an older analysis on file, but was told that there probably wouldn't be one, as the collection of electronic analyses on a national level was a very recent development. There could be local records but that would take some time. He promised to see what he could find.

Dr. Rigoni was the doctor who had worked with Vijay Patel when Vijay discovered his early cancer through the analytical capability of his watch invention. He had attended Vijay's funeral where he met and spoke with Alek Belikov and Jason Patel. Rigoni wondered if Vijay's technology might be able to help with this disease, too, so he called Beli-Tel and shared what he had learned from the Russian blood analysis. Alek, Jason and Nadya went to work.

As the days passed and the deaths grew, so did the understanding of the condition's symptoms. They weren't unusual at first: tiredness, mild headaches, nasal drip, slightly elevated temperature. The headaches then grew in intensity and type, changing from dull aches to throbbing aches to severe pinpointed aches in the forehead region. Toothaches, earaches, and backaches were also reported.

The CDC began urging everyone on their contact lists to self-isolate, escalate their hand hygiene, stop sharing of utensils, and avoid mouth to mouth contact. They were hopeful that their actions would slow the deaths, but each day brought higher death tolls. Unlike the earlier pandemics, this condition, at least for the moment, offered no opportunity for recovery, so it was the morgues, not the hospitals, that were inundated.

FINAL CHANCE

So when, very quickly, Beli-Tel was able to upload new capability to the embedded chips that would detect the bacteria, it was only to advise the infected victims that they would die within five days. The irony was that this notice, essentially a Final Notice, was not dissimilar from Vijay Patel's first health watch, the VT2. It was not lost on Alek, who had worked with Vijay on its development.

***

Given what was known, everyone was doing everything they could. However, one week after the AIA conference, almost twenty thousand people had died.

***

Chapter 28 – Alphabet Soup

CDC Headquarters. At the beginning of the second week after the conference, the CDC received a call from Maharishi Pharma, a pharmaceutical company in Pune, India. They had a vaccine that was ninety-five-percent effective in preventing and stopping the progression of the Arctic Flu, as the disease was being called. They had one million doses that they would provide within twenty-four-hours for one thousand dollars a dose. Results guaranteed.

***

The White House. Assembled in the Oval Office were the heads of the CIA, FBI, NSA, HHS, NIAID and the CDC's Preparedness and Response team. A real "Alphabet Soup." President Sanders and Erika Ruiz arrived and got right down to business. Sanders asked, "Assuming that this vaccine is authentic, how is it possible that they developed it so quickly?"

Dipika Krishnan, Secretary of Health and Human Services flatly stated, "There is only one possible answer. They've been working on it for some time ... before the outbreak. Months, at least."

Sanders grilled back, "How can that be? Everything I've heard is that no one has ever seen a bacterium like this."

Heidi Butler, CIA, replied. "Well, if the vaccine is real and if the bacteria is really something new, I wouldn't rule out a new, unique form of germ blackmail."

Everyone looked at Butler, trying to understand what she'd just said, and Sanders asked, "Explain what that would look like."

"Well, the plan is pretty simple. First, develop a new, highly contagious and dangerous bacteria. Second, develop the antidote or vaccine. Next, launch the infection and let it wreak havoc for a while and then pick out your blackmail targets."

Joe Strickland, FBI, asked, "Have any of the other affected countries been offered the vaccine?"

Ollie Barth, NSA, replied, "Good question. We haven't heard anything, but then we've not shared it either."

Sanders asked Erika to immediately call the heads of state in the other affected countries.

Erika left and Sanders asked the status of the latest results.

Dr. Amy Ellingson, the Leader of the CDC's Preparedness and Response team replied, looking at her tablet, "There are twenty-five-thousand dead and another forty-thousand to fifty-thousand with symptoms on our contact reports."

Sanders asked for confirmation that the vaccine from Maharishi would stop cases in progress and Dr. Ellingson replied, "They say it works, but they won't share any test results. And even if it does, many of the people currently with symptoms will be dead by the time we get the vaccines."

Dr. Ahmed Talib, the Director of the National Institute of Allergy and Infectious Diseases (NIAID), added, "What is certain is that each day thousands more will develop symptoms and thousands more will die. Mr. President, blackmail or not, we don't have a choice. Even with very good luck, we are months away from a vaccine. If our guidelines are followed, the cases may decrease, but ..."

Erika returned and everyone turned to hear what she had to say.

"I haven't been able to reach the Russians yet but no one else has been offered the vaccine."

There was complete silence as everyone in the room pondered Erika's statement.

Strickland broke the silence. "There could be a straightforward answer in that we have by far the largest exposure because of the conference."

Heidi Butler asked the doctors in the room, "How would we roll this out and test it, given the risks for both a quick and slow roll out? I'd be very concerned about doing it too quickly."

Dr. Ellingson countered, "So far no one has survived once the symptoms develop so they have nothing to lose. I'm in favor of giving it to anyone who definitely has the symptoms. Besides, the vaccine may be able to reduce the inevitability of death and reduce the symptoms."

Sanders replied. "Good points. I don't like this, and I want to get to the bottom of how this vaccine was developed, but for now, unless someone has a better idea, I'm for going ahead ... urgently. Dipika, can you arrange the deal with

Maharishi, committing to pay but withholding payment until we can assess the efficacy of the vaccine? How long do you think it will take before we know if it works and is safe?"

Dr. Krishnan confirmed the action and said, "We should know if it works within a few days if it stops the symptom progression. Ahmed, how long before we know it's safe?"

"Hmm. Good question. If it stops the progression and the victims check out to be free of the bacteria, another week or two should do it."

Sanders asked Erika to contact General Chavez to ready military transport to pick up the vaccines once Dr. Krishnan gives the green light.

Barth suggested using a plane based in the UAE to pick it up, saving time.

Sanders excused the health services people and asked the CIA, FBI and NSA to remain.

***

Sanders opened the discussion with the three security heads. "Something about this doesn't smell right. I understand blackmail. Hell, I deal with Congress every day! But this is different. It appears to have been planned months ago, many months, and I can't help remembering that the one lone survivor of the Arctic mission – even though he died later – was a Russian. Heidi, thinking about the scenario you described earlier, how crazy would it be for this guy Volkov to have been involved with the creation of a bacteria and a vaccine against it through a collaboration with someone in India? They could have planted the bacteria on the Arctic expedition, using someone who was in on it and had received a vaccination against the bacteria, only to be silenced later. And by using an Indian company to offer the vaccine, it would draw attention away from Volkov."

"Not very farfetched and a billion dollars is a prize worth going for. Do we know the Russian's cause of death yet?"

Sanders replied, "I don't think so, but the doctor at Hopkins who looked at his blood analysis is convinced that he'd been vaccinated."

Butler said, "We'll look into Maharishi Pharma and see if we can establish any links to Russia and Volkov. I'd like to nail down the Russian's cause of death, although I suspect I know why, just not how."

***

The Following Day. The next day there was a cornucopia of "news" to fit everyone's needs: conspiracy theories, partisan theories – for whatever, against whatever. You name it.

There was the actual story carried by the mainstream news that the U.S. had secured a million doses of a vaccine against the Arctic Flu. A military transport had landed at Washington Dulles Airport and was met by dozens of other aircraft and ground transport to speed the vaccine doses to potential victims in various cities around the country. It would be a controlled roll out with closely monitored data to assess effectiveness and any side effects.

The vaccine had been developed in India in an amazingly short timeframe. Some of the media had questioned how it could be done so quickly, and what kind of testing had been done in that short timeframe, but for the most part, everyone was just happy that it had.

From that root of the actual story, there were offshoots, including stories that the vaccine did stop the disease, but it also turned the recipients into vegetarians – as part of a government plot to reduce animal farming. There was one that accused the government of buying from India because it was cheaper, thus hurting U.S. pharmaceutical companies and jobs. And there were some who claimed the U.S. had been negotiating the price while people were dying.

Finally, there were also a number of stories that the disease itself was an ongoing threat and that the vaccine would offer only temporary immunity so that everyone would be re-infected, and the world would end.

But the disinformation story that seemed to resonate with many was the one carried on Faux News and other conservative outlets – that President Sanders' team had miscalculated the risk and, as a result, over fifty-thousand people had died. And in Edinburg, Pennsylvania, that was exactly what Grover Nerdkist II had hoped for.

***

CDC Headquarters. Within three days of the vaccines arriving at Dulles, every person on the CDC's extended Arctic Flu contact list had been vaccinated. And those who had been vaccinated on the first or second day found their symptoms were decreasing. There continued to be a few additional cases where there was no traceable connection to an infected person, but their upgraded embedded chips detected the symptoms, and they were vaccinated.

Following the payment to Maharishi Pharma of a billion dollars, the company began to donate vaccines to other parts of the world affected by the Arctic Flu. When asked why the company had singled out the U.S. to charge, a representative from the company said that the quantities needed elsewhere were small and that the shelf life of the vaccine was short. He was unable to answer how short.

The CDC, with full backing from the White House, immediately shipped samples of the vaccine to all U.S. pharmaceutical companies and told them to proceed urgently with developing their own, even if they simply copied the sample.

***

The White House. The president had made a nationwide broadcast that the outbreak had been contained. He didn't hint at possible foreign interference but did say that the infection, although contracted during the Arctic Expedition, did not pose a recurring threat.

President Sanders met with the heads of the CIA, FBI, NSA and also the Director of Homeland Security, Althea Crawford.

Heidi Butler (CIA) reported back on the Russian's cause of death – heart attack. He added, "It's amazing how unhealthy it can be for a fit, thirty-five-year-old Russian who carries out a clandestine job for someone." She shared a photo of the deceased participating in a recent decathlon.

"But there's something else. The doctor at Johns Hopkins, Dr. Rigoni ... He received two blood analyses from the Russian heart attack victim. One was at his time of death – and the other was six months ago. The significant difference was that the recent blood test showed the presence of cells that were specifically designed to fight the Arctic bacteria – a vaccine."

That made the room go quiet for a moment as the group realized the implication.

Sanders then repeated Maharishi Pharma's explanation and decision to give away their vaccine to other countries. "As weak an excuse as this was, our concern is that they could do it again, leaving us exposed. So, I okayed the CDC sending the vaccine to other U.S. vaccine manufacturers. Given India's liberal interpretation of drug patent law, our own companies should be able to come up with equivalents very quickly by simply tweaking. I asked Althea to join us because of the concerns expressed the other day that this outbreak was not about an ancient zombie pathogen, but one that had been manufactured. Heidi's information about the blood analysis backs that up."

Ollie Barth shared that the NSA had begun targeting telephone and internet communications between the Pune area of India and St. Petersburg. "It should begin to produce data shortly."

Butler added, "Maharishi Pharma is owned by Naresh Argawal. He's one of the richest people on the planet with extensive holdings in oil, chemicals and pharmaceuticals. We haven't found any obvious connections between him and Volkov, but we're monitoring communication as much as we can."

When Butler had said the word "chemicals," Sanders' mind flipped to the White House bomb with poisonous gas. He wondered, "Could there be a connection?"

***

Chapter 29 - Open Season on Senators

The State of Washington, D.C. Kari's election to the Senate six years ago was during the circus they called a presidential election year. The Senate, while critically important, received scant media attention during a presidential election and funding campaigns meant competing with your own Party colleagues who were running for president. A midterm election was definitely lower profile, but it was still a big deal.

Kari approached the election with some doubts, mostly about herself and her enthusiasm for the race. It would mean a lot of time away from Otis and Yogi, and also, from doing the work of a senator. Kari's sense of responsibility was spelled with a capital 'R,' and while some of her colleagues seemed not to care about missing the chance to vote and debate issues, Kari did.

As she started to attend meetings and rallies with her constituents, her doubts were soon dismissed – partly because the connection with people invigorated her and partly because they were behind her. She was a shoo-in to win, especially given that her opponent was Laurence Donald. She actually had to shake his hand once at a debate and it took everything she had to smile.

To no one's surprise, Kari won with a huge margin. But, back home with the two men in her life, Otis made a huge mistake when Kari asked if they could have a low-key life for a while:

stay at home, eat at home. Otis agreed, and he even cooked dinner one night. Kari was blown away with his cooking and when he repeated his performance the next night with an equal or even better meal, they both realized that he'd blown his secret, and the kitchen became a shared space.

***

Edinburg, Pennsylvania. Grover Nerdkist's gathering on New Year's Eve of 2062 was an emotionally mixed affair. Georgi Volkov was there as usual, despite his ban from entering the country, and he was again in an unusually good mood; but Naresh Argawal had been stopped as he passed through U.S. immigration at JFK International Airport. Nerdkist explained what he had heard: that the FBI had been called in and Argawal was interrogated. He refused to answer any of their questions and an accompanying member of his party got word to the Indian government who applied pressure. Other than being considered a blackmailer of sorts, although not legally so, Argawal was released and sent back to India immediately and banned from entering the U.S.

Georgi bragged, once again, that he and Argawal seemed to be the only ones doing anything. He didn't need to go into detail explaining what he meant by that. The group knew; and while a few of them were bothered by fifty thousand of their fellow Americans being killed, all of them were impressed and jealous of the billion-dollar ransom.

Karen Rover, perhaps to show Georgi that the Americans were equal to the task, listed a few of the politicians who posed a potential threat. One of those she mentioned was Kari Patel-Graham.

Nerdkist had a personal grudge against Kari and her family for having the audacity to threaten him over the pictures he had. He tried to reinforce Rover's mention of Kari and he reminded everyone about the compromising pictures he had of her.

Volkov scoffed. "You Americans are very funny. You use nuclear bombs and other bad things, but sex is not okay?"

Gerry Failwell, who had started listening at 'compromising pictures,' disagreed. "I don't know. Photos sure screwed me over."

Volkov laughed menacingly. "I think being stupid did it."

Rover re-focused everyone on the idea of targeting politicians. "Patel-Graham is only one to watch. Even better, we could target senators who will be replaced with Republicans — appointed by conservative governors — if something should happen to those senators."

Creud started to interrupt but Nerdkist cut him off. "That's a great idea!"

***

Montgomery, Alabama. Just one year into her term, a rare liberal U.S. senator from Alabama was killed. The Governor, Semper Creud, appointed a conservative to fill the position. The newly appointed senator would serve for the remainder of the six-year term.

***

FINAL CHANCE

Topeka, Kansas. A month after the murder of the U.S. senator from Alabama, another liberal U.S. senator – this one from Kansas, and just as rare – was also shot to death. The Governor of Kansas, Chester Cobolt, appointed a new conservative senator who would also serve out the balance of the six-year term.

***

The White House. President Sanders met with Joe Strickland, Ollie Barth and Heidi Butler. He joked with them that he spent more quality time with them than he did with his family. Much of that time had been discussing and chasing leads about Volkov and Argawal, and today was no exception, although it was prompted by the senator shootings. After the second murder, Sanders had given Strickland and Butler the authority to monitor Governors Creud and Cobolt's phone calls and e-mails, with a narrow scope of communication relating specifically to the murders.

In their informal mode, Sanders asked Joe what, if any, progress they'd made.

"We're pretty sure that both murders were carried out by local militias, but we haven't been able to pinpoint exactly who did it. We also think they were coordinated from the outside, by Glen Slade … the guy who's been conducting militia training around the country. His father, Harlan Slade, started the business, the 'Right to Bear' militias, in the twenties. They help militias get started with training for everything from recruitment to buying weapons, training, and even battle simulations. Gives them a chance to wear their hazmat gear outside the domes."

"Jesus! How much of this is going on?"

"More than we'd like, but nothing that the National Guard couldn't handle. We'd like your okay to keep tabs on Slade, though."

"Anything between the governors and Slade?"

"Not that we've found, but there's been communication between the governors and Grover Nerdkist II."

"That asshole?"

Joe smiled, "Rich one, though. He and Creud talk a lot, nothing specific. Cobolt has had a couple of brief conversations with Nerdkist, too. If there was coordination between the two militias, I'd put my money on Slade being the coordinator, and if there was a motive and money to back it, Nerdkist is the one."

Sanders nodded, "I'm okay with you watching Slade, and add Nerdkist, too. I know he's aiding the Republicans so it's not unusual, but I want to be sure he's aiding them legally. If it is a concerted effort, do they realize that they'd have to kill over twenty more senators to even get close to a majority?"

Butler chimed in, "Well, let's hope that's not their plan."

Sanders asked, "Heidi, any reason to think there might be overseas involvement?"

"No. Nothing we've seen."

"Okay. Keep me posted on this. Ollie, I understand something was picked up in Russia."

FINAL CHANCE

"Yes, we picked up a number of calls from Pune to St. Petersburg, and two of those were made to the same number we ID'd in relation to the bomb attempt at the White House. Those calls preceded the Arctic Flu incident. The phones used are not traceable and since the last call between them, neither number has been used again."

Sanders had been at the edge of his seat until Barth's last sentence. "So that's it?"

"No, we've found thirteen phone calls between the areas. It seems that the phones are used once or twice and then a new pair of phones are used. All untraceable."

"When were the calls made?"

"That's where it gets interesting. The first call was made on January 21st, 2061, from St. Petersburg to Pune."

Sanders' thoughts took him back to that day and quietly he replied, "A day after the bomb was meant to detonate."

After a brief period of silence to let Sanders process his thoughts, Barth continued. "The other calls were made starting in March of 2061 through June of 2062 – a time span that could accommodate the planning and execution of the Arctic Flu event."

Barth's revelation kick-started a wave of thought amongst the others and he gave them a few moments to think before he added, "The Archaeological Institute of America announced the Arctic expedition on February 25th, 2062."

Heidi Butler thought out loud what the others had understood, "Enough time to invent a disease and a vaccine."

Sanders' head was spinning. "Okay, so it's a good bet that Volkov and Argawal are connected. But how? Why? Is a billion dollars a big enough prize for these guys?"

Butler replied. "If it was just the money, possibly not. But both these guys made the bulk of their money in oil and they know that if the U.S. could be tempted to make some exceptions, others would follow. The hacking into our power networks is consistent with that, plus Volkov has an axe to grind with us for the sanctions and banning. And as for Argawal, from what we found, he was angry about being cut out of the COVID vaccine loop. So, neither are big fans of ours."

Sanders needed to wrap it up. "Okay. We know the Russians won't help us with Volkov, but let me check with State to see if India can help with Argawal. If you get anything else on either the Senate shootings or the Argawal-Volkov connection, let me know. Thanks, guys."

***

The State of Washington, D.C. Otis and Kari talked about the senator murders. They agreed that if they were carried out because a conservative governor would refill the seat with a conservative, then Kari wouldn't be a target.

But Otis was still concerned and said solemnly, "If. What if it's more random? Like for intimidation? Divisiveness?"

He wanted Kari to stay in D.C. until more was known. "At least if you stay here, the Capitol Police can protect you. In Massachusetts, you're just another person."

Kari was more concerned about doing her job, which was representing the people of Massachusetts. "I need to spend time there. It's why they elected me."

FINAL CHANCE

"But you can't run again anyway."

"I'm termed out for the Senate, but there are other jobs," she said coyly.

"Wow! It wasn't long ago that you weren't sure you'd even stand for re-election to the Senate and now you're talking about going big-time!" Otis was teasing now.

"I could change my residency and run as a D.C. senator. We live here more than Massachusetts anyway."

"You could do that? Start over running as a senator from another state."

"Yes. According to the new rules."

Now serious, Otis said, "No! Let's stay focused on the big prize. Ever since we talked about this a couple of years ago, I've wanted to live in that big white house. Hell, that's why I asked you to marry me."

Kari quipped back, "No. You just wanted a free place to live. You didn't care where!"

"Well, yeah. Okay, so I'm frugal."

"Nice word for cheap. But I guess it also means you're cooking dinner tonight instead of taking me out."

"Hmm. Maybe not that ... cheap."

***

Frankfort, Kentucky. For the third month in a row, another conservative governor appointed another conservative U.S.

senator following the murder of the state's liberal senator. But this time the shooter was caught, and he quickly confessed and cooperated to avoid the death penalty. He named the head of his militia as initiating the assassination and offering a reward.

The leader of the militia, Grady Quaid, was obviously built of sterner stuff, so it took almost a full day before he named the person who'd named the target and offered the reward money. Interestingly, the reward offered to the shooter was about half of what the leader of the militia was offered, and even more interestingly, the offer came from Glen Slade.

The FBI brought Slade in and he denied his role and claimed that the money he gave to the militia head was a refund from a training contract. The FBI decided to hold Slade without bail on a Federal Crime. As they kept him sequestered, they put pressure on the militia leadership in both Alabama and Kansas and they hit the jackpot. First one and then the other admitted that Slade had asked for their cooperation to kill the senators and had offered the rewards.

The militia leader in Alabama, Rufus Wade, confessed that he'd asked one of his militiamen, Zeke Wesley, to do it. Wesley denied it but the FBI offered him some leniency if he confessed, and he confirmed that Wade had asked him to do it. Wesley hesitated, but when the FBI told him that the reward offered was about a quarter of what Wade was given, he agreed to help. The FBI believed that while Slade was behind all three deaths, he was working on someone else's behalf.

The militia leader in Kansas, Wayman Virgil, tried to blame the murder on one of his men who'd carried it out just to gain favor. Again, the disparity of the reward given the militia leader versus what was received by the shooter, along with a promise of some leniency, were the catalysts to get a full confession and further incriminate Slade.

The FBI also uncovered large sums of money from overseas banks to numerous accounts that Slade controlled. Slade and the six militia members were all charged with murder and domestic terrorism.

The terror continued, but now Grover Nerdkist II, Karen Rover, and the Honorable Governor from Alabama, Semper Creud, were the ones in the crosshairs and the ones trembling by its effect.

***

Chapter 30 – A Chilling Message

The Planet, Earth. All over the world, the winter of 2063-2064 would be remembered as the worst on record, but like climate change warnings, most people, living comfortably in their domes, didn't care or even know about the weather unless it affected them. And this time it did – severely.

Record snowfalls, even in places where it didn't normally snow, dramatically impacted power generation from solar collectors, which had been built into almost every possible surface. Now roads, domes, roofs were covered for days at a time, causing brownouts and blackouts even more severe than the power hacking was causing. The outages affected almost all manufacturing, as well as transportation, hospitals, technology and anything electrically driven – which was pretty much everything.

The message was loud and clear to scientists, if not the masses: environmental healing had a long way to go. The politicians who embraced science were proven right, but that didn't help the mood of the people. Fossil fuel backers' PR teams ramped up the volume of demands for fossil fuel backup power generation, especially in light of the growing number and severity of weather-related power outages. The fact that 2064 was also a presidential election year contributed to the vitriol.

Republican opposition joined in the fray – some might say they created it – calling for an immediate move to utilize the U.S.'s significant fossil fuel capability and for the removal of the Energy Secretary.

The Sanders' government was unmoved and worked diligently to restore power as well as encourage affected countries throughout the world to remain steadfast in giving the environment the breathing space it obviously still needed.

***

Edinburg, Pennsylvania. Georgi Volkov mingled with his fellow plotters at their annual New Year's Eve gathering on that last day of 2063. Volkov seemed to enjoy these events and – despite the ban on his entering the U.S. and the record snowfalls that seemed to close most airports – he seemed more ebullient than usual. He also brought regards from Argawal, who decided that his own ban from entering the U.S. was reason enough not to attend.

Volkov actually complimented Nerdkist and expressed approval of the senatorial murders.

He sneered, "So much better den stupid pictures of girl, but need take out whole lot more den three."

The group discussed potential plans and Volkov pressed for greater efforts to get the U.S. to agree to fossil fuel back-up power.

"If U.S. do it, others do it, too, and prices go up."

Nerdkist explained that it was an election year and that he hoped to add more members to the House and Senate. He also stated that Sanders would easily be re-elected.

Volkov's smile disappeared. His expression contorted into a dark and evil visage and he growled back, "Not if he dead!"

***

The State of Washington, D.C. The new rules, confining election campaigning to the calendar year of the election itself, had been welcomed by the public, but it all but guaranteed that far less work would be undertaken in Washington once the year began. Of course, most people wouldn't notice the difference.

President Sanders ran unopposed by his own party and he wasn't overly concerned about the race. He'd won by a large margin before and from what he could see, he felt that the opposition candidates were pretty non-threatening.

As the candidates attacked each other, they also attacked Sanders. The power outages were high on the attack list, followed by the Arctic Flu deaths and Sanders' refusal to let up, even a little bit, on coddling the environment. He was also taking flak about his generosity to many poorer nations. The messaging was significantly financed and therefore unrelenting. However, it largely fell on the deaf ears of an almost fully employed labor force that had most of what it needed. Things had been going so well that the challenging politicians and their attacks were largely ignored.

The only fly in Sanders' game plan ointment was that his Party wanted him to stay with Doug Johnson as his running mate. Sanders tried to make them realize that Johnson would be a weak candidate in four years' time, but with time running out, he gave up, surprising some.

The fact was that Sanders felt sorry for Johnson, whose wife had been murdered five years ago. It had happened during the early stages of the 2060 presidential campaign. Johnson was running for the Party's nomination against Sanders and Patel-Graham. They were on the campaign trail and Johnson's wife was at home, alone. An intruder broke into their house and shot Mrs. Johnson, killing her. Johnson dropped out of the race a couple of months after Kari did and, after Kari turned down Sanders on the vice president's job, Sanders offered it to Johnson.

Sanders recalled Johnson refusing the job at first because the murder investigation was still ongoing. No suspect had been identified. Johnson also seemed less focused than he'd been during the primary, but Sanders understood. He'd waited a while, giving Johnson some more time and ensuring that his third choice would accept; but before that happened, Johnson called, almost begging for the job.

And so, Sanders accepted Johnson again, but not before admonishing the Party movers and shakers about their perceived need to balance the ticket with a more conservative vice president. "Even though I may be a progressive, there are very few – if any – progressive wish list items left to consider. What we need is a very electable understudy."

He wasn't far off. Indeed, all Americans enjoyed medical, dental, vision and hearing care, as well as paid maternal and paternal leave, and a guaranteed minimum wage. And, thanks to Otis' efforts, pre-school through university or vocational education were also part of everyone's benefits.

As the election campaign ground through its phases, the Sanders-Johnson ticket got an unexpected and frankly unnecessary gift. The power hacking program had been cracked. It was indeed Russian originated and, as expected, the Russian government denied any role in the long and damaging program. Of course, winter was a distant memory, and many voters welcomed the less humid and more comfortable dome temperatures. And so, to no one's surprise, the Sanders-Johnson ticket was the winner again, by an even larger margin than their first term.

***

Shortly after new year, Sanders made a snap decision for himself and Johnson to visit a newly re-invented manufacturing dome near Fredericksburg, Virginia. This high-profile event was emblematic of the country's biggest challenge.

For the past fifteen years, full employment had been virtually guaranteed as a result of the transformation from fossil fuel to solar and other renewable energy sources. That shift, along with the breakneck pace of constructing domes, required enormous engineering and manufacturing efforts, placing huge demands on the U.S. labor force, as well as hundreds of thousands of imported workers.

As the demand for new doming lessened, the country was being pro-active to ensure that new jobs would be available to take their place. The "Fredericksburg Domeworks" facility currently employed over twenty-thousand people making integrated dome panels. These panels were like smart puzzle pieces that, when put together, carried the solar energy along integrated circuits.

Taking advantage of the manufacturing capability of the facility, the operation was transformed into making solar road panels as the U.S. continued to replace asphalt and cement roads with the high-tech composite solar energy producing surfaces. Orders were also building up for what promised to be a robust export market.

FINAL CHANCE

The fifty-five-mile journey from the White House to Fredericksburg along I-95 was entirely along a newly surfaced, solar energy-producing road. The Fredericksburg run was a longer motorcade journey than usual, but Sanders also wanted to mention the great ride down on roads manufactured at Fredericksburg.

The route skirted a number of domed towns and cities, but in between, the effects of climate change could be seen through the leafless branches of dead trees and the absence of even a single bird.

As the thirty-two-vehicle presidential motorcade approached the Angela Parkson Memorial Bridge over the Rappahannock River, en route to the industrial dome, three camo-clad men – safely hidden in the trees on a hill overlooking the bridge – received a call. The call came as they watched the first advance car, or "Route Car" of the motorcade, cross the bridge. They'd seen a number of other vehicles and motorcycles earlier, ensuring that the route was clear and that all entrances to I-95 were closed. Earlier they'd observed a chopper and a drone or drones in the area as well.

The voice on the phone said, "We're just behind the motorcade, which is about two miles out from the bridge, travelling at a steady sixty-five miles an hour. Limo three in the outside lane is your target."

The three men on the hill quickly made their final preparations. At the same time, an analyst at Homeland Security made three calls even more quickly. The first was to dispatch an attack helicopter from Quantico Marine base to the Parkson Bridge. The second was to the drone pilot surveilling the area to look for activity near the bridge; and the third call was to Secret Service command about the call she had just intercepted.

The Viper-II chopper lifted off within a minute for the twenty-mile flight, pushing hard to reach its top speed of three hundred miles an hour. The drone pilot circled his machine gun equipped UAV back to the area near the bridge. He hadn't seen anything during the past hour but now he was laser focused on possible assault areas.

Secret Service command radioed the Agent in Charge in the ID car just as the motorcade sweepers were approaching the bridge. The AIC immediately radioed all vehicles to scramble – changing lanes and positions.

The chopper was getting close and the drone pilot's enhanced view spotted activity in a clearing on a hill, overlooking the bridge. He steered his UAV directly to the area, arming the fifty-caliber machine gun. He had a good view of the men on the hill, and he watched as they aimed their shoulder fired rockets, just seconds before he was in range. The machine gun fire took the three men down before they could retreat into the cover of the trees, but the rockets had been launched.

The Secret Service Electronics Countermeasures vehicle was travelling just in front of the president's vehicle and two "Spares," one of which was carrying the vice president. The Countermeasures vehicle was equipped with electronic warfare sensors and when it detected the inbound rockets, it detonated smoke grenades to confuse the rocket tracking system. The deception worked with two rockets, but one hit its mark, practically disintegrating the vehicle and its occupants.

The motorcade picked up its pace and raced ahead to a safe exit from the freeway. Coming to a stop and checking in all around, without anyone leaving their vehicles, they assessed the personnel damage. The scramble had worked, and the president was safe. There were three casualties though: two secret service agents and the vice president.

FINAL CHANCE

Units were sent to the hill where the three men had been shot. All three were dead. A vehicle was found nearby, and it belonged to one of the dead men. All three belonged to a Virginia group calling themselves the "Real Militia."

***

The Homeland Security Analyst who intercepted the message knew that the call she'd listened to came from one of the cars now "trapped" behind the motorcade. The problem was that the phone used couldn't be traced to an individual and the number of cars now backed up numbered in the hundreds.

Despite the task, the Secret Service Agent-in-Charge decided to process all the cars before allowing them to proceed. Based on the wording of the phone call, Secret Service Agents, FBI Agents and some local law enforcement processed the cars across the three lanes, looking for two or more people in a car with at least one male driver or passenger. All others were waved through.

Those that met the criteria were asked for their identification and their cell phones, which were quickly checked for a match against the number identified by Homeland Security. About forty minutes after the processing began, the Viper crew radioed-in that there was a stationary car on the road, just before the bridge, and that the other cars were going around it.

Motorcycle units were sent back and determined that the car was abandoned. Nothing was found however, and a forensic team was dispatched to see what they might find. The car was traced to a doctor in Manassas, but it had been stolen from the Manassas Dome garage. Security footage from the garage provided a facial identification match to another member of the "Real Militia,' and prints from the car matched an additional member.

Being a fugitive in a domed world wasn't easy. Survival for periods of greater than twenty-four hours meant entering a domed environment; and to do that, a chip was required. The two men in the car were apprehended the following day as they entered the Dale City Dome, just south of D.C.

***

Chapter 31 - Right to Bear

The White House. Sanders' first order of business was finding the perpetrators. The threat of the death penalty easily motivated the two men in custody to implicate their Militia commander, Aiden McCoy. As lieutenants, they were able to describe the entire operation in detail, including the acquisition of the rockets used.

McCoy, for his part, identified Glen Slade as the initiator and funder of the operation, who assisted with the operation, even while in prison. But the big questions remained unanswered: who was ultimately directing this, and was it related to the earlier assassinations and/or attempts?

Sanders and Erika Ruiz were in the Oval Office with Heidi Butler and Joe Strickland, along with Althea Crawford, Homeland Security, Ollie Barth, National Security Advisor and Luther Rawlins, Secret Service.

Strickland gave them an update on the FBI's questioning of the suspects. They had picked up a few more details but everything so far seemed to stop with Slade.

But then he dropped their biggest discovery. "We found these text messages on the phones of the two guys following the motorcade and on the phone of one of the attackers on the hill." He handed a document to Sanders.

Strickland provided commentary. "This was from the phone recovered on the hill to the phone found on the guys in the car following the motorcade, at eleven-ten on the twenty-fifth."

"Sent:02-25-2065/11:10:27 To: +1.434.646.1851
Message: In position
Received:02-25-2065/11:10:30 From: +1 434.646.2345"

Sanders visibly shuddered as he read it.

Strickland continued. "The next message was also received on the phone we recovered from the two guys in custody. It was sent from an untraceable burner phone twenty-three minutes before the attack. The burner phone was acquired in the D.C. area."

"Sent:02-25-2065/11:21:37 To: +1 434.646.1851
'Limo 3 outside lane'
Received:02-25-2065/11:21:41 From: +1 771.251.3375"

Sanders' eyes widened as he read it and grasped the implications. "This came from someone in the motorcade?"

Strickland replied. "We think so. We've checked and there were no drones in the area nor was the motorcade passing any areas with good oversight, so no one else could have known the car position. In addition, the Service had already made a shift since departure, so it had to have come from the motorcade, or at least with info from the motorcade."

Strickland regained Sanders' attention. "The next message is a call from the two guys in the car to the hill lasting eight seconds. It was two minutes and twenty seconds before the attack."

FINAL CHANCE

"Outbound call:02-25-2065/11:41:17 To: +1.434.646.2345
'Limo 3 outside lane'
Call ended:02-25-2065/11:41:25 From: +1.434.646.1851

He gave Sanders some time to read before adding, "Given the absence of any other communication received by the 'Hill team' around the time of the attack, we think the call was probably giving them the target details. Critically, that call was made seconds before the motorcade was scrambled, prompting this final message.

"The final message was from the burner phone."

Sanders sat frozen as he read the last communication.

"Sent:02-25-2065/11:42:48 To: +1.434.646.1851
'scrambling! stand by'
Received:02-25-2065/11:42:45 From: +1.771.251.3375"

Ollie Barth exclaimed, "Jesus! Seconds before the attack! So, it had to be someone in the motorcade!"

Strickland replied, "So it seems. And the attack happened sooner than they thought, so they didn't have time to issue new details."

Althea Crawford added dryly, "Because they became the target."

Sanders jerked around to face Crawford and angrily demanded, "Are you implying that the messages were coming from the vice president's car?"

Crawford stated flatly, "I'm just saying it is a distinct possibility, particularly because there was no further communication."

And then she directed a question to Luther Rawlins. "Luther, how much time was there between the scramble command and the attack?"

Luther looked at his notes and said, "Twenty-three seconds."

Barth thought out loud, "So the command to scramble was given, and a few seconds would go by while someone grabbed their phone, typed the message in and sent it off."

Rawlins added, "It would probably take three to five seconds just to realize what was happening. Then another five plus seconds to type in and send the message. And then another five plus seconds to know what the car positions were. And all of that in an unexpected and very high-pressure environment. If it came from the targeted car, I'm not surprised that they didn't get off another message. On the other hand, if it wasn't the targeted car, they may have had time."

Sanders asked, "And there's no way to know who sent those messages?"

Strickland shook his head, "No."

Sanders asked Rawlins and Strickland to work together to look into any anomalies in the motorcade staffing and security that might shed some light on the leak.

***

It was no secret that Doug Johnson wasn't Bo Sander's first choice as his vice president, but now, there was a big cloud over Johnson's honor and morality. Sanders actions and behavior, however, following the assassination did not reveal those feelings. The funeral, Sanders' eulogy, his concern for Johnson's remaining family, and his respect for Johnson's service presented a sincere feeling of gratitude and loss.

FINAL CHANCE

To those who knew Sanders, and even those who also knew about the motorcade attack details, they weren't surprised. To Sanders, the jury was still out, and Doug Johnson was innocent.

***

On top of Sanders' list was appointing a new vice president. He knew whom he wanted, and he spent a great deal of time listing the reasons and framing an argument against the pushback he was sure he would get from the Party. He asked Erika to get Isabelle Martin on the phone and when he was told she was holding for him, he grabbed his list and steeled himself for the fight.

Isabelle thanked him for his thoughtful handling of Johnson's funeral and asked him if he'd thought about a replacement. He confidently told her whom he had in mind and before he could launch into his long list of reasons Martin said, "Perfect. I agree. Have you discussed it with her?"

Sanders replied, "No." He simply hadn't had time, but he said with a smile that Martin couldn't see, "I wanted to run it past you first."

***

Kari waited in the West Wing Lobby. She was pretty sure she knew why she'd been invited but until she spoke with the president, she tried not to rule out other possibilities. She just couldn't think of any.

Kari and Otis had discussed it and Otis's only complaint was that the Naval Observatory was further from his office. He added that the plus side included a bigger yard for Yogi to run in – and the possibility that they might get some secret service agents to pick up poop – a swimming pool and a chef!

Kari's mind was swirling with thoughts, and Erika Ruiz had to step into her line of vision to get her attention.

Sanders was easy to like and easy to talk with. A great listener, he was informal and down to earth, but beneath that homey character was an incisive mind and a world- class bullshit detector. He was able to sift through the ideas he openly welcomed and separate out the good ones from the not so good.

Sanders and Kari spent only a couple of minutes off-topic, Sanders complimenting Otis's work in Education and Kari sharing her admiration for Sanders' moving tribute of Doug Johnson. She asked if there was any progress into the investigation that he could share with her and he smiled and said, "We'll get to that, hopefully, in just a minute, but first let's discuss what I'm sure you know is the reason you're here — the vice presidency. It's yours if you're up for it."

Kari immediately replied, "I know you're busy so ... yes."

They were both smiling broadly, and Sanders asked, "No reservations? You're accepting a job that just ended someone's life."

Kari responded with respect and sincerity. "I know the risks and I also know and have a great deal of respect for the men and women who risk their lives to protect us. I'm also ready to assume the responsibility to help the millions of Americans who rely on us for our leadership and judgment."

Continuing the tone, Sanders looked squarely at Kari. "Thanks, Karima. I am really looking forward to working with you. What does Otis think about it?"

Kari quipped, "Well, Otis was concerned that the Naval Observatory was further from his office."

Sanders burst out laughing. "Tell him I said that he'll just have to get his lazy ass up fifteen minutes earlier!"

He buzzed for Erika, and both he and Kari were still laughing when she walked in and said, "I guess the answer was yes?"

Sanders replied, "Yep, so get started on the paperwork. Last time I checked, we still have super-majorities in both houses so there shouldn't be any issues. I want this done ASAP."

Erika took her boss at his word and left to start the process.

Sanders waited until he heard the door click shut and said, "The two guys we captured and the three that were killed were all members of a Virginia militia group. But they got their orders or directions and reward from Glen Slade. The senator murders were also orchestrated by Slade, but we're convinced that there's someone else pulling the strings. Also, and this is very confidential, someone in the motorcade sent information to the attackers. We're investigating everyone and every aspect of the motorcade."

Sanders paused for effect and continued, "We can't rule out the possibility that the messages were coming from the vice president's car."

Kari was shocked. "Why do you consider that a possibility?"

Sanders picked up two files, and opened one, handing Kari a single sheet of paper. "These are phone records during the time immediately before the attack.

Kari looked at the four records and Sanders explained each one.

"There was never a fifth message. It could be that the sender saw it was too late ... or the sender was in the vice president's car. And so far, that's all we know. I'd like you to take a good look at this as well as the senator murder files with a fresh pair of eyes, especially with any thoughts about who could be behind the crimes."

"Sure. Anything else I need to know?"

"You've heard of Grover Nerdkist?"

Kari felt sick. She'd all but forgotten about him and the pictures. But now she realized that she had to come clean. "Yes, I know who he is and before Erika gets too far along with the paperwork, there's something you should know."

Kari took Sanders through her brief relationship with Laurence Donald, the photographs, and the Beli-Tel break-in, which Donald had attributed to Nerdkist.

Sanders wasn't concerned about the photos, but he was definitely interested in Kari's comment about the break-in.

Kari asked, "Why did you ask me about Nerdkist?"

"We know that there was some communication between Nerdkist and Governors Creud and Cobolt around the time of the murders."

Kari countered, "Blackmail photos, break-ins and theft are pretty tame compared with attempted presidential assassination."

Sanders corrected her, "That should be assassinations, as in more than one; plus a successful assassination as in President Parkson."

FINAL CHANCE

Kari's eyes opened very wide. "Are you serious? You think he's involved in all of that?"

"We can't prove it … yet. But we think it's possible. That's why I'd like you to look at the files."

***

Sanders' request for a "soon as possible" vice presidential appointment materialized, and less than a month after their meeting, Karima Patel-Graham was vice president of the United States.

***

Chapter 32 – A Good Move

Number One Observatory Circle. Kari, Otis and Yogi moved to their new residence, Number One Observatory Circle, and everyone was happy with most, if not all, it had to offer. Yogi was happy with the thirteen acres of grounds. Kari loved the look and feel of the hundred-seventy-year-old Queen Anne style home with its series of rooms connecting to each other, its round turret rooms, inglenook fireplaces, and broad verandas that wrapped around the ground floor. And Otis loved the fitness room, pool and circular library.

It did take them some "getting used to" the omni-present Secret Service and housekeeping staff, but it was obvious that they were all chosen for their warmth and friendliness as well as their specific professional skills.

Jennifer, Jason, Nadya and the Belikovs were very proud of Kari, and they visited as often as possible, helping to fill the thirty-three-room house with laughter as Adam and Vijay Jr. frolicked with Yogi. The one room that was off-limits was the bunker.

Kari and Otis realized that now, even with their very heavy workloads, they could extend their outreach to many others through gatherings and parties. Their respective secretaries soon found themselves quite busy managing invitations and coordinating catering requirements with the staff at Number One.

Unsurprisingly, Kari's life changed dramatically. In addition to her new home, she also had to get used to having two offices: One at the White House, and her main office at the Eisenhower Executive Office Building (EEOB) on the White House Grounds.

She had spent the past month thinking about her key focus as vice president as well as reviewing the assassination and murder files. She accepted that someone in the motorcade had sent the messages, but so far, no further progress had been made.

The president agreed with Kari that the most pressing issue was the environment. He hoped that Kari would succeed him in four years, and this would give her a running start in dealing with their greatest challenge. He acknowledged, too, her scientific background, which would enable her to help manage the U.S. and the world in taking the right steps at the right time.

***

EEOB. Getting thrown into the deep end as VPOTUS carried with it a very steep and intense learning curve. The POTUS included her on virtually all of his meetings to get her up to speed, get acquainted with the key people, and after the meetings, get Kari's assessment of the individuals and the situation. Those opinions often differed dramatically from his own.

Kari had asked former Vice President Johnson's Chief of Staff, Kristine Robin, to stay on for a month – both for continuity and to consider whether she and Kari could work together. The experiment lasted less than two weeks, and that was only because Kari gave Robin a huge benefit of the doubt. If you'd asked Kari to explain why she decided to make a move, it boiled down to trust. It was just a feeling, to be sure, but it was a strong feeling.

So, Kari appointed Cyndi Burt as her chief of staff. Ms. Burt had been her COS for almost ten years at the Senate, and one thing was certain. She knew she could trust her. Energetic, organized, personable and tough as nails, Cyndi had served in the Army for eight years, including some combat duty. With her red hair and freckles, she may have looked like the girl next door, but anyone who underestimated her was in for a big surprise.

***

The White House. President Sanders was in California and he asked Kari to meet with the Secretary of State, Erin Millan, to discuss word of a joint venture between GazProd of Russia and SheikOil of Saudi Arabia.

As Secretary Millan explained it, the services included construction of oil-fired power plants – both fixed and mobile – capable of supplying complete domes or factories with a non-solar power source.

Kari asked if she thought this was a true private industry deal or a front for the two governments.

Millan couldn't be completely sure but offered what everyone already knew – that in those two countries there really weren't any completely private enterprises. She explained that GazProd was owned and run by Georgi Volkov, who was no friend of the U.S. There were sanctions against his company, and he was banned from entering the country.

SheikOil was chaired by Prince Ibrahim Al Saud. Prince Ibrahim was also the Crown Prince of Saudi Arabia.

FINAL CHANCE

The announcement was a surprise on two counts. First of all, it would be in violation of the international agreements in place to protect the environment. That would mean, in theory at least, any development, anywhere in world, that included the use of fossil fuel would be in violation. Both the country allowing the construction and the company building it could be fined and banned from any activity, legal or otherwise, worldwide. Hardly a model business plan.

The second surprise was that the two countries had never shown any affection for one another. Quite the opposite, they'd competed fiercely and unscrupulously right up to the final banning of fossil fuel use.

Kari suggested that it might be a public relations event, meant to stoke some lingering embers from the protests of last year's severe winter. At first, neither of them could understand what the game plan could be, but then Kari had an idea.

Kari asked Erika if Lorrie McIntyre, Chief Counsel, was in and could she join them.

McIntyre arrived and both Kari and Secretary Millan briefed her about the joint venture. Kari asked if simply constructing oil-fired power plants was considered a violation, or was it based on actual use of the facility.

McIntyre wasn't certain but thought that construction alone would not be a violation as long as all other aspects of the agreement were followed. The three discussed it and McIntyre agreed to look more closely at the agreement.

The next day, an announcement with details of the joint venture was made. An editorial in the Wall Street Journal about the closed-mindedness of the current Administration accompanied the announcement, lamenting the loss of jobs and leadership. Grover Nerdkist was quoted in the scathing attack, warning everyone about the prospects of enduring another cold and dark winter.

In her role as the Administration's leader on the environment, Vice President Patel-Graham blasted the actions of the two countries and companies, pointing out that should any country be tempted to use fossil fuel power, they would be held accountable for their actions. Privately, she mulled over the role of banned and sanctioned Georgi Volkov in the deal.

Nerdkist, with assists from Karen Rover and Semper Creud, attacked Kari as out of touch with real people. Without evidence, they pointed out that she and her family weren't forced to endure freezing conditions due to the power outages. While that was true, the attack sounded better than it was, as very few people in the U.S. actually suffered freezing conditions within their domes.

***

The joint venture proceeded, and a number of oil-fueled electricity power plants were built in Russia and Saudi Arabia. None of the units had been used as yet. Governor Semper Creud tried to have some built in Alabama, but even his State legislature rejected the request.

***

Not only had the public relations attempt by the "Gang of Seven" been a complete failure for the promoters, but it also exposed a potential relationship between Volkov, Nerdkist, Creud and Rover that the Administration and federal law enforcement found very interesting.

***

FINAL CHANCE

EEOB. Cyndi Burt entered Kari's office to tell her that the president asked her to come to the Oval office at 9:00 AM for a meeting with the Secretaries of Health and Human Services, Dr. Dipika Krishnan, and Homeland Security, Althea Crawford.

***

The Oval Office. Kari knew and liked both secretaries, and the feeling was mutual.

Kari had an obvious connection with Dr. Dipika Krishnan through their shared Indian heritage, but they were also about the same age, and Kari had a deep appreciation of Dipika's mind on all things medical. The secretary of Health and Human Services' parents were British Indians who had immigrated to the U.S. shortly before Dipika was born. Kari recalled an evening when her father was in D.C. for a couple of days. They'd bumped into Dipika at RASA's, a hip Indian restaurant, and Vijay and Dipika really hit it off.

Dipika had been thrilled to meet Dr. Vijay Patel, the inventor of the infamous VT2 watch, or "Death Watch," as it had often been called because of its "Final Notice" feature.

The Russians had also engaged Final Notice recipients to carry out assassinations during the 2020 election, which was the source of Kari's connection with Althea Crawford, the head of Homeland Security.

Althea was the adopted daughter of former FBI Agent, Zoe Brouet, and Secret Service Agent, Demi Magret. Both agents had worked with Vijay in relation to his VT2 watch. Althea was African American and about Kari's age. As with Dipika, they had last met at Vijay's funeral.

Sanders entered the room and although he was wearing his warm smile and demeanor, Kari had a feeling that this was not going to be a light-hearted meeting.

Sanders got right down to business. "Dipika, tell us what you know."

"Although we try not to think about worst case scenarios 24/7 at the Department, we can never really not think of them. The Arctic Flu was certainly a reminder of that. At the moment, we're investigating a tragic and disturbing outbreak of what may be a virus in southern India. In a small town – Chittur – in the Indian State of Kerala, almost three-thousand people have died within the past two days. That's half their population. We're investigating and attempting to get valid blood samples so we can understand its progression and structure to stop it or slow it down and possibly develop a vaccine. The Indian authorities are cooperating fully."

Sanders prodded. "Dipika, your office mentioned something else, too."

Dipika swallowed and took a deep breath. "Yes. The outbreak is, simply put, mysterious. It doesn't seem to behave in the same ways other viruses have. And I'm not talking about mutation. It's hard to explain, but if we can keep this between the four us – it seems more synthetic. Manufactured. More Arctic Flu than COVID. We've spoken with our Indian counterparts, and they're baffled, too. So far, it seems to be contained to that one town. We hope to have some additional information soon, so we'll let you know. I'm confident that we'll figure out how to deal with this ... virus. But we need to be able to act swiftly."

Sanders turned to the Homeland Security Director. "Althea, my concern is that this may be another criminal act, like the

Arctic Flu, that is in the disease test phase. Perhaps whoever is developing it carried out a test that went haywire. Otherwise, why call attention to it with a big incident?"

Sanders saw the puzzled look on Kari's face, and he realized that their theory about the Arctic Flu being manufactured by Argawal's company was never released beyond the Administration and law enforcement.

"Kari. We believe that Naresh Argawal and Georgi Volkov conspired to develop the Arctic Flu virus and a vaccine, and then held us for ransom."

Now Kari understood Sanders' reference to a test. "So, their next steps would be to infect the U.S. or other countries?"

Sanders answered. "Probably just us unless someone else has pissed him off. Sorry."

Althea asked, "What do we know about the Indian government's relationship or view of Argawal? They can't be happy with him if he killed half a town."

Sanders answered. "After the Arctic Flu, when we realized we'd been blackmailed, State approached the Indian Government. Our proof was largely conjecture, with a pretty hefty dose of logic, but it was felt that there was no love lost between Delhi and Argawal. I'll ask Erin to make sure they're aware of our suspicion."

Dipika added, "We'll press forward to learn as much as we can about the virus and perhaps how it got out of hand, if that's what happened. We'll also proceed with the assumption that this virus might still come knocking on our domes at some point, so we'll get as ready as possible to do what we can to prevent or thwart an attack. I'll keep you posted. And Kari, it's great to have you on the president's team."

Althea chimed in, "I'll second that."

Sanders and Kari remained as the two cabinet secretaries departed.

Sanders said, somewhat apologetically, "I guess that was another file I should have given you. It will be on your desk shortly."

Turning more serious, he added, "These are the things that really scare me. We lost over fifty-thousand people to the Arctic Flu, and if it hadn't been a blackmail scheme, we might have lost millions before a vaccine was ready. The assassinations are small potatoes compared with these situations.

"I'd like you to run point on this one. Talk with Erin and see if we can get Argawal shut down. To me, he's the most dangerous loose cannon out there."

***

Chapter 33 - Currying Favor

The White House. Kari received Secretary of State, Erin Millan, at her White House office. Kari got down to business and asked about the secretary's dealing with India's Minister of External Affairs with respect to Maharishi Pharma's Arctic Flu vaccine.

Millan confirmed Sanders' comment about the Indian government's less-than-sterling opinion of Maharishi in general and Naresh Argawal in particular. Argawal was considered opportunistic, an exploitive employer, a polluter, and generally unethical.

Kari actually smiled and asked facetiously, "What do they really think about him?"

Absolutely straight-faced, Millan answered, "He's very religious."

Both women laughed, but quickly Millan turned serious, "I spoke with the Minister very early this morning and it does appear that Maharishi Pharma was responsible for the deaths and the toll is rising. They're not sure if anyone in the town will survive, but it's even worse. Chittur is actually part of a greater, interconnected domed area centered around Coimbatore, with over three million people. They're trying to isolate the virus, but they know so little about it that they don't know its infection process."

"Can't Argawal help them?"

"They can't find him."

Kari asked, "What's known about the outbreak?"

"Apparently two employees of Maharishi Pharma were tasked with infecting a small number of people in a slum area outside the main area of the town. They were told that people would become sick – although not terminally – and to remain there, discretely, for an indefinite period and observe. They were also told that when the people did become sick, the two employees would reveal that they were clinicians, and offer to help, injecting them with a vaccine and taking blood samples.

"Something obviously went wrong, possibly because of language barriers. Apparently, people in Chittur speak a language understood by only a very small percentage of Indians. Anyway, the Maharishi employees panicked when people started to literally drop dead, so they jumped on their motor scooter and fled."

Millan paused and said, "Kari. I'm not making this up and the Minister wasn't either."

Kari replied, "My father told me many stories about India, and while this is far wilder, it's not beyond belief."

Millan said, "But I'm not done yet! As they raced away and went through town, their scooter crashed and the vials of the virus broke. Scores of people crowded around the accident to gawk, help, or scavenge and then the local police arrived, and the two employees confessed everything, just in time. They both died hours later. Of course, the people who came to the accident scene became infected, and then the police, and then the virus ripped through the town.

FINAL CHANCE

"The police found an unusual amount of cash in the possession of the Maharishi employees and they surmised that it had been given to them to pay volunteers, but perhaps the employees either paid less or even nothing. The virus is highly toxic so maybe they found ways to cut corners and keep the cash. In fact, that might be why it got so out of control.

"Maharishi executives, except for Argawal, have been detained and are being brought to Delhi for questioning. Early word is that there in an untested, unproven vaccine but nobody trusts anyone there enough to use it yet."

Kari didn't know whether to laugh or cry, but her real emotion was anger. Extreme anger. "I can't abide testing on animals! How those people could do this on unsuspecting people is just horrific!"

Millan offered, "If it's any consolation, my contact said that this is Argawal's demise, when they find him. It seems to some that India's threshold for cruelty is high, but this time, it's been breached. And the Minister told me that Argawal will be facing a very long prison sentence, probably in something called a 'Special Jail,' where special has a dark meaning."

Kari took a very deep breath to come back to their real world. "Let's hope that they can contain it to a very local area and also that perhaps the vaccine does work. If that happens, and Argawal's unique skills can be taken off the table, we can breathe easier ... for a while. Can I ask you to reach out to your contact for another reason?"

Millan replied, "Sure. Is it about the Arctic Flu and the bomb on Inauguration Day?"

Kari smiled, "Yes. I was pretty certain you knew about those but I'm still the 'new kid,' so I had to ask. If the gig is up for Argawal, maybe he'd confess and name a collaborator."

"Like maybe a charming Russian with a name like Volkov?"

Kari rose and, holding out her hand, said, "Wouldn't that be nice. Madame Secretary, thank you very much. Thank you for your detailed report."

Shaking her hand firmly, Erin Millan smiled. "I'll let you know immediately if I hear any more news."

***

Over the following weeks, the vaccine that Maharishi had developed was found to work and the virus was eradicated. But not before almost ten thousand had people died.

The investigations into Argawal and Maharishi Pharma went on for almost three months. Close to twenty executives, including Argawal, were sentenced to long terms in "Central Jails" located in the State of Tamil Nadu, the State where they killed almost ten thousand people.

The evidence gathered during the investigation included vials of the Arctic Flu and the Indian Flu, along with vaccines for both. Argawal was still missing and none of the other Maharishi executives admitted any involvement or wrongdoing with respect to the Inauguration Day bomb attempt or the Arctic Flu event.

***

EEOB. Secretary of State Millan asked for a meeting with Kari and Dr. Dipika Krishnan to be held at Kari's EEOB office. Secretary Millan explained that she wanted to meet there as it was a little less public.

FINAL CHANCE

At the meeting, she explained that following the investigations at Maharishi Pharma, the Minister of External Affairs called her with some disturbing news.

"He told me that when they discovered the vials of Arctic and Indian viruses and vaccines, the inventories didn't match with what the records showed. There were seven vials of the Arctic Virus and six of the Indian Virus missing. The records indicated that twenty vials of the Arctic Virus were originally manufactured in June of 2061 and that five were removed for 'Testing' in January of 2062."

Both Kari and Dr. Krishnan mentally calculated the date in context to the Arctic Virus pandemic a few months later.

Dr. Krishnan articulated it. "So those vials could have been used to seed the infection. Did the Minister mention the date of the vaccine production?"

Millan looked at her notes. "November 2061."

Kari asked, "So there are seven vials of Arctic Virus and six vials of the Indian Virus out there ... somewhere ... with someone? Do we know when the Indian Virus vials were produced."

Millan checked her notes again. "April, 2065 and the vaccine in May."

Kari ran the dates through her mind, "We can assume that the missing virus vials and vaccines disappeared sometime after the vaccine was produced in May and before the raid on Maharishi in late June. The botched Chittur test and raid could be the start date for whatever plan they had in mind."

Millan agreed that Kari's theory was reasonable, and Dr. Krishnan observed, "We have ample supplies of the Arctic Flu vaccine on hand and at least here, in the U.S., the microchips will detect any infection from that flu. The Indian Flu appears more aggressive, and we don't have the chips programmed for that, nor do we have the vaccine on hand. Can we obtain samples of the virus and vaccine so we can immediately update our chips and produce and test a vaccine?"

Secretary Millan replied, "I don't see why they wouldn't cooperate. I'll ask."

Kari added. "It's urgent. Whoever has the stuff will not wait until we're ready, and they've known that we've known for at least three months."

***

The Situation Room. Two days after the meeting with Secretary Millan and Dr. Krishnan, Sanders invited Kari to a meeting with Joe Strickland, Heidi Butler, Althea Crawford, Ollie Barth and Luther Rawlins. She was about to see President Sanders become 'Bo.'

Sanders asked, "Kari, I think you know everyone here so Luther, why don't you kick it off."

Rawlins reported that they had concluded the investigation into potential irregularities and suspicions surrounding the motorcade communication. There were none, leading them to the possibility that the texts originated from the vice president's car.

Rawlins' report inevitably was never going to deliver good news, just news of various degrees of bad. It was obvious, seeing the look on Sanders' face, that this was one of the worse degrees.

Rawlins continued. "So, that means one of the three people in that car was a traitor. Either one of my guys or the vice president. It's theoretically possible that it was more than one of them, but I'd bet my life it was just one."

Sadly, Sanders spoke, "And Luther, I'm guessing that you'd bet your life it wasn't either of your men."

Luther paused and then said, "Yes Sir."

Sanders smiled and corrected him. "Luther, in these sessions in this room, everyone is on a first name basis. Understood?"

"Yes Sir," came his automatic response, followed by chuckles from the others.

Luther recovered, faked a surprised look and asked, "What? Isn't 'Sir' your first name? 'Sir, Mister President, Sir'?"

That brought out some real laughs, but they were short-lived.

Sanders said, "I knew both of your guys and I wouldn't bet against them either. But what the hell was Johnson doing, then? Was he really impatient to get this job?"

Ollie Barth said, "As part of this investigation, we've re-vetted the former vice president and see nothing that would point to anything treasonous, but our remit doesn't get down into the psyche of an individual."

Joe Strickland weighed in. "We've done the same thing and the only negative mark we see is the incident with his wife's death."

That shocked everyone and got their full attention.

"There were a couple of timing issues around the incident that could possibly have provided a way for him to be involved, but there was never any motive. And all signs pointed to a forced entry and a burglary gone wrong. But even if he was guilty of that, why ... do this?"

There was almost a minute of silence while everyone pondered that question.

Sanders finally broke the silence, "Okay, let's move on. Anything happening with the wiretaps and phone logs?"

Strickland said, "That's me again and I'd like to add another name to the watch list – Karen Rover. Seems like Nerdkist and Rover talk a bit, mostly about the power generation protests, but we picked up one little nugget when Nerdkist said, 'Argawal's in trouble.' She asked why and Nerdkist just said that he'd tell her when they meet. So, okay to add Rover to the list?"

Sanders' thoughts were elsewhere but he said, "Yes. How do they know Argawal, and more importantly, why?"

Althea Crawford said, "His name was in the news, both for the Arctic Flu and the Indian virus epidemic, but that comment suggests it was more personal.

Sanders got the meeting back on track. "Anything more on Slade, Volkov or the dimwit in Alabama?"

Everyone tried to suppress their smiles but there was nothing else to add. Sanders asked Kari to present an overview of the meeting she'd had regarding Maharishi Pharma and Argawal.

FINAL CHANCE

With the exception of Luther Rawlins, the other attendees were aware of Argawal and the Indian Flu, but they hadn't heard the story and importance behind it. So, Kari explained about the botched virus test, deaths and investigation into Maharishi. She then detailed the missing virus vials.

She finished with the recently received and disturbing news. "When the Indian Government Minister tried to obtain a supply of the virus so it could be studied, they were told that in the interest of safety, it had been destroyed. So now, the only supply of the virus is in someone else's hands."

Althea Crawford asked, "Ahh, so, that's the back story to the alert at ports of entry for suspicious vials. But couldn't the Indians just make some more?"

Kari agreed, "We asked that, but they said no. This incident has been very painful for them. We still might be able to get some details – a recipe – but my concern is that depending on who has those vials, they may know that speed is important."

Strickland asked, "Can't we draw some blood from the victims?"

Kari wore a wry smile and slowly shook her head. "Not in India. Cremation takes place the next day or second day at most. Unfortunately, the Hindu religion doesn't understand our scientific needs. They believe that after death, the body serves no purpose, so a quick cremation is the quickest way to release the soul and help with reincarnation."

Strickland tried some light humor – "They must have a lot of coroners" – which was met with some eye rolls and looks of 'seriously?'

Sanders added, "HHS and CDC are trying to reverse engineer the virus from the vaccine, but I'm told that's a long shot. From what we know, even if we have a good supply of the vaccine on hand, the speed of this virus is unlike anything we've seen. So, keep your ears and eyes open. As he adjourned the meeting, Sanders asked Kari to join him in the Oval Office in fifteen minutes.

***

Chapter 34 – Arctic Bad. India Worse.

The Oval Office. Kari joined Erika and Sanders in the Oval Office.

Sanders said, "Ollie Barth just called, and they intercepted a message from an unidentified phone in the St. Petersburg area of Russia to an unidentified phone in the Tallahassee area. Here's the message." He handed Kari a single piece of paper.

"Sent:10-25-2065/21:22:40 To: +1.878.234.5119
Arctic bad India worse
Received:10-25-2065/21:22:59 From: +7.9585.852.436"

Sanders explained, "The message was sent to a phone issued in the Pittsburgh area, but the message was received in Tallahassee."

Having received the initial, and more detailed, report about the incident in India, the message shook Kari.

Her mind racing, she said, "Getting a vial or even vials into the country won't be difficult. I presume that all airports and ports have a physical description of the vials?"

Sanders replied, "Yes, they do. And if an infected person arrives, they can be detected if they have a fever. But from what little we know about the virus, early stages may not include a fever. That same lack of information makes identification via the microchips impossible."

Kari asked, "Are there any clues about who the recipient of the text might be? Or any internet chatter about a potential location? Does the fact that the phone was issued in Pittsburgh and is now in Tallahassee tell us anything?"

Sanders shook his head. "So far we've not picked up anything. All we know is that the vials have been missing for a few months and that if our hunches have been right, the text message is from Volkov."

Hopefully, Kari added, "Maybe the message was an indication of finalizing their plan and that their target date is still down the road."

Sanders looked at her and said, "After five years in this job, it's getting harder to be an optimist. That's what I wanted to talk with you about before Barth called."

Kari looked at him and saw the worry, sadness and aging – the gray hair invading from south to north and the tired eyes.

"I'm sorry, Bo, other than having the weight of the world on your shoulders, what's the matter?"

Sanders hesitated and began, "I'd been thinking about Doug. You know he wasn't my first choice in either my first term or second, but he always seemed like a decent guy. And I felt for him, losing his wife the way he did. But now I believe that my trust and sympathy have allowed me to be played and frankly, I'm embarrassed and angry. And yet I also hope I'm wrong.

"I know this Indian Flu thing is too important to get us off course, but I was wondering if you'd had any thoughts about Doug and his role, if any, in the attack?

Kari had given it a lot of thought, but it was all conjecture. She just said, "I don't have an opinion yet, but let's both of us stay focused on the virus. And I'll keep an open mind on Doug."

***

Number One Observatory Circle. Kari confided in Otis that evening about Sanders and how much older and more tired he looked.

Otis asked, "Given your career path and trajectory, does that worry you?"

"I think gray would look good on me, don't you?"

Otis recognized the trap and purred, "Sweetheart, you look great in any color!"

***

Thanksgiving, Chestnut Hill, Massachusetts. Jennifer had orchestrated a superb Thanksgiving dinner with gourmet 'contributions' that included Alek and Sophie's roasted Brussels sprouts, Jason and Nadya's Bourbon Cranberries, and Kari and Otis's curried black-eyed peas. Yogi contributed, too, by keeping Adam, now eight-years-old, and Vijay, Jr, seven, occupied and on their toes with his defensive soccer moves. It was a warm, loving family gathering, yet they still missed the man who had made the scene possible. Vijay Patel.

This Thanksgiving, in addition to the eight invited guests, there were four uninvited ones: Vice President Patel-Graham's Secret Service detail. Jennifer and Kari insisted that they rotate through so that they could each enjoy even a brief holiday meal, while maintaining their protocol outside the house. The youngsters were thrilled and couldn't wait to tell their friends.

After dinner, when the kids were off playing with Yogi under the watchful eyes of the backyard Secret Service detail and grandparents, Kari was discussing the non-classified aspects of the Indian Flu investigation. She mentioned the frustration with unregistered phones, making it impossible to identify the conspirators.

Jason stated, matter-of-factly, "You could correlate the known numbers of people you suspect with an unknown burner phone. It's probably only circumstantial, but if you suspected me and saw that I was in Chicago, based on my known phone number, and a call or text was made or received by a burner phone in Chicago, that would at least place me at or near the scene of the burner call."

Kari made a big mental note to discuss that with Sanders and then she asked Jason and Nadya a question about the flu itself.

"Are you aware of the efforts to reverse-engineer the Indian flu from the vaccine in order to understand the virus structure and update the microchips?"

Nadya answered. "Yes. We've been working with the CDC scientists. It's all hypothetical as we have no way to test for it, and if we design too wide a profile, it could result in everyone being stopped."

Jason asked, "Appreciate that it may be confidential, but who do you think might want to weaponize the virus and why?"

Kari decided to deflect the question and simply said, "We don't have any credible threats or known motives. We're just being cautious after the Arctic Flu."

Jason asked, "Please tell me that guy's in jail, right?"

"No. They're still looking for him and we don't know if there are others that he was working with."

That conversation was scuttled when the kids burst into the house full of energy and stories of their mini-soccer match, including Adam's boast of scoring against one of the Secret Service agents!

***

The Oval Office. Kari shared Jason's idea about correlating a known phone's location with that of a burner, and Sanders asked her to pass that along to the CIA and FBI. She also told him about the less than enthusiastic hope from Nadya regarding the chip update potential.

Despite their ensuing conversation about the devastating possibilities that the missing vials might cause, Sanders seemed upbeat and more relaxed after the long, and uneventful weekend. It had been almost seven months since the virus was produced and sometime between then and three months ago that the six vials had disappeared. Anything could have happened, even a mistake in the inventory, or perhaps the employees in Chittur had more than was believed.

Kari mentioned that the CDC was coordinating the production of millions of vaccines, just in case. The Indian version had been tested and it didn't have any adverse side-effects, but no one knew if it was effective against the virus.

**

December 18th, 2065, Los Angeles International Airport.
The Christmas holiday travel season was in full swing
and LAX was teeming with people arriving and departing.
British Airways flight 209 had landed almost an hour ago,
but even with the expedited process afforded flight crews,
British Airways flight attendant, Gillian Wood, was in a long
line slowly approaching the engulfed immigration control
checkpoint. The slow pace gave her plenty of time to think
and argue the pros and cons of her next actions. As the
immigration agent mechanically called, "Next," Gillian made
up her mind and, as the immigration perfunctorily stamped
her British Passport, she asked to speak with the police.

She was startled when almost immediately a uniformed
police officer was at her side and she panicked momentarily,
second-guessing her decision. Then she quickly stated –
more like blurted out – what she had decided to say.

The officer seemed to immediately grasp the importance of
what she'd said and escorted her to a nearby interview room.
He asked her to wait and left her alone with her thoughts.
Within a few of minutes a supervisor from the Transportation
Safety Agency arrived and Ms. Wood repeated her earlier
statement to the officer.

Fifteen-minutes later, Supervisor FBI Agent Louise Sandoval
arrived, and Gillian Wood got to tell her whole story. It began
two days earlier at a strike rally staged by British Airways
flight attendants at London's Heathrow Airport. The flight
attendants were angry and felt they were being bullied by
management, who were stalling to extract a pay and working
condition deal that was far worse than their present working

agreement. The strike action was well into the third month and the workers were feeling the financial pain. Because of the reduced pay as a result of the strike action, many had been forced to alter their living arrangements, and some were even facing mortgage defaults.

Gillian explained that she'd been approached by a young woman, who she thought was a fellow flight attendant. They began talking and the young woman told her that she could offer Gillian a chance to give management a black eye.

All she had to do was surreptitiously spray a mist onboard her flight. The mist would make a number of people mildly ill and as a result, British Airways would be blamed, and the union would fan the PR flames. The offer was worth a hundred thousand U.S. dollars.

They'd spoken for a while and the woman assured Gillian that the mild, flu-like illness, although not dangerous, would be enough to get attention. Gillian asked if she'd get sick as well, but the woman explained that before her flight, at the airport, a doctor would meet her to inject a vaccine-like antidote that would protect her. He would then give her the aerosol cannister and deposit the money into her account. The woman asked Gillian if she had a cell-phone app that could confirm the transfer, which she did.

The doctor who met with her was a nice, well-dressed young man. He gave her the injection and the cannister. He showed her how she could simply walk down the aisle and unobtrusively spray the mist downward. It was important to do this no sooner than one hour before landing. He then asked her to access her bank account on her phone and provide him with her account details. He used his cell phone, tapped some keys and asked her to refresh her phone. She looked and saw the hundred-thousand-dollar deposit. It wasn't as much in Sterling, but she remembered giggling when she looked at her account. She'd checked it twice more before take-off and revisited her internal conflict of having all her problems solved by making people sick.

Ms. Wood then went on to explain that after almost twelve hours with the passengers, she began to feel really badly about making them sick just before Christmas, especially all the children. There were so many children. And so, as the hour approached, she kept stalling and then decided she couldn't do it.

Agent Sandoval asked Gillian to access her banking app. Gillian complied and then outraged, said, "How did they know I didn't do it? The money isn't there!"

***

Agent Sandoval immediately reported the incident along with a photo of the canister. Massive searches were carried out at airports around the country, looking in trash collection points used by the airlines as planes were cleaned. Hazmat clad FBI staff took the canister that Ms. Wood had carried into the country off for analysis.

***

The Situation Room. It was just before midnight on the eighteenth that President Bo Sanders assembled the vice president and heads of the FBI, HSA, HHS and NSA. A grim and bleary-eyed Althea Crawford kicked it off, briefly explaining the story from Los Angeles. She then detailed the massive trash search and ominously related the news.

"Cannisters similar to the one at LAX were found in airline trash collection points at Miami, O'Hare, JFK and Dulles. All were empty or near empty. The flights involved were from London, Warsaw, Dubai and Istanbul, carrying over two thousand passengers and crew. Dipika can explain what's happening now."

"First of all, we're rushing supplies of the vaccine out to all the airport areas involved. We're still pretty early into our vaccine production process and although we have plenty for the people on those flights, many of them have connected to other cities. We're busy tracing them and will be sending supplies to those cities. But we still don't know if the vaccine even works."

Joe Strickland picked it up. "We're contacting the flight crews of all the flights where the aerosols were found to find the distributors and see if we can get additional information."

There was a pause and Sanders jumped in. "Ollie, are you monitoring the internet and phones for messages?"

"Yes sir. Nothing yet." No one corrected the 'Sir' comment.

Kari asked, "What do we know about the content of the cannister? Is it the virus? How much did they hold? I mean, would each cannister represent a vial?"

Strickland answered, "Good questions. We don't know. And no, we can't be certain that we've found them all."

Sanders said, "This night is going to get longer and unfortunately, very painful. Does anyone need anything that requires my help? If not, I'm going to try to get some sleep, but have me woken if we learn anything I need to hear. I suggest all of you get some rest, if you can."

***

The White House. 3:15 AM. Sanders sat up and swung his legs out from his bed as he picked up the phone. "Yeah, Joe. Waddya got?"

"The cannisters. We've got five of them. It's the Indian Virus and based on the vial description we got from the Indians, a cannister would hold about one vial. So, that makes five of the six vials accounted for. We don't know if we missed one or if a flight attendant took it and kept it or disposed of it.

"We've interviewed all the flight attendants. Two confessions and dozens of denials. We're holding the two confessors and the entire crews of the other flights. The airlines are not happy."

"Okay. Anything else?"

"No. Go back to sleep."

"Thanks, Joe. I'll try."

***

Chapter 35 – The Day After

The Oval Office, 7:05 AM. Kari and Sanders were looking at the updates from the airline attacks. Sanders had taken calls from the presidents of Turkey and the United Arab Emirates about holding their flight crews. In both cases, he advised the leaders that all except the guilty parties would be released, once cleared by the CDC. They had matched fingerprints to the cans.

Kari had spoken with Dr. Krishnan at CDC. The vaccines were in place, including at the cities that passengers from the affected flights had connected to. Vaccinations had already begun with the flight crews, although tracking people down in the middle of the night was slow going.

Dr. Krishnan had also issued a warning. She explained that the flight attendant, Gillian Wood, in Los Angeles had agreed to a blood sample draw so the effects of the vaccine she had received in London could be studied. They wanted to make sure they weren't doing more harm than good in vaccinating others. What they found was nothing other than a puncture mark. They were waiting for samples and results from the other flight attendants.

Kari had asked, "Do you think she was lying about the injection?"

Krishnan said, "Her story matches that of the others, so no."

Kari asked, "Medically, can you explain that? Could it be completely benign in some?"

"It could be benign but there should still be evidence. Compared with the vaccine we've produced; we see no indication of anything similar in Ms. Wood's blood."

Sanders and Kari took a call from Ollie Barth. The NSA had picked up a text from a burner phone in the St. Petersburg area of Russia to a burner in the Pittsburgh area. The message reads, "Let games begin! Look forward to great New Year party. Have present for you."

The president and vice president looked at each other, speechless, and then Ollie's voice came through the speaker again.

"There's more. We took Kari's correlation suggestion and turned up a hit. Grover Nerdkist's known phone number."

Sanders was excited. "Have you told Joe yet?"

"No. I called you as soon as I got this."

Sanders asked, "How physically close were the two phones?"

Ollie replied and you could almost hear the smile in his voice, "Both within his private dome."

Sanders thought for a moment and said, "I'll call Joe. Thanks, Ollie! Great work!"

The country's two top executives sat in silence for a moment.

Kari asked, "By his comment about a great New Year's party, do you think they have plans to meet?"

Sanders was quick to know where Kari was going with this and replied. "Perhaps, but Volkov can't come here."

"Well, he's not supposed to come here. That's different. But even if it is somewhere else – and I mean outside of Russia – it could be a chance to grab Volkov, assuming that's who sent this."

Sanders thought out loud, "What about grabbing or questioning Nerdkist? He may have information about the sixth vial."

"Could that be the present?"

Sanders looked like a deer in headlights and said, "Let's call Strickland."

Sanders explained to Strickland what the NSA had found and also the immediate thoughts that he and Kari were sharing.

Strickland considered the options and said, "That sixth vial could be anywhere. Destroyed, miscounted, given to a flight attendant who got cold feet and didn't say anything, or yes, it could still be in play. Or ... it could be the present. And if Volkov is the bearer, Happy New Year! But let's not grab Nerdkist yet."

Sanders looked at Kari who nodded and gave him a thumbs up.

Sanders asked Strickland, "How should we proceed?"

"I'll put a twenty-four-seven watch on Grover and in addition to the NSA's surveillance, we'll tap all his phones, with your approval. I'd like to request an even broader wiretap to also include Karen Rover, and the governors of Alabama, Kansas, and Kentucky. That way we can make sure that we get invited to any of their parties."

Sanders and Kari continued their discussion when Erika came in to say that Dr. Krishnan needed to speak with them urgently.

Dr. Krishnan's worried voice crackled from the speaker. "We finally tracked down the last remaining flight attendant from the Dubai flight. That was the first arrival of the five flights, so she was one of the earliest to be exposed. And she arrived before we knew about the attacks, so she wasn't held. She stayed with a boyfriend in New York and when he woke up this morning, she was dead. A sharp 911 dispatcher called the FBI. We've quarantined her boyfriend and he's helping trace others who may have been exposed. We've drawn a blood sample from the flight attendant to be able to verify the cause of death and also see if she received a fake vaccine."

Sanders interrupted, "What do you mean by a fake vaccine?"

"All of the flight attendants who'd claimed to have gotten a vaccine hadn't received a real one – or certainly not an effective one. They might have even been given simple saline solutions."

Kari verbalized both her and Sanders' thoughts, "That way the witnesses would all be dead."

Sanders looked at her sharply and said to Dr. Krishnan, "The news on this attack will probably break soon if it hasn't already. I'm going to need a detailed update on what you're doing, have done, and still need to do. How bad do you think it's going to be?

Dr. Krishnan replied, "We've had some good luck. The Polish flight was delayed so we were able to isolate the passengers, and the flight attendant confessed quickly, so we vaccinated everyone before they were released ..."

FINAL CHANCE

Sanders interrupted, "But you don't know that it works!"

Dr. Krishnan politely replied, "Mr. President, you cut me off. The passengers and crew from the Polish flight were bussed from the plane to an unused emergency ward that's been in place since the pandemics. But let me just answer your question. Of the twenty crew members from the Dubai flight, the only one we weren't able to vaccinate was the one that disappeared to her boyfriend's apartment … and she died. All the other crews are fine. Also, we're way ahead of where we were with the Arctic Flu concerning tracing. I'm confident that we'll do better than we did with that one."

Sanders erupted again. "Better than fifty-thousand deaths?"

"I'm sorry, Sir. I'm tired and there are so many variables, but it should be less than half that. We'll know more later today or tomorrow."

And then, sadly, resolutely, and with obvious weariness in her voice, she continued, "In the meantime, there are people whom we haven't found yet and if they're infected, they will most likely die. And it's too early to understand the transmission characteristics. That's another variable. But I'll send you the available details you'll need to address the situation, and I'll keep you informed."

Kari jumped in and said, "Thank you, Dipika. Sounds like you and your team are doing everything possible. Try to get some rest."

The line went dead.

Sanders looked contrite and apologized. "I'm sorry. I could blame it on sleep deprivation but that would be too easy."

Kari returned to her EEOB office and called Jason to thank him for his correlation idea.

Jason was pleased and asked, "How close were the phones?"

Triumphantly, Kari answered, "Nerdkist has his own dome and both phones were within it."

"Great! Still circumstantial but someone is guilty." And then he remembered something. "Ask your FBI guy to contact Jeff Hepple at SHARE in California. During their experiments with phone networks within domes, they were recording all calls to assess quality. It's a long shot but they may have recorded something of interest."

***

The White House, December 19, 2065. President Sanders held a press conference at noon, detailing the incident and issuing an appeal.

"Ladies and Gentlemen. Yesterday, five flights arrived in the country carrying passengers infected with a potentially dangerous virus. Thanks to very quick and effective action by the TSA, CDC, and FBI, most of the potential contamination spread has been contained. It is extremely important, however, that any passengers from the following flights arriving yesterday, who have not already been contacted by the CDC, or people who have been in contact with passengers on these flights, get in touch immediately with the CDC on this special number: 12345. I'll repeat that: 12345.

"The affected flights are: Emirates flight 201 from Dubai to New York, JFK Airport ... Turkish Airlines flight 7 from Istanbul to Washington Dulles ... British Airways flight 209 from London to Miami ... British Airways flight 269 from

FINAL CHANCE

London to Los Angeles ... and Polish Airlines flight 3 from Warsaw to Chicago, O'Hare.

"An effective vaccine is available that will prevent the virus from advancing. It is free to anyone who needs it. And we must contact everyone concerned."

And then, to the clamoring press, he added, "Any questions?"

As expected, almost everyone's hands shot up along with their pleas to be recognized. The questions were mostly anticipated.

Washington Post reporter: "Have there been any deaths and if so, how many?"

Sanders: "Sadly, yes. Seventy-seven."

CNN reporter: "Is this possibly a new pandemic and do you have plans for containment?"

Sanders: "We don't believe it will become a pandemic and our personal microchips are in the process of being updated."

New York Times reporter: "Let me get this straight. We have what appears to be a new, dangerous, and highly contagious virus that arrived from five countries on the same day ... and for which a vaccine already exists. But it is not considered to be an early indicator of a pandemic?

Before Sanders could reply, another reporter shouted out, "Was this a planned attack?"

There was now pandemonium in the room with questions being screamed from almost everyone.

Sanders stood perfectly still, silent and smiling until the noise receded. "If we can keep this session under control in an orderly fashion, I will attempt to answer everyone's questions as best I can."

That silenced the mob and Sanders began by explaining about the outbreak of the virus in India as a result of a laboratory accident. The laboratory and those responsible had been shut down but it appeared that some viral material remained at large. It was also possible that unknown perpetrators have used the material to attack the United States.

The room broke out again and, once more, Sanders stood silently until the noise subsided. "Last chance. Next time I disappear. Yes, the attack seems planned, but we don't know who carried it out. As for the presence of the vaccine, when we first learned about the virus some months ago, even though it had been contained in India, we decided to produce a vaccine, just in case. Turns out that was a good idea. There's not a whole lot more I can tell you and I sincerely ask you to get my message out to all corners of the country so we can cut off further contagion. There'll be another full briefing at six PM."

***

The Oval Office. Kari congratulated Sanders. She felt the press conference had gone well. Plus, they had just gotten an update from Dr. Krishnan. The good side of having virus victims was that it gave them the information they needed to update the microchips; and just one click later, the entire country's chips were updated to detect the presence of the "Indian Flu."

They had now found and contacted everyone except for six people from the flights, and everyone else had been vaccinated. Dr. Krishnan surmised that those six probably lived alone and had already become victims. Undoubtedly there would be some others who would have been or will be infected, but not many.

The victim total was ninety-seven, which included almost two-dozen through transmission from passengers. While having people die is never something to boast about, containing the situation as quickly as they did was something to be proud of, and Sanders heaped most of the credit on Dr. Krishnan and the CDC.

Joe Strickland called with news of a few new hits from the wiretaps. There was a text message from (probably) Rover to Nerdkist between burner phones that the death toll seemed very low. And then there was one from (probably) Nerdkist's phone to one in St. Petersburg, Russia, echoing Rover's message. And finally, a reply from St. Petersburg with a comment that the death rate was probably way understated.

As the day went on and with the realization that they may have escaped a huge disaster, the tension and adrenaline that were keeping Sanders awake started to subside, and he asked Kari to take the 6:00 PM press conference.

Although the crowd of reporters was pretty much the same as it had been at noon, they were somewhat calmer. Kari explained that the incredible effort of the CDC had kept the potential death toll of more than three thousand passengers (plus their contacts) to under a hundred. The CDC had also updated the microchip file so that anyone with symptoms will be alerted. "And," she added, "we have plenty of vaccines available."

They asked questions, but Kari's personable demeanor and down-to-earth style disarmed them, shredding away the combativeness the press often displayed. This was their first meeting and they liked what they saw.

***

The White House, Christmas Eve day. Kari, Otis, and Yogi were doing last-minute packing for their flight up to Boston when the president called. Fearing a last-minute emergency, Kari held her breath as she took the call.

Sanders was ebullient. "We got our Christmas Present. At least I did. A message was intercepted that the person with the Russian phone number would be arriving in the U.S. on New Year's Eve. So, have a very Merry Christmas up in Boston. When are you back?"

"That's great news! I was planning to return on New Year's Day, but I'd like to join you for what will hopefully be a memorable New Year's Eve! So, I'll see you then."

***

Chapter 36 - Happy New Year! (2066)

Edinburg, Pennsylvania. The FBI had a small army assembled around the private dome in the rolling hills of Pennsylvania. There were also a half dozen agents stationed at the Newcastle Municipal Airport to await Volkov's private plane from Montreal.

Joe Strickland was pleased that this would be a large gathering, too, as Semper Creud, Karen Rover, and Gerry Failwell had recently arrived. Another attendee that took some digging to identify was Prince Ibrahim Al Saud. Strickland thought that this might be his best New Year's Eve ever – at least during his law enforcement days – and he was pretty sure that Sanders would feel the same. He had assigned an agent to live-stream the event to the Situation Room at the White House, where Sanders would be watching.

The FBI had Federal warrants for a breach entry as well as complete plans showing the layout of the dome and the huge house. This was 'payback' for the government doming of Nerdkist's entire estate, including a stable block, staff quarters, and a huge garage with over fifty vintage cars. They knew exactly how to get in, and exactly how some might try to escape.

The team from the airport advised them that they were on their way and that they were following the "package" at a safe distance.

The plan was to wait twenty minutes after Volkov's arrival before disabling the dome's security systems. They could then see – using their electronic gear – exactly where the group was gathering before launching the attack.

***

Volkov had arrived to great fanfare but he simply waved and went to his room. Ten minutes later he returned bearing a lavishly wrapped gift. He was offered his favorite vodka and looked around at the group of people that he privately viewed as somewhere between weak and dumb. He'd often wondered how the United States was as strong as it was if people like this could be influential.

Volkov seemed moved that Argawal wasn't there to celebrate. After all, Argawal was the only person other than himself who'd contributed to the effort.

Volkov told the group that Sanders was lying about the deaths. Twenty thousand Indians had died in a much more limited venture. He praised the assistance of Naresh Argawal for developing the virus and he implored Nerdkist and Rover to expose Sanders' lies.

Creud began boasting about helping to kill a senator when all hell broke loose from all sides. Explosions and the sound of shattering doors seemed to come from all sides of the large room at the same time. And before anyone recovered to even think about moving, four teams of fully battle-clad FBI agents carrying serious weaponry and the smell of the explosives streamed in.

A bullhorn blared. "FBI! Lie face down on the floor!"

Everyone did except Volkov. He had removed the wrapping paper from the package he had and was waving around a canister.

"I tink dat you drop your guns and lie down, or I spray dis virus and kill you all with much pain."

Strickland said, "Go ahead and spray."

Volkov laughed and said, "You tink you so smart but you know nothing, like all Americans." And he began spraying a mist.

Strickland smiled and said, "Cuff them all."

Creud had wet himself, the Prince was demanding diplomatic immunity, and Failwell said he didn't know what was going on. He was just attending a party. Both his comments were true.

They were all taken to the FBI office in Pittsburgh to be charged and questioned. Everyone except Volkov asked about the virus. Georgi's comments had scared them. Strickland told them that it was a deadly and painful virus developed by their friend Argawal, but that a vaccine existed. When they all demanded and then pleaded to be vaccinated, they were told, "as soon as we're finished questioning you."

They had many answers to the questions that had been put on hold over many years. On the assumption that Nerdkist was the hub of everything, they milked his fear of the virus simply by saying, "We'll let you think about that while we question the others." Only when they were fairly certain they had gotten everything, did they vaccinate him. His testimony incriminated everyone, including himself, and there was one more piece of evidence that made it impossible for anyone to deny their involvement.

Jason's tip about calls within domes being recorded during the test period paid off, and the bonus was that the recording process had never stopped. Ironically, Nerdkist had signed off on the approval to record his calls when the dome was first built. He never got around to canceling it. They had Nerdkist's conversations with all of them on tape, as well as recordings with a number of people who weren't there, including Naresh Argawal, Glen Slade, Governor Cobolt of Kansas, Governor Connell of Kentucky, the CEOs of various agri-businesses whose companies were involved with the strikes, and Laurence Donald. There was one other person implicated through the recordings, but Strickland kept it under wraps.

Volkov didn't lose his cockiness, even after they told him that the vaccine he'd used was not effective. A day and a half later, as the onset of the virus began to take hold, he began to talk.

Volkov didn't so much confess as he did brag. He bragged about killing President Parkson, he gloated over the long string of power outages, and he spoke with pride about killing fifty-thousand Americans with the Arctic Flu. He laughed about the mistake that killed Vice President Johnson, and he expressed regret that although he killed several Secret Service agents on Necker Island, he missed killing President Metcalf again. He also railed against what he called Sanders' lies about the Indian Flu deaths. He claimed there were many more and he was proud to make fools of the Americans with his clever airplane attacks.

Volkov capped his list of atrocities with a vague, dark, and threatening remark. "I have big regret not to kill President Sanders in White House, but that not over yet."

***

FINAL CHANCE

The Situation Room. The president's and vice president's eyes were glued to the screen and when Strickland ignored Volkov's warning and Volkov began spraying, Kari gasped, but Sanders smiled and said, "The whole team's been vaccinated."

As the FBI team left the house with their prisoners, the pair clapped and high-fived. Sanders retrieved a bottle of champagne from an ice bucket. He popped the cork, poured two glasses and he and Kari toasted to a new and happier year. Neither one of them truly believed it.

Sanders's phone rang. It was Strickland. Sanders heaped compliments on him, and the team and Strickland thanked him for suggesting the vaccinations. He laughed as he told Sanders that Volkov's threat about a painful death had proved to be a powerful incentive to Nerdkist and his comrades to fully and truthfully answer all their questions.

Strickland reported that in addition to Volkov, Nerdkist and Creud were very much implicated and that the Prince and Failwell only marginally so. Volkov had admitted to the previous assassination attempts, the Parkson assassination, the motorcade attack, both the Arctic and Indian Flu attacks, and the power outages. Strickland did not tell him about Volkov's final comment.

***

The Oval Office, January 1st, 2066. Sanders smiled as he hung up the phone after his call with Shamalov. The Russian president had been screaming during much of the call, demanding the return of Volkov. Sanders resisted the urge to say "Nyet," but he did give him the English translation.

Shamalov had slammed the receiver down after Sanders told

him that he'd make a deal. The next time Russia captures an American in Russia who admits to assassinating a Russian president, attempts to assassinate two other Russian presidents, assassinates a Russian vice president, and kills over fifty-thousand Russians on Russian soil, Sanders will not demand his or her return.

Kari and Erika were in the Oval Office during the call and they were trying to keep their smiles under control. When Sanders put the phone down, he said with feigned surprise, "He hung up on me! Perhaps it was something I said."

Kari quipped, "He was probably upset about thinking there could ever be more than one Russian president."

Erika said, "Are you ready to take the call from the Saudi Foreign Minister?"

"Ready? I guess I don't have a choice. What is he going to demand and threaten us with? Any ideas?"

Kari and Erika looked at each other and Kari offered, "Expel our Embassy staff? Buy Russian weapons?"

Sanders shook his head and groaned, "Put him through."

"Good evening, Abdul. I suppose you're calling to wish me a Happy New Year."

"Good morning, Mr. President. Actually, that wasn't the reason for my call, however, please allow me to do that now. I would like to wish you a Happy New Year, and now to the reason I am calling you, which I expect you know. Our King has asked me to convey two messages. The first is to send his regards." The Foreign Minister paused.

Sanders was rolling his eyes and grimacing. "And his second message?"

"He said to tell you that we waive our right to diplomatic immunity regarding the Prince and that we will not be posting bail when it is set. All the King asks is that he receives a fair trial."

Sanders was speechless while Kari and Erika had to hold themselves back from applauding and shouting.

Sanders regained his composure, thanked the Foreign Minister, and asked that his thanks and regards be communicated to the King. He finished with, "I assure you that the Prince will receive a fair trial."

Sanders looked at his two colleagues and said, "I guess dad wants his son to grow up a little."

***

January 2nd, 2066. To say that the news of the dramatic New Year's Eve raid dominated the media would be a major understatement. Readers, viewers, and listeners around the world learned the details about the arrest of Georgi Volkov, who was being charged with carrying out a multitude of crimes including assassinations, mass murders from the Arctic and Indian Flu, as well as the power disruptions. Naresh Argawal's heinous contributions were also covered. Playing second fiddle, from a news perspective, were the arrests of his cohorts, Governors Creud of Alabama, Cobolt of Kansas, Connell of Kentucky, along with Grover Nerdkist II, Karen Rover, Gerry Failwell, Prince Ibrahim Al Saud of Saudi Arabia, and several American CEOs.

Bail had been denied for all as they were considered flight risks.

***

The White House. At 6:00 AM, Joe Strickland met privately with President Sanders. Strickland had requested the meeting and Sanders had been puzzled by what seemed to be an awkwardness in Strickland's manner.

Sanders listened to many of the recordings from Nerdkist's dome that Strickland played, his mood sinking. He asked Strickland who else knew and was told that only one analyst had heard it.

They discussed it for a while and when Sanders asked if it could be kept quiet, at least for a while, Strickland agreed.

***

The White House had been focused on Sanders' State of the Union address on January 13th, until the Secretary of State, Erin Millan, requested an urgent meeting with President Sanders on January 4th. The Russian President, Vladimir Shamalov, had ordered all Americans out of the U.S. Embassy in Moscow and he was recalling all Russian Embassy staff in the U.S. home as well. All attempts to contact anyone in the Russian government had failed.

As the day wore on, the reports started to flow in that the Russians had commenced aggressive military naval operations close to the U.S. borders in the northeast and northwest. Reports of long-range bombers flying close to U.S. airspace were also being received.

The United States went into full alert and readiness to defend against and counter an attack, should one be launched. Both the president and vice president were completely consumed with evaluating the changing situation and discussing options to end what appeared to be a stalemate over Volkov.

FINAL CHANCE

Assistance from other nations was requested but as the days went by there was still no communication between the U.S. and Russia. The media added to the uncertainty with non-stop reporting from a wide variety of pundits offering their opinions about possible outcomes. A common question centered on whether it was worth the risk over a single person – Volkov – but Sanders was adamant. So were the Russians, and their aggressive and dangerous provocation continued.

Sanders' State of the Union address focused on the Russian threat and he made a pretty compelling case against trading Volkov for a resolution. But with no hope in sight and a planned weekend trip to Camp David with his wife and children just two days away, he ignored his instincts to remain in Washington – mainly, so that the children could play in the snow. After all, he'd only be thirty minutes away.

***

Chapter 37 – Sleeping with the Secretary

The White House, February 1, 2066. It was four-thirty in the morning as the president stretched and turned beneath the warm comforter, cuddling against the still sleeping Secretary of Education. Wondering if this was the first time a president slept with a Cabinet Secretary in the White House brought a wry smile to her face, as her mind refocused on the planned and unplanned events of the day.

***

The days that followed the assassination of President Sanders had been the darkest days of Kari's life. The calls she received from all the world's leaders were a combination of condolences and good wishes, but the messages of condolence far outweighed any positive feeling the leaders tried to convey.

Following Sanders' assassination, Volkov bragged that he had been behind the murder, supplying enough detail to prove it.

That prompted the first and most meaningful call she received – a call from President Vladimir Shamalov.

"Madam President. I congratulate you on this sad day. I want you to know that Russia had no part with killing of President Sanders. I am sad President Sanders dead and I am sorry I

played the games with him and make worries until he died."
Shamalov paused and Kari just listened. She heard him take a deep breath and continue. "I know Volkov not good man but I not know how bad he was. All of Russia ashamed. You can feed him to pigs if you want."

"Madam President. I hope we work together. I believe USA try to do good for world. Goodbye."

Kari sat there for a couple of minutes trying to interpret the meaning and level of sincerity of what she had just heard.

***

Situation Room. President Patel-Graham had just received her daily security briefing, which included another update about the assassination. There weren't many unknowns remaining.

The FBI had pinpointed the launch site of the fatal UAV missile near Thurmont, Maryland; and by using satellite imaging, they had identified the vehicles and ultimately, the perpetrators, who were members of a Maryland Militia. Where they got the "Switchblade" UAV, however, was still unknown.

The investigation uncovered that a small camera had been attached to the dome, via a micro-UAV. It would have been able to observe the late president enter the pool area and to transmit that information. The gas was probably for insurance in case the explosion didn't kill him. It was widely known that Sanders was an avid swimmer and that he used the pool frequently on his visits.

During the investigation feedback, it was also revealed that the poison gas that killed three Secret Service agents was a form of Botulinum neurotoxin, similar to the gas contained in the assassination attempt on Inauguration Day, five years ago.

Kari reacted. "I want to keep the type of gas confidential. Understood?"

She made sure she received affirmatives before she continued and switched subjects.

"General Chavez, why wasn't an anti-UAV laser weapon system installed at Camp David?"

Looking uncomfortable, Chavez said, "Madam President, we had been led to believe that the dome would provide adequate protection."

"What led you to believe that?" Kari asked.

More uncomfortably, Chavez had responded, "It was an assumption by the Secret Service, SHARE, and the Joint Chiefs."

Kari asked Luther Rawlins for his view.

"Madam President. General Chavez is correct. Both the White House and Camp David are heavily protected from missiles and have been for some time. We discussed the level of dome vulnerability with SHARE, and their engineers felt it would take a sizeable missile to penetrate a dome – a missile of the size that we currently protect against. Obviously, there was an error in that calculation."

Kari had replied, "Obviously," before asking Emma Steadman, "Assuming that all of our domes are equally vulnerable, how difficult and costly would it be to protect them?"

Steadman replied that she would discuss the dome reinforcement options with her engineers and pull together the cost estimates, grouping them by dome type. "I understand it's a high priority and as soon as that's done, we can get some cost estimates pretty quickly." She added, "The private sector reacts and responds rapidly when there's a chance that we might be buying something."

In the days after the assassination and Kari's swearing-in, Joe Strickland had requested a private meeting.

He seemed to be taking Sanders' death harder than anyone, but he never said why.

"Madame President, when we searched Nerdkist's house we found this piece of paper and eleven SIM cards. There are two lists of card numbers. One labeled 'Me', and the other 'DJ.' The SIM cards we found at the house are listed in the 'Me' column. Some numbers have been crossed off and we believe those are the ones he'd used already. One of the crossed-off numbers is the phone used in Tallahassee when it received the Indian Flu reference from a Russian phone.

Kari asked, "And the 'DJ' list?"

"Doug Johnson."

Kari asked, "How do you know that?"

The phone used in the motorcade attack was from one of these numbers.

Kari studied the list for a while, more for an excuse to think.

"Who else knows about this?"

"Just me. I haven't revealed who 'DJ' is."

"Can we keep this quiet for a bit?"

"I can try, but when Nerdkist spilled the beans, he told us that when Johnson was campaigning for the Presidency, Nerdkist had him followed, just on the odd chance they could gain some leverage. He hit the jackpot. Johnson had gone back to his house at the time of his wife's death, although he always denied it. Nerdkist blackmailed him but he only got some minor intel, apart from the motorcade. Nerdkist confessed that he had to press Johnson hard on that. Sanders was the target and Johnson went along with it."

Kari had wondered about Johnson's loyalty, but there was never proof. Still, hearing it without speculation was a bit of a shock. "Wasn't President Sanders advised of Johnson's involvement with Nerdkist?"

"Yes, Ma'am, he was, but he asked me to keep it confidential."

"Okay. I'm asking you to do the same. And Joe, all of us have been devasted by Bo's death, but you seem to be taking it very hard. I know you worked closely with him and he had enormous respect for you. Are you okay?"

Strickland looked twisted with pain and then he paraphrased Volkov's words following the New Year's Eve raid. "My big regret was not to kill President Sanders in the White House, but that's not over yet."

Kari tried to reassure him that there was nothing in those words that could have changed the outcome. She hoped he would realize that at some point.

FINAL CHANCE

Strickland left, thinking about what Kari had just said and hypothesizing actions that might have protected Sanders.

He was also feeling guilty that he hadn't mentioned the photos of Kari and Laurence Donald. He felt even more guilty for having seen them. He'd stared at them for a long time, not recognizing or even imagining who it might be. As soon as he realized who he was looking at, he'd put them in his pocket and destroyed them as soon as he had the opportunity.

Kari was also feeling guilty. When they were moving out of the vice president's residence, she'd accidentally pulled out the center drawer of her desk all the way and, wedged in the joint, at the very back, was a similar list of numbers and SIM cards. Kari's photographic memory – a genetic gift from her father - had immediately recognized the SIM number from the motorcade. She wasn't sure what to do then and she still wasn't sure what to do now.

***

After the security briefing, the new president looked out across the Rose Garden from the Oval Office, deep in thought. The roses were in full bloom, but she didn't see the flowers. Her head was spinning. Doug Johnson was a traitor. How should she handle it? It seemed like yesterday that this room was Bo Sanders' Oval Office. Had it only been two weeks since Bo's State of the Union address, and four days less than that from the assassination? Both seemed lifetimes away.

She was pulled away from her thoughts by Erika Ruiz, now her chief of staff, as she entered the room. Erika was a keeper. A bundle of upbeat energy with an encyclopedic grasp of rules, protocols, events, and most importantly, knowledge of the personal histories of almost anyone that President Patel-Graham would need to interact with.

"Good morning, Madam President," Erika said, with a little more lightness emerging through the aftershock of the assassination – just enough to make Kari almost believe it.

"I hope so, Erika. Or at least better than yesterday."

Actually, yesterday wasn't bad, just rather sad ... and very hectic, and very long. There were dozens of phone calls from leaders throughout the world offering condolences, or more accurately, ticking that box and hoping to start a good relationship with the next POTUS; and then, even more, phone calls from governors, senators, House members, and countless others, flooded in, ranging from the very sincere to, "How can I turn this changing of the guard to my advantage."

The door from the private study and dining room opened and the secretary of Education entered, casting a compassionate smile in place of his usual wide grin and balancing two mugs of coffee on his briefcase.

"Hi, Erika. I've brought the president's coffee. It's the least I could do for letting me sleep with her." The big grin returned briefly.

A big, floppy-eared apricot-colored goldendoodle – tail wagging furiously – ran over to the two women, oblivious to the details of all the recent events, except for a sense that the humans were sad.

Yogi's antics worked and Erika even laughed. She looked at Otis and said, "That's the worst kept secret ever." And then, cuddling the furry White House resident, "Good morning to you, too, Yogi!"

Handing Kari a mug, the secretary kissed her on the cheek and said, "Good morning, Madam President. Did you sleep well?"

"I did. Set a new record, too. Four hours!"

"Excellent!" Gulping down the rest of his coffee, Otis Graham quipped, "I will leave you two amazing women to save the world so I can be sure that its human inhabitants, at least those in this country, are educated enough to appreciate your work." And then addressing Erika he asked, "What time will Madam President be free for dinner tonight?"

"She should be free at eight and she'll be hungry because she's having lunch with senator Blake," Erika said with a knowing look. "And don't forget, we're expecting a huge snowstorm tonight."

"Thanks for the heads up! Let's just hope the dome holds. Bye, Yogi. Don't bite any foreign dignitaries! That goes for you two, as well. Ciao."

Otis left and Erika said, "Your husband cracks me up. Is he always in a good mood?"

Kari replied quickly, "Yes. Bo's death changed that, but Otis never lost his optimism and bright outlook. It really tested him. He loved Bo."

The two women reflected on that for a while and then Erika changed the direction and said, "My dad's a big college football fan and Stanford was one of his favorites. He was really upset when Mr. Graham didn't go pro."

Kari replied, "Otis has few regrets, and going to Oxford instead of playing pro ball is not one of them. He is absolutely passionate about education."

That prompted Erika to ask, "I'm assuming then that there'll be no change at the Department of Education?"

"Smart lady! And since I didn't appoint him, he can stay, according to our legal eagles. Besides, given his work there so far, removing him might be an impeachable offense."

Erika laughed. "Okay, let's go over your day."

***

Chapter 38 – Picking up the Baton

Oval Office. Kari's dilemma over Doug Johnson had forced its way back into her thoughts. She needed to make a decision and decided to talk with Otis – tonight.

She also knew she needed to decide on a vice president.

The efforts of the past twenty years were finally beginning to bear fruit in many ways, the most important being environmental. And while the environment was improving, it was still fragile, and it was still way too early to let up. The air quality was better but still not healthy. The warming trend of the oceans had abated, but the water was still too warm and the state of marine life still healing.

It was true that the United States and the world, in general, were enjoying their highest-ever quality of life, measured not by the outdated GDP, but in terms of ESEP – Economic, Social, and Environmental Progress. It had taken almost a hundred years since Robert Kennedy stated in his 1968 campaign speech, "GDP measures everything, except that which makes life worthwhile."

But how sustainable were these achievements? She knew that not everyone was happy with the status quo of living life in an upside-down fishbowl. When will their patience run out and what will be the consequences? She needed to forestall that possibility – both in the U.S. and abroad – because she truly believed that this was everyone's final chance. This is the job that she chose for herself, and for the moment, it was up to her.

***

Erika announced that the secretary of Health and Human Services had arrived.

Dr. Dipika Krishnan had brought with her Drs. Ahmed Talib and Amy Ellingson from the CDC's Preparedness and Response.

Kari felt that this wasn't a simple "welcome to the big job meeting." She remembered Dr. Krishnan's colleagues, so she half-listened to the introductions. It was when Dipika said that there was something specific that they wished to discuss, that she was fully alert.

"Although we try not to think about worse case scenarios 24/7 at the Department, we can never really not think of them. The Arctic and Indian Flu were certainly reminders of that. We can't say for sure that pandemics like those of the twenties and thirties will never happen again; but if they do, the good news is that we'll be better prepared than ever to fight them, thanks to the embedded chips and enhanced tracing capability."

Kari was very young during those two turbulent pre-dome decades, but she remembered the masks, social distancing, and remote schooling. Her mind was on full alert based on Dipika's "something specific to discuss" comment.

Warily she said, "I have enough worse case scenarios to think about right now, so I hope you're not here with another one."

Dipika turned to face the young, earnest male doctor to her right. "Ahmed, please explain the outbreaks to Madame President."

Dr. Talib was young and serious, leading Kari to muse that perhaps he did think about worse case scenarios 24/7.

He said, "Madam President, we're monitoring a disturbing viral outbreak in Zimbabwe at the moment. So far it appears to be small and contained, but also extremely aggressive."

Kari asked, "When a virus like this is identified, what does 'monitoring' entail?"

Talib replied, "We attempt to get valid samples so we can understand its progression and structure, to effect prevention and develop a vaccine. We learned with the Arctic and Indian Flu how powerful chip detection of a disease can be once we understand the disease."

Dr. Ellingson added, "That information is then shared with the entire Preparedness and Response Team so we can see if the new disease creates gaps in our ability to cope with outbreaks. For example, how is the disease transmitted, incubation period, specific demographic susceptibility, et cetera."

Kari nodded her head and asked Dipika, "Okay. So, is there something specific that I need to be aware of?"

Dipika smiled. "You want to 'cut to the chase' as they say in the movies. Yes. The outbreak is mysterious. It has some similarities to the Arctic and Indian Flu in that regard."

Dipika paused and looked uncomfortable. She lowered her voice and said, "It's hard to explain but — if we can keep this between the four of us – it seems more synthetic. Manufactured. We've sent a team to get additional information as soon as possible, so we'll keep you posted. I promise you that we'll figure out how to deal with the virus. We just need to be able to act swiftly."

Kari appreciated that the vast majority of major cities throughout the world were already domed, but not many countries were using chips yet. So, any pandemic, if not quickly contained, could wreak havoc within the closed environments ... which brought her back to the security meeting earlier that day.

"What do you know about Botulinum neurotoxin?" Kari asked. The three HHS members looked at each other briefly and Dipika answered. "It's extremely dangerous. Why do you ask?"

"How could it be weaponized in a dome environment and what could be done to defend against it?"

Dr. Talib's answer confirmed him as a 'walking encyclopedia of terror.' "Assuming an average weight of one-hundred-fifty pounds for each of the almost six billion people on the planet, less than two ounces of pure BoNT could eradicate humankind. The most likely delivery systems in a dome environment would be through contamination of food, beverages or via an aerosol release."

The thought of Talib's answer paralyzed Kari for a moment. "Is there any way to protect against ...BoNT?"

Talib glibly replied, "Sure. Immunization."

Kari asked, "So why do we get vaccinated against smallpox, measles, COVID, etcetera, but not BoNT?"

"Cost versus current risk. The incidents of death are extremely rare." And he added with a smile, "Besides if we immunized everyone, Botox treatments wouldn't work."

The three women all laughed, and Dr. Ellingson exclaimed, "So I guess that ends that!"

And then they all laughed, but Dipika came around first. "Madame President. You didn't answer my question. Why are you asking?"

"It was nothing. I'd heard about it being very deadly and it kinda stuck with me, so when we were talking about diseases, it popped into my mind again."

She hoped her lie worked and she wrapped up, "This meeting has been a success in that you definitely have my attention. I'd like to get started with as wide a group as possible, so let's make sure we discuss our readiness plan, probably not including BoNT, at the next Cabinet meeting. Dipika, I'll see you there and Dr. Ellingson, Dr. Talib, thank you very much. I look forward to seeing you both again as we develop plans to improve our odds against diseases. And keep me posted on the Zimbabwe situation. I don't want a Zimbabwe Flu added to our deadly flu collection."

Even Dr. Talib smiled as they said their goodbyes.

***

Erika entered the Oval Office to advise Kari that Senator Blaydon Blake, the Majority Leader, Representative Cara Khan, Speaker of the House, and Isabelle Martin, Chair of the Democratic Party, had arrived for lunch. Kari gave the briefing report from Erika a quick re-read before heading to the president's Dining Room.

She was pleased that item one of the agenda was filling the vice president's job. The other agenda items were about the 2066 and 2068 elections. She couldn't believe that her party was already talking about and plotting for 2068.

***

Despite the power at the table, it was Isabelle Martin who led off with business after the greeting formalities. Kari and Martin had an uneasy history, but Kari was fairly certain that was now behind them.

"Madam President, we need to discuss the vice president vacancy. Who do you have in mind?"

Kari rattled off three names. "Senator Hughes, Governor Welti, and Representative Telles."

Martin looked pleased. "Excellent choices. I have three general criteria that I feel are important to consider. What vacancies they create, their electability – both as a running mate as well as a line of succession – and finally, their propensity to challenge you in a primary."

Kari asked, "Is that last point a plus or a minus?"

"For whom? You or the Party?"

Kari replied, "I was thinking the country."

Martin smiled. "Touché! I think a robust primary creates enthusiasm and, of course, it gives our members a chance to express concerns with an incumbent."

Senator Blake chided, "The term 'incumbent' in this case is purely a technicality. And even in a technical sense, Madam President was appointed as vice president. She was not elected to either position."

Kari smiled and used his first name purposefully, "Blaydon's correct, and the primary will establish what kind of world our constituents want and who they want to lead them. I'll be ready when the time comes." She wanted to add, Blaydon, please chew with your mouth shut and don't talk with your mouth full.

Martin gave her opinions of each candidate. "Hughes has four years left and choosing her would almost certainly cost us a Senate seat. It was a tough win. She probably wouldn't be a threat to challenge you in a primary either, as VP.

"As for Governor Welti, good choice. The lieutenant governor is a Democrat and I'm pretty sure Welti will have his hat in the 2068 ring."

Kari asked, "And Craig Telles?"

Martin answered, "A little inexperienced, perhaps. Probably not a primary challenge."

Speaker Khan spoke, "What Craig lacks in experience he more than makes up for with intelligence. And he doesn't intimidate easily."

Martin gave her a disapproving look but said nothing.

Kari wanted to get this over with and she was determined that she did the choosing. With a combination of defiance and sarcasm, she demanded, "Are there any others I should be considering?"

Martin didn't hesitate. "That's a good shortlist." And sensing Kari's determination, "Consider the Senate seat situation, although our majority is pretty robust. And let me know what you decide."

Kari was surprised. She remembered Sanders telling her about the pressure on him. Could it really be this easy?

Martin said that there was more to discuss. The 2066 elections in particular.

Kari said sarcastically, as she shifted her gaze from Martin to Blake, "I will make myself available to help any way I can, although as an unelected vice president and president, I doubt I'd be very helpful."

Facing re-election himself, Blake's face reddened, and he squirmed but said nothing.

Speaker Khan jumped in, "I'd love your support. I've got a tough fight ahead."

Kari smiled. "You got it! Let me know where and when."

Martin tried to talk about 2068, the key battleground states, vulnerable members, Party platform, and some other general campaign topics, but Kari stood up, prompting them to do the same.

Kari said, as sincerely as possible, "I'm sorry. As you can imagine, I have a lot on my plate right now. Thank you very much for your thoughts. I look forward to discussing things in more detail once we're closer to the election."

***

There was one more meeting on Kari's agenda, and she wasn't looking forward to it.

The assassination of an American president is a catastrophic event with the potential to affect virtually everyone in the world. It has the power to stop and derail even the most important plans, events, and lives; but apart from those obvious, consequences it also affects individuals in large and small, personal and impersonal ways.

While Kari was being hurriedly sworn in at the White House following Bo Sanders' death, Molly Sanders, Bo's wife, and First Lady stood by, reeling from the unfathomable grief and effects of the loss of her husband. She also needed to be a strong mother to two children who had just lost their father in a violent and craven act.

People who knew Bo and Molly felt their hearts ache for Molly and her daughters, unable to imagine what they were feeling. And yet, as soon as the White House staff were advised about the assassination, they set about packing up the Sanders' possessions as though they were packing up the forgotten items of a departed hotel guest who had neglected to check a drawer. It was their job.

Following Kari's taking the oath of office, Molly and her children had gone to her parent's home in California. But the next day, they'd returned to Washington to attend Bo's funeral.

Molly was coming to the White House to meet with Kari and the White House staff to cover the details of the funeral.

Kari had interacted many times with Molly and the children during her time as vice president. In public, Molly was quiet and formal; but in private, she was very warm, funny, and down to earth. Whenever she saw the very blonde, blue-eyed Molly with Bo, they reminded Kari of her parents.

Molly and the kids, Patricia and Katharyn, arrived at the Oval Office as any normal guests would, even though this was her house less than two weeks ago. Kari and Molly embraced, each of them fighting back tears. Slowly, they broke away and sniffled in unison, and Kari shook hands with the girls. She commented about how well they looked after the long flight but left her observation of reddish eyes unspoken.

When the funeral plans were made, Kari suggested that they stay at the currently vacant vice president's residence, where both children had been born. Molly had loved the idea and appreciated the privacy.

Molly said, "Thanks again, Kari, for offering Observatory Circle. It was like coming back home. I always liked it better than the White House. Memories of these two monsters joining us there will always make it special."

The kids giggled at their mom's label of themselves and then, just as Kari had arranged, Erika came in and took Patricia and Katharyn to the president's residence so they could watch TV, play video games, or frolic with Yogi.

Kari asked, "How're you doing?"

"I cry a lot. I've been so angry these past few days ... more than I've been in my entire life. Other than that, okay."

They looked at each other, laughed, hugged, and then shed a few more tears.

Molly asked, "How about you? Talk about a major life change. You've just been thrown into the very deep end."

Kari replied, "I don't have a lot of time to feel much. I'm sure you know. It's one problem to the next one and one call to the next and one meeting, function, activity to the next. And then I try to relax and get as much sleep as I can and hope it's longer than a couple of hours."

Molly smiled and said, "Bo thought the world of you, and I know that he wanted you to pick up the baton."

The unsaid words – "But not in this way." – weighed heavy on both of them and they took deep breaths to quell the tears.

Kari changed the subject and tone. "Did Bo ever say anything about Doug Johnson? I mean, anything that might involve trust?"

Molly looked at her, "Yes. And I don't mean at the end, after the motorcade attack. There was always something that Bo sensed but couldn't put his finger on. Doug seemed unsettled and removed at times when certain situations were discussed."

"Like what?"

"Nerdkist. Whenever Bo and Joe Strickland were discussing Nerdkist, Doug looked nervous, even guilty. Those were Bo's words."

Following a few seconds of silence, while Kari absorbed what she'd said, Molly changed the subject. "Speaking of vice-presidential roles, who is Queen Isabella trying to push down your throat?"

Kari laughed. "Surprisingly no one yet. I met with her, Representative Khan, and the charming Senator Blake today. He's a piece of work."

"He wasn't Bo's favorite either. Especially if they were eating."

Kari burst out laughing. "So, I'm not the only one!"

The two women talked some more, and Kari pressed Molly to stay in touch and never hesitate to call if she needed anything.

Later on, Kari wondered about Molly's change of subject away from Doug Johnson. She suspected that Bo had told Molly in confidence, just as Kari planned to do with Otis this evening.

***

Chapter 39 – Endings & New Beginnings

The White House Residence. Kari and Otis met for their dinner date at 8:15 PM. The White House chef wanted to please Kari, but he struggled with vegan cooking. His effort with Indian food resulted in a similar, dismal, outcome, so Kari steered him to some Julie Morris recipes, which he executed quite well. Tonight, the chef had made a garlicky butter bean soup, followed by Portobello mushrooms with spinach and a pomegranate glaze. Sadly, for Otis, it was a glass of wine – not a beer – meal; but luckily, for Yogi, there were some crunchy vegetable off-cuts.

After catching up on how their respective days had gone, Kari told Otis everything she knew about Doug Johnson, including Bo's hunches as related by Molly.

Otis listened until Kari asked, "What should I do? What would you do?"

Otis laughed and said, "What I'd do is tell you that I'm glad I don't need to make that decision.

"I'm not even sure whom you'd tell. He can't be tried – for his wife's death or his own. Besmirching his name doesn't help anyone. And if you did tell, you'd also be implicating Bo, although 'incriminating' may be overstating it.

"The only risk is that when Nerdy's trial comes up, he could spill the beans, although I'm not sure why he would unless he thought it would benefit him."

"Thanks," said Kari. "You made some good points. I don't even know if I'm obligated to share what I know unless it was relevant to something specific. And speaking of Nerdy, as you call him, I wonder if he kept my pin-up pictures around. Strickland didn't say anything, but I've had visions of FBI agents all over the country with copies in their wallets."

"The only danger there is if one of them ever said anything to me about it," Otis interjected. "You'd have to grant me a presidential pardon."

"The Republicans and the press would have a field day with that! But changing the subject, I met with Isabelle Martin today."

"Wow, you really do get to have all the fun! So, how was Queen Isabella?"

Kari laughed. "That's what Molly called her!"

"How is Molly?"

"Considering what she's just gone through, pretty good, but …" Kari's mind wandered off, trying to imagine what Molly was going through.

Otis read her mind. "I'm pretty sure you'll never have that experience. Nobody bumps off Education Secretaries, although there've been some that should have."

"We talked about my new vice president."

"So, who is it?"

"That was why I changed the subject. I wanted your advice."

"I think I'll have to start charging for these services. No money though."

"Ha, ha. Hughes, Welti or Telles?"

Otis snapped back, playfully. "Hughes! She's hot!"

Kari sneered and commanded, "Yogi! Bite your daddy's ankle!"

Yogi half rolled over and wagged his tail from his upside-down position.

Otis reached down to rub Yogi's belly as he asked, "Is Telles the one from New York who wants to give everyone two thousand a month guaranteed income?"

"Yes. And several cities have been doing that for quite a few years. The results seem to support the scheme but even though plans like that have been talked about for years, it still defies my logic."

"So, who's your choice?"

Kari smiled, "Telles. I want someone smart, thinks differently and isn't afraid to challenge me or the status quo."

"Are you planning to go radical progressive?"

"No. My plan is pretty much what Bo and I put together before … his death." Kari took a deep breath as the reality of that washed over her. Then she continued.

"I just want someone to keep my head in the future; plus Craig's a climate junkie, and that's our number one priority." Otis got up and took Kari in his arms. "Thanks for talking with me and asking my advice. I'm honored!"

Otis held her for a very long time, until she planted a kiss on him, wiped her eyes, and said, "Thanks. I love you and I need to tap into your wisdom to help me through it. And I will get through it."

***

The Oval Office. The funeral of Bo Sanders was, as expected, a respectful and solemn affair, without as much pomp and ceremony that often accompanies high-profile funerals. That was Molly's wish and what Bo would have wanted. Molly held her head high and – it could be said – her emotions in check, except during most of the many speeches lauding her late husband. But even then, through a quiet stream of tears, she exuded dignity. The children, too, were subdued, but seeing their mother cry triggered similar reactions.

Of all the speeches, it was the one by the Secretary of Education that elicited the most praise, and tears.

"I met Bo Sanders about twenty years ago when we were playing college football – against each other – and we certainly weren't rooting for each other. But I remembered him as a team player – always thinking of others, on and off the field: his teammates, those less fortunate than himself, kids who needed some guidance.

"Bo and I, as two Black men, owe so much to our forebears who we mostly know only through reading and hearing about. Men and women who have paved the way for us, like Martin Luther King, John Lewis, Barack Obama, and Angela Parkson.

"When Bo chose me to be on his team five years ago, I was honored, and I've worked harder than I've ever worked before because he inspired me, encouraged me. I owe more of myself to him than anyone I have ever known.

"I'd like to borrow some words that another former President, Bill Clinton, once used to honor John Lewis. Bo Sanders 'was a man, like all other humans, born with strengths that he made the most of when many don't. Born with weaknesses that he worked hard to beat when many can't.

"One of Bo's many strengths was his ability to listen to the many sides of a situation, and seize the right way forward while never losing sight of the goal. His main goal was one that he knew he might never live to see, but he wanted it for his children and all the children in the future. He wanted to nurse the environment back to health so we could return to those freer lives that many of us remember, with the ability to fully enjoy our beautiful planet as it once was.

"Bo Sanders knew that the path we are on is the right one, and he believed in us to carry on."

***

The Oval Office. Kari hung up with the last of her list of proxies who were connected to her three vice president candidates. She smiled at the realization that everyone she called was unsurprised as to the reason for her call. Their preparedness during their brief discussions gave her no doubt that the three candidates knew they were being considered. And she wondered how many others felt the same – but wouldn't get the call.

Kari knew that Hughes would say no, but Kari would meet with her anyhow – if for no other reason than to convey her esteem for a woman who was willing to pass up a big role to keep the Senate seat. Welti was interested and Kari had a feeling that he would be giving as much thought to how it might help his primary run as to the job itself. It didn't matter, she wanted Telles, and he was interested.

***

Within a week, Kari had met with the three candidates and called Isabelle Martin to advise that she had selected Craig Telles. Isabelle's subdued "okay" spoke volumes.

***

The White House, March 1st, 2066. Craig Telles was sworn in as vice president one week after the trials of Volkov and the other defendants were scheduled. All of them were charged with Federal crimes in the murders of presidents, a vice president, senators, and Secret Service agents, as well as over fifty-thousand deaths from the two manufactured virus attacks.

The vast majority of people were clamoring for the death penalty, but there was an extremely vociferous, although smaller, group who stood against death, even for someone as loathsome as Volkov.

It had been another long day, but Kari was looking forward to delegating some responsibilities to her new VPOTUS and giving her more time with Otis and Yogi. She'd just gathered up some reading for the evening when her phone buzzed. Erin Millan was on the line.

"Hello, Erin. You're working late. What's up?"

"Madame President, I just received a call from the Foreign Minister of India. They've located Naresh Argawal."

"That's great news! Are they bringing him in?"

"No."

"What! Why not?"

"He's in Zimbabwe."

***

The End
(Almost)

EPILOGUE

United States District Court - Middle District of Pennsylvania, Harrisburg, Pennsylvania, April 1st, 2066. It was decided to hold two trials, one for the assassinations of the U.S. senators and the other one for the presidential, vice presidential, Secret Service agents, and virus-related deaths.

The first trial was complicated and featured nine lawyers. Nerdkist, Rover, Creud, and Slade were found guilty and sentenced to serve three sequential life sentences. Cobolt, Connell, and the local militia leaders were each given a single life sentence, without parole.

The second trial was more of a circus and the results were varied and quite controversial. Gerry Failwell was given a single life sentence for conspiracy to commit murder. His lawyer had argued, somewhat successfully, that he didn't know what was going on with respect to any of the murders and assassinations. That was probably true, but it didn't affect the outcome.

The Prince's lawyer offered a similar argument and he, too, was given a single life sentence. The Justice Department offered to return him to Saudi Arabia to serve his time, even though they expected that the King would release him early. To their surprise, the Saudis said to incarcerate him in the U.S. for at least five years, returning him, if his behavior warranted, after that, to serve out his term.

FINAL CHANCE

Volkov, Nerdkist, Rover, Creud, and Slade were sentenced to death and the "anti-deathers" went on a rampage. The four male prisoners were first taken to the U.S. Federal Penitentiary, USP unit, in Allenwood, PA, and the throngs of protesters – both for and against – created havoc in the town. Except for the Allenwood Café, Weaver's Ice-Cream & Pizza take out, Michael's Beverages, and the Holiday Inn Express, most everyone else in the Allenwood Domed area was quickly tired of the commotion and shortage of ice cream, pizza, and beer.

Meanwhile, Karen Rover was sent to the Federal Penitentiary in Alderson, West Virginia. Business immediately boomed at the Alderson Big Wheel Take Out and Moia Wolf Cosmetics.

Guantanamo Bay Detention Camp. Officials at all levels of the Federal Government tired of the aggravation caused by the protestors so, by some sort of legal-political maneuver, in the middle of the night, all five were sent to Guantanamo. No protestors, no media, just a firing squad. And, given the crimes, a long list of volunteers to do the firing.

On their final day of reckoning, no media coverage was allowed; but, to no one's surprise, a leaked video covered the executions. All five were lined up against the wall and it took a while to strap Nerdkist and Creud to the wall because their legs would not hold them. Both had soiled themselves, making the area around them slippery for the service members to get the straps in place. But then it was "Ready. Aim. Fire." And the bawling was silenced. The videos trended for weeks and advertising revenues on every social medium soared. Then, just as quickly, it was over.

***

The White House. Kari had called to Shamalov to advise him of Volkov's death, not knowing what to expect. However, he was understanding, saying that if an American had done that to Russia, he'd also face a firing squad. The call ended with Shamalov inviting Kari to Moscow, commenting that the two countries could do so much more if they worked together.

Kari reflected on the call with their greatest adversary. She knew that the global actions taken thus far had yielded some modest gains but if that progress could not be sustained and if the world slipped back, the next atmospheric decline could be more like falling off a cliff.

Kari's mind drifted to the ominous threat from Zimbabwe when Erika came in to say that Erin Millan was on the line. Kari had looked at Erika, took a deep breath, and almost whispered, "Yes, Erin."

"They found Argawal near Bulawayo, in southwestern Zimbabwe. That was near where the mysterious deaths had occurred."

Erin hesitated to give Kari a chance to get her bearings, and Kari cautiously asked, "Yes?"

Erin continued, "Apparently, much as he did in Chittur, Argawal had infected a local village, inhabited mostly by an ancient, primitive tribe. But unlike Chittur, the relatively few survivors of the village grabbed Argawal and dealt out their primitive form of punishment. We have no more to fear from Mr. Argawal."

Kari asked, "What was the punishment?"

Erin told her and all Kari could say was 'Ewww!"

***

The Capitol Building, The State of Washington D.C., January 20, 2069. The crowds were gathered for the presidential inauguration. Outside the dome, the sun was shining, and the sky was a bright blue. The newly elected Vice President, Craig Telles, kept looking at his watch, counting the minutes to his inauguration, and then it was official.

The Marine band played high-spirited brass-infused music as the crowd cheered wildly. Telles, his wife, and the Chief Justice stood solemnly as Kari Patel Graham strode to the podium, to be sworn in for the first time as the elected president of the United States.

Otis, Jennifer, Jason, Nadya, Adam, Vijay Jr., Alek, and Sophie looked on with pride. Yogi was just happy to be amongst so many people, getting so many pets.

***

The Very End

ACKNOWLEDGMENTS

Sadly, I'd like to acknowledge our real climate crisis for the inspiration to write this book. I wish I'd written faster because real events and technology outpace my imagination.

Writing requires a lot of help, and I am grateful for the abundance I've been given, especially from my life partner, Jackie Morris. Her love, encouragement, support, and editing, have all helped make FINAL CHANCE and the entire FINAL SERIES, a reality.

Jackie has written and recorded a song, "Money to Burn," which in many ways reflects the environmental struggle that many of the characters in this book, and all of us, must face if we want to ensure our survival. A download copy of the song is available at: https://jackiemorris.net/track/2093128/money-to-burn

I also want to thank my beta readers – Bonnie Sloan, Irene Becker, Amy Ellingson, and John MacPherson – for their advice. I took it!

A shout-out, too, to AJ Bongiovi, for his ideas and suggestions to keep the book moving. Excellent insights.

Last but certainly not least, I want to thank the many (more than expected) readers of FINAL NOTICE and FINAL ACT and for those of you who have just finished FINAL CHANCE, for your acceptance, liking, and particularly your openness in considering new and different positions on important issues raised in these books.

Feel free to contact me at van@vanfleisher.com or visit my website: www.vanfleisher.com.

***

ABOUT THE AUTHOR

My journey to becoming an author took over seventy years, and it started in high school – a requirement if I wanted to play football and baseball. Mr. Smith, my literature teacher, was intrigued when I aced his essay test after six weeks of saying nothing in class. And so, he asked me how I did so well. My answer was simply that, "I'd listened." He asked if I read books, and I answered honestly, "No." So, he handed me a copy of a book, "The Catcher in the Rye," suggesting I might like it. I took it and actually read it, anxiously waiting for the baseball part that would surely be in a book with that title. I'd been tricked but kick-started to a lifetime of reading.

I've enjoyed two careers over fifty years that afforded me not only the opportunity to read voraciously on my thousands of flights (seriously) but also to learn so much about people, cultures, business, and life. I worked for an international airline and lived in five U.S. cities, three countries, and worked all over the world. My other career was as an international management consultant, working in and flying between thirty plus countries.

Not surprisingly, upon retirement, I decided to write. FINAL NOTICE was my first thriller, followed by its sequel, FINAL ACT. FINAL CHANCE rounds out the trilogy.

I live in Carpinteria, California, with my partner (and editor), Jackie Morris, and our goldendoodle, Yogi.

***

FINAL CHANCE QUESTIONS FOR BOOK CLUBS

Following are some suggested discussion questions for book club moderators. The author is happy to consider special book club rates and engage in discussions, as possible. I would love to hear about your conversations and any comments you may have. van@vanfleisher.com.

1. Overall, do you think that the author was open-minded in his dealings with the major issues?
2. What did you like, love, or hate about Final Chance?
3. Regarding the references to the VT2 watch, how would you feel about knowing when you will die, and what would you do with your last days?
4. Could you envisage a situation where you could kill, knowing you would never live to stand trial?
5. Based on the premise of Final Chance, what do you feel are the country's most significant issues?
6. What are your views on embedded microchips?
7. Did you agree with Kari's final decision on Doug Johnson?
8. How do you feel about law enforcement surveillance?
9. What are your thoughts on the threat of climate change?
10. Did you like the author's writing style?
11. Would Final Chance (along with or independent from Final Notice and/or Final Act, if you've read them) make a good movie?
12. What actors would play the main characters?
13. Having experienced a pandemic, how concerned are you about other, even more deadly episodes?
14. Who were the most likable characters? Least likable?
15. Did Final Chance influence your views on anything?
16. Your overall rating: 1-5 stars.

Made in the USA
Las Vegas, NV
07 December 2021